Praise for the works of Kat Jackson

Golden Hour

Kat Jackson has written another excellent book! If you've not already, check some of her other books out. *Golden Hour* is no exception, I love her writing style and her books have "drawn" me in.

-Jo R., *NetGalley*

Rapidly becoming one of my favourite lesbian authors, she writes intelligent books that explore more than just a romance.

-Claire E., *NetGalley*

I am coming to find that I really love books by Kat Jackson, she manages to pull me in on an emotional level and I enjoyed the pairing between Lina and Regan very much. The way Lina's PTSD was handled and described gave the book more depth than the average romance novel and when it's done in the way Jackson does it, it's very much lifting the book to a next level. *Golden Hour* can be read as a standalone, yet Lina was first introduced in an earlier book (*Across the Hall*) and that couple has a role in this one as Lina's best friends. Highly recommended!

-Dominique V., *NetGalley*

The Roads Left Behind Us

5 star, 5 star, 5 star...did I like this story...yes! The writing is beautifully filled with so much emotion and intelligent dialogue, I was sad when it ended. The environment is academia which makes the content of many conversations slightly elevated over other romance novels. Yet very understandable and warm. The characters are real, interesting, and distinct. I liked all of them. I highly recommend this story.

-Cheryl S., *NetGalley*

That was some marvelous writing; the vocabulary alone was spellbinding. The two MCs and every single supporting character are so well fleshed out that you feel as if you stepped into a room full of your friends and are catching up on all the gossip. The "will they, won't they" makes quite a pull at your heartstrings, but the end result makes the shipwreck all the more survivable. Their love story is charming, it's refreshing, it's as stormy as it is placid, and you will find yourself smiling hard at the MCs' antics throughout. A play at the Student/Professor fantasy, but you'll find these two are on equal footing in the PhD program where a delicious age-gap and big, beautiful brains war to find shelter.

-Alice G., *NetGalley*

Across the Hall

I loved Kat Jackson's first book, *Begin Again*, and I've been not-very-patiently awaiting the release of her second. I was not in any way disappointed! If you're looking for a layered tale of wonderfully flawed people, look no further. What enchanted me so much about *Begin Again*, and what runs through *Across the Hall* is one of the things that makes humans so interesting is that we are not perfect.

Mallory and Caitlin are complex characters with great depth, who I alternately wanted to hug and shake. Their stories are carefully crafted, and I am so thrilled to hear that Lina is getting her own book!

-Orlando J., *NetGalley*

Kat Jackson's *Begin Again* was an incredible debut and she became my favorite new author of 2020. Needless to say I was really looking forward to this sophomore effort. It didn't disappoint.

It's a workplace romance featuring two mains with a lot of baggage to bring to a fledging relationship. This story is really told in third person from Caitlin's POV, so we don't really know what's going on in Mallory's head. I really enjoyed following the ups and downs of the relationship and it was hard to tell where it was going. I started reading and next thing I knew, I was finished. That's what I love about a book.

-Karen R., *NetGalley*

I completely enjoyed this book from start to finish. I thought Caitlin was super charming and I really felt for her when she was trying to get back on the dating horse. Of course she picks a woman who's a bit of an ice queen! They are always the hot ones!! What I loved even more, though, was that Mallory was actually a great equal to Caitlin. I really felt the ying/yang and their chemistry.

I don't want to spoil it, but there is a bit of angst between the two that I wasn't expecting, but it made it that much more entertaining. And go Caitlin for calling Mallory out when she was, in part, being led on. I may have cheered a little.

Overall, a very fun read with great characters, excellent chemistry, and just the right amount of story. Can't wait for the next one from Kat Jackson.

-T. Geist, *NetGalley*

Begin Again

This debut novel was well written, with a good pace, and I could sympathize with the characters.

-Michele R., *NetGalley*

Begin Again is one of the most beautiful, heartrending, and thought-provoking books I've read. Kat Jackson manages the rare feat of making a lesfic novel that toys with infidelity meaningful and elegant. While this all might sound a bit grim, it does have plenty of lighthearted moments too.

-Orlando J., *NetGalley*

Begin Again is one of the most thought-provoking, honest, emotional and heartrending books I've ever read. How the author managed to get the real, raw emotions (that I could believe and feel) down on paper and into words is amazing. If you read the blurb you will know, sort of what this story is about. But it's much more than that. As other reviewers have stated, it's not a comfy read but was totally riveting. I read it in a day, I just couldn't put it down. Definitely one of the best books I've read and if I could give it more stars I would for sure! Superbly written. Totally recommend.

-Anja S., *NetGalley*

The Missing Piece

Kat Jackson

Other Bella Books by Kat Jackson

Begin Again
Across the Hall
The Roads Left Behind Us
Golden Hour

About the Author

Kat Jackson is a collector of feelings, words, and typewriters. She's a teacher/behavior coach living in Pennsylvania, where she enjoys all four seasons in the span of a single week. Kat's been consumed with words and language for essentially her whole life, and continues to spend entirely too much time overthinking anything that's ever been said to her (this is a joke, kind of, but not completely). Running is her #1 coping mechanism followed closely by sitting in the sun with a good book and/or losing herself in a true-crime podcast.

The Missing Piece

Kat Jackson

BELLA BOOKS

2023

Bella Books, Inc.
P.O. Box 10543
Tallahassee, FL 32302

Printed in the United States of America on acid-free paper.

First Edition - 2023

Editor: Alissa McGowan
Cover Designer: Heather Honeywell

ISBN: 978-1-64247-445-9

PUBLISHER'S NOTE

Acknowledgments

First and foremost, thank you to everyone at Bella for providing the space and opportunity for writers like me to bring their dream stories to life. I'm grateful and still a little stunned every day that I get to do this.

Alissa, thank you endlessly for another editing journey together, and thank you for loving these characters as much as I do.

Many thanks to everyone who puts up with me when I send texts that say something like "Yeah, cool, I'm writing, bye."

Dedication

For all the late bloomers out there,
brushing off the soil as your petals reach toward the sun

CHAPTER ONE

The unmistakable sound of the main door smashing against the wall behind it halts Renee Lawler's manicured nails over her keyboard. She feels her brows crease and quickly widens her eyes, as she's certain the repeated furrowing is *the* contributing force behind the new, uninvited, and unwelcome wrinkles on her forehead. So invested is she in this careful, practiced routine that she misses the sudden hush falling over the gentle buzz and hum of the English department offices, followed immediately by lumbering yet surprisingly purposeful footsteps drawing nearer to her office door, which is, regrettably, more than ajar.

"Renee."

She jolts to attention, wrinkles momentarily forgotten. "Franklin."

The Dean of Liberal Arts takes up the entire doorway, leaving little space for light from the hallway to leak in. Renee forces her eyes to stop from rolling—her body's honed, natural response to even seeing Franklin Malnor's name, let alone having him appear unannounced in her office. Instead, she pastes a bright smile on her face, hoping its superficiality isn't too obvious, but also not caring enough to make it seem more genuine.

"You're over budget. Again."

Renee sighs heavily, the drama of the action intentional. She stands and presses her navy-blue skirt down to ease potential wrinkles (not much less offensive than the invaders on her forehead), then slowly makes her way around to the front of her desk and perches on the edge, dangling one five-inch canary-yellow high heel while the other digs into the worn wooden floor. She levels her eyes on the space between Franklin's bushy eyebrows, yet again wondering why his wife doesn't suggest he tame the overgrown thickets.

"Franklin," she starts, her tone edged with honey.

"No," he says immediately, crossing his arms over his broad chest. "It's the third year in a row. I understand math is not your forte"—Renee cringes at his *for-tay* pronunciation—"but this is becoming a habit. A fiscally problematic habit."

Renee ramps up the wattage of her smile. She isn't worried about the budget—clearly, she never is—but Franklin's presence in her office is something she does not enjoy under any circumstance. As far as bosses go, he could be far worse, but the personality that oozes from him is not one that Renee appreciates. Franklin is a schmoozer at his best, a sycophant at his worst. She wants to trust him, has tried to for years now, but something inside of her refuses to let it happen.

Truth be told, that little something inside of her has a long history of refusing to let things happen. Even at the evolved age of forty-seven, Renee still isn't sure if this is a good thing.

Straightening her posture, Renee gazes at Franklin, allowing a mask of sincerity to fix itself on her features. "I'll figure it out. I always do."

He grunts. Renee can tell he wants to come further into the office, but thankfully, a carefully constructed invisible fence of her authoritative feminine energy keeps him at bay. "You always say that."

"And," Renee says, pushing firmness into her tone, "I always follow through with what I say."

The split second of hesitation from the dean is enough to secure yet another yearly win for Renee. She mentally pats herself on the back even though she knows she'll have to at least make it *look* as though she's attempted to cut back on some of the department's spending for next year. Per usual, Franklin will somehow forget this conversation ever occurred and the miniscule over-budget amount (what was it, a cool $5,000 this year?) will slide through, no more questions asked.

Renee wonders, as she does every year, how that works. And just as quickly as the thought appears, it's mown over by the sheer joy of sticking it to the man. Oh, how she delights in sticking it to the man.

"All right then." Franklin tugs on the end of his standard black tie, lifting it off his barrel-shaped torso before letting it listlessly flop back down. His eyes flick around the office, never settling back on Renee. She's fairly certain he's afraid of her. And she likes it. "I'll be waiting for your revised budget. It better not include any aesthetic items meant to enhance your drab surroundings."

The pathetic parting shot doesn't land, and as Franklin leaves without a goodbye, Renee waves gaily at his retreating form. She waits for the stubborn main door to be flung open and creak out an unsatisfying groan as it lumbers toward closing. The door has never slammed and it never will. Renee's office door, however, can slam with an intensity that shakes the classrooms on the floor below.

She resists the urge to summon an earthquake, not wanting to upset the tender-hearted scholars on the first floor. Instead, she releases a long-held breath and arches her neck backward, letting her eyes scan the beige ceiling tiles.

"Fucking Franklin," she mutters to the tiles, blinking long and slow. "Holier than thou piece of steaming raccoon shit covered in maggots and—"

A low whistle interrupts Renee's colorful rant. "I take it that went well."

"As always." Renee rolls her neck to the side and looks at her second-favorite hire of all time, Dr. Courtney Wincheck-Rodriguez, who is hovering in the doorway.

"So now isn't the best time to ask for some favors?"

Even Renee's sideways vision can't smear the wickedness of Courtney's grin. "I believe you already know the answer to that." She runs her fingers through her hair as she resumes normal posture. "But ask anyway. You know I love to screw with that sad excuse for a man."

"Actually," Courtney says as she walks into the office and drops into one of the chairs across from Renee's imposing black walnut desk, "I'm more interested in knowing why you chose raccoon shit."

"Easy. It's rated one of the top smelliest animal shits."

"According to?"

Renee shrugs. "The Internet." She flicks her wrist in Courtney's direction. "Limited time here, Courtney. What do you want?"

"A TA."

"No."

Courtney tilts her head, adopting an expression that's meant to look innocent and wholesomely needy. It nearly hits the mark but Renee knows it's a facade. "Please?"

"No," Renee repeats. "While I'm thrilled that you cut to the chase, as you often do, you know there's not a chance in hell that I can even consider granting that request."

Courtney crosses her arms and fixes Renee with her characteristic penetrative stare. "You got Kate a TA."

Another flick of the wrist. Renee idly wonders if others consider that her characteristic move. She very much wants a signature move, she realizes. "You and Kate have completely different course loads. Would you like me to expound upon all the intricacies of how she is, quite simply, more deserving of a TA?"

"I'm pretty sure you misspoke and want to use a word other than 'deserving.'"

With a huff, Renee slides off her desk and returns to her chair. Far from drab, it's a luxurious, ergonomic rolling cloud. Fine, perhaps it isn't in the "beautiful" category of office furniture, but it is the most comfortable seat Renee has ever sat upon. Fuck Franklin. Who is he to snub her office? His entire wardrobe is the epitome of drab and—

"Well?"

Renee looks at Courtney. "What?"

"I'm waiting for a better word than 'deserving.'"

"You may continue waiting."

Courtney laughs. "Seriously, Renee. No chance?"

"Seriously? Doubtful." Renee taps her password into her sleeping computer. "I would have to cut something, or someone. And you know how much I loathe cutting."

"Yes, I do, but you've seen my schedule for next year." Courtney leans forward, resting her elbows on her thighs. "Hell, you *made* my schedule. Can I handle it? Obviously. Would it be supremely helpful to have a bright, young scholar under my experienced wing to guide through the intricacies of academia whilst simultaneously taking just a tiny bit of grading obligation off my plate?" She nods, her sharp gaze never wavering. "Yes. Yes, Renee, it would."

"And my priority is keeping my professors happy." Renee steeples her fingers. "I'm five thousand over budget."

Courtney taps her pointer finger against her chin. "Weren't you seven thousand over last year?"

"That's entirely possible, but—"

"And didn't it slide through anyway?"

Renee clenches her jaw. She wonders if that action contributes to around-the-mouth wrinkles. "I regret telling you things."

"Oh please," Courtney says as she stands to her imposing 6'3" height. "I'm your favorite confidant. You'd be lost without me and we both know it." As though a thought has suddenly occurred to her, she raises her hand before Renee can counter. "And don't even say what I think you're going to say, because I've been here longer, ergo I have seniority plus the prolonged experience with handling all of"—she gestures toward Renee—"this. In conclusion, I'm your favorite and I'm more *deserving*."

Renee lifts one shoulder, a coy move that doesn't often grace her frame. "Second favorite."

Courtney shakes her head as she leaves the office, a mumbled "Ridiculous" floating back to Renee, who merely smiles.

It's not that Courtney is wrong; she was Renee's first official hire after her appointment to department chair following a mess of inner-departmental shenanigans that no one speaks of. Renee was only thirty-seven when she suddenly rose to the top rank in the English department and she wasted no time in weeding out the last remnants of the previous chair's misguided hiring practices. Courtney showed up at the exact right moment and Renee jumped on the opportunity to bring her bright, sarcastic, loyal light into the department.

And truly, she was Renee's favorite for many years.

Until, of course, Kate Jory's résumé appeared in her inbox and Renee nearly wept with joy. Bringing Kate into the department and learning that she was even better in person than on paper is by far Renee's greatest accomplishment as of yet. Too, she thoroughly enjoys encouraging Kate and Courtney to battle it out for top position, especially since Kate could care less and that drives Courtney crazy, leaving the war lopsided and hapless, but quite impassioned on one side. As the duel waxes and wanes, Kate merely shakes her head and rolls her eyes, though Renee imagines Kate secretly enjoys having a dig to jab at Courtney when needed.

Renee sits back in her chair and crosses her legs, allowing herself a quiet moment of pride. She has worked hard over the last ten years, and she's confident she has the best department in the entire university. Though it is small, it is mighty. Competition and over-confidence run rampant throughout the university's departments, but Renee never worries. Her professors are a reflection of her: determined, hard-working, passionate, and just a touch arrogant in all the right ways.

Yes, she thinks as she brings up the budget and prepares herself for the onslaught of numbers and formulas, everything is exactly as it should be.

CHAPTER TWO

"What do you mean, you forgot?" Renee hears the thinly veiled horror in Kate's voice but chooses to wait her out instead of replying. "How does one *forget* they're attending one of the most prestigious literary conferences on the East Coast? And not just attending. You're moderating one panel *and* presenting years of research on another, which, by the way, has actually been advertised."

Renee continues bustling about her office. She registers an exasperated sound coming from the general area in which Dr. Kate Jory sits, but her laser focus is preoccupied with finding the binder that holds the materials she needs for that aforementioned highly publicized panel.

That thought momentarily stops her movements. A firework of excitement shoots through her and explodes low in her belly. She'd deny it to anyone who ever dared ask, but Renee loves, absolutely thrives on, being the center of attention. Especially in situations where, like the one looming in the very near distance, she's considered an *expert*. She wiggles her hips before remembering Kate is still in the office. *Focus*, she commands herself. *Find the damn binder.*

It sounds like Kate has continued to talk as Renee pushes books and folders aside. She would never refer to herself as a packrat or a hoarder, but the amount of material in her office suddenly seems more problematic and unnecessary than helpful. She should make a point to clean out and organize when she comes back from the conference. Right. Because that will fit into the schedule that she makes as demanding and tight as possible.

Renee stifles a laugh, but apparently it wasn't stifled quite enough as the room goes silent behind her.

"Did you just…giggle?" The horror is less veiled now.

Renee spins around on the tall, thin heel of her blood-red shoes. "I did not."

Kate's normally pale face is tinged with an amused blush. "You absolutely did."

"Fine, I may have, but if I ever hear that you told *anyone*…"

"Honestly, Renee, even if I did, no one would believe me."

Renee crosses the space—bigger than most offices in the department, but still on the small side as offices go—and sits down behind her desk. "I may be slightly unprepared."

Kate's hazel eyes widen. She blinks three times, rapidly. "You're what?"

"I know." Renee huffs out a breath. "Unprecedented. Uncharacteristic. Troubling."

She doesn't need a response or an agreement from Kate: they both know that Dr. Renee Lawler thrives on being prepared—not only for the task at hand, but also for all tasks that could spontaneously appear at any given time. Renee functions with order and order alone. She spares no time or attention for chaos, uncertainty, or surprises. Her life, mirrored in her job (or, honestly, the reverse is more accurate), is highly structured and precise in every measure.

It is for these exact reasons that it is beyond mind-boggling that Renee cannot find that one damn binder.

She narrows her eyes at the professor—her favorite, for many reasons—sitting across from her. "Did you take my binder?"

"Why in the world would I have your binder?"

"Why wouldn't you?" Renee counters.

"Because it has zero value to me." Kate leans back in her chair. The maroon blazer she's wearing hugs her curves, as does all of her tailored clothing. Renee admires Kate's dedication to her wardrobe, envies it a bit, despite the fact that they have contrary opinions on footwear. "Where did you last have it?"

"Right here." Renee gestures toward her desk, which is a step beyond neat and could not hide a stuffed, hulking bright-blue binder. "I was going over Callie's notes—"

"Wait a minute. You let Callie read your tome?"

Renee stiffens, not because she accidentally let it slip that she had, in fact, allowed Callie Lewes (who happens to be Kate's younger, extremely intelligent girlfriend who is also a professor in the English department) to review her dissertation-length essay, but rather because she chafes every single time Kate and Courtney refer to her masterpiece as a "tome." It deserves a much more enticing nickname, one Renee hasn't come up with just yet.

"She didn't tell you?" Renee pairs the conversational spike with a sugary smile.

"She didn't. It must not have been that inspiring." Kate's grin, carrying shades of glee slapped up against wickedness, crinkles the nearly invisible wrinkles around her mouth. "Anyway, go on. You were reading her notes, and…"

Renee bites back the multitude of retorts she desperately wants to volley back at Kate, just to keep the rousing verbal game in play, and decides instead to stick to the more pressing issue: the binder. "Yes. She's quite smart, you know. I did take her notes into consideration, but ultimately"—Renee spreads her hands over the smooth wood of her desk—"why mess with perfection?"

"Why indeed," Kate murmurs, that happily evil grin not wavering.

"And so, after I removed her Post-its and walked them to the trash can—" Renee stops as the realization dances in front of her. "Oh."

"Oh?"

The amused, vaguely embarrassed sound that escapes Renee's lips is not quite a giggle but not the full-bodied laugh she lets loose when something truly regales her. "I know where the binder is." She flicks her wrist toward the door. "You can leave now, thanks for your help."

Kate stands and brushes nonexistent lint from the front of her charcoal-gray pants. "Always a pleasure. But I do need to know where the binder is, since it didn't magically appear on your desk. For the sake of ensuring you're prepared," she adds.

"I am quite prepared, thank you very much." Renee nearly buys the lie before remembering how badly she needs to spend some time with that binder.

When Kate waits at the door, her posture determined and a touch haughty, Renee relents. "It's at home," she mumbles.

"Okay," Kate says slowly, drawing out each vowel. "Then I suggest you wrap things up here and go home." She glances at her watch. "Especially considering you're due in Vermont in four hours."

CHAPTER THREE

It isn't that Renee is late. "Late" isn't a word in her vocabulary, especially when applied to her own actions. After spending the morning ensuring everything would run smoothly in her absence from the university, she'd hustled home and packed, which had taken just as long as she'd anticipated it would. Her ability to pair high heels with business-professional attire is a finely honed talent, one she delights in putting on display at every opportunity. Was it worth the extra fifteen minutes bustling in and out of her oversized closet? Absolutely. It always is.

Finding the damn binder exactly where her brain had eventually pictured it had been a relief. Renee had shot the inanimate object a glare of contempt before sliding it into her leather bag, giving it an extra push to ensure it was snugly encased. If it leaped out before she got into her car, she would have been utterly screwed in Vermont.

True, she's technically scheduled to attend a cocktail meet and greet at 6:00 p.m. Also true, the traffic gods were on her side and she made the trip to Burlington in just over two hours. Renee has, as Kate likes to say, a bit of a lead foot.

It's the part where she didn't leave her house in New Hampshire until 4:30 p.m. that causes her to be a bit less than punctual, and Renee doesn't want to steal anyone's thunder by making a late, grand entrance into a likely otherwise dull cocktail hour. So, it seems appropriate that she shuffles into her hotel room around 7:00 and promptly orders room service along with a chilled bottle of chardonnay.

With a sigh, Renee settles into one of the firm armchairs positioned by the floor-to-ceiling windows in her room. She sips the icy wine, rolling the subtle pineapple flavor over her tongue, and takes in her surroundings. They are, in a word, drab. Tans and creams, the standard furniture, no vaguely interesting artwork. The curtains are heavy and an unflattering shade of ecru. At least the room is clean and the bathroom houses an oversized tub that Renee was not expecting and is thrilled to discover.

"Drab," she mutters, shaking her head. "Fucking Franklin."

Not wanting to give the overbearing dean more attention than he requires, Renee turns to the blue binder that sits on the table before her. She distractedly taps the front cover with one finger. While it's true that she mixed up the dates of the conference in her overwhelmed brain, she hadn't exactly *forgotten* about it…nor is she unprepared by an average person's standards. She spent months fine tuning and overanalyzing her own writing. She has a long list of talking points coupled with a bulleted list of thoughtful answers to questions she's fairly certain might be asked of her. Everything is ready to go, including her moderator's notes; she simply thought she had two more weeks to over-prepare.

Alas, as infrequent as it is, she was wrong.

Renee smiles as she looks out on the darkening city. There was something highly amusing about allowing Kate, whom she really does adore, to believe that she was ill-prepared and forgetful. Part of Renee knows that Kate didn't buy a second of her dramatics, but the idea that she had, even for a moment, thought Dr. Renee Lawler was not on her game is hysterical. She considers calling Kate to check in and have a good laugh but stops herself before she so much as touches her phone.

Kate belongs to someone else. And it's not that Renee wants her for herself—not in *that* way, at least. But she let Kate in, something she loathes to do with the general population. There's something about Kate's personality—she feels like a warm, oversized sweater that Renee can pull around herself and burrow into. Kate has become familiar with some of Renee's idiosyncrasies, a few tender threads of her past. Kate knows things that others never have (and, yes, likely never will). Renee trusts her, and while the word "trust" makes every inch of her skin crawl, she has to admit that Kate makes it easy. Comfortable, even.

But Kate has Callie, and Renee respects their relationship; she understands her second-place position in Kate's life.

It's the only place in her life where she accepts not being number one. Besides! She has other…people…in her life. Right. Plenty of people.

Renee twirls her empty wineglass between her fingers and looks at her phone, marveling at how dark and silent a phone can be.

"Dr. Lawler! So great to see you. We missed you last night at the meet and greet!" Keisha Caldwell, conference facilitator extraordinaire, embraces Renee then holds her at arm's length and looks her up and down. "As usual, we are killing it in the wardrobe department."

Renee casts her eyes down and takes in the sleek, flattering lines of the deep red blazer that sits atop a silky black camisole showing just enough cleavage to keep it interesting. She decided against the matching skirt, feeling it was a bit too short for comfortably sitting on a low stage in front of dozens of professors and other literati, and went with black pants that hug her thighs and firm calves. Plus, she was able to use the black to break up the matchy-matchiness of the scandalously high heels that do, in fact, perfectly match the hue of her blazer.

Red, Renee's second-favorite power color, is a hard color to pull off. But she knows the shade compliments her chestnut-brown hair and skin tone (once described by an overly enthusiastic Sephora makeup artist as "medium-light with cool undertones"). White, saved for important meetings, is her secret-weapon color. It makes her cobalt eyes cold and determined. She's watched grown men wilt beneath their power when she illuminates her eyes with a bright white top of some sort.

"I so wanted to join you all last night," Renee says, smiling grandly. "Unfortunately, I had a scheduling issue at the university that kept me a bit later than I'd intended."

Keisha smirks. "Is that what we're calling it these days? Scheduling issues?"

Renee barely holds in the laugh that threatens to jump out. She and Keisha have run in the same professional circles for years, and yet she still forgets how well Keisha knows her.

"That excuse might work on our male counterparts, but you and I both know you spent a little too long in the closet." Keisha bumps against Renee. "If this outfit is a predictor of what's to come, I'd say it was worth it."

"Did I miss anything riveting last night?"

"No more than the usual pandering and ego-massaging," Keisha replies, taking the change in subject in stride as she always does. "You did miss the opportunity to meet with the other presenters on your panel, though."

Renee nods slightly. "I'm assuming it's too late for that, considering my tight schedule today." She glances at her watch, confirming that the panel she's moderating begins in twenty minutes. Once that ends, she'll have just fifteen minutes to regroup before presenting.

"You'll be fine. Besides, you'll have the chance to dazzle everyone at the mandatory happy hour this evening."

Renee tilts her head, assessing the smirk that has once again appeared on Keisha's full lips. She idly catalogues the stunning shade of dark-pink lipstick Keisha selected for today, a hue that highlights the golden undertones in her rich umber skin. "Mandatory? Since when?"

"Since you didn't show up last night. And don't even try to tell me that you won't want a nice glass of wine and the opportunity to collect new fans."

She can't argue either piece of Keisha's claim. Most people Renee knows shy away from networking, but she has a knack for making connections in order to get what she wants. According to her parents, Renee is a born leader; her mother still makes a point to bring up how Renee commandeered all the girls in fifth grade to refuse to interact with the boys for an entire week. Her mother claims the goal was to solidify Renee's position as Boss. Renee remembers it being more about the immaturity of the boys and not liking the attention her female friends were suddenly giving them. This contrast in opinions is one of several hundred reasons why Renee speaks with her mother... infrequently.

But yes, the truth is, Renee is talented when it comes to schmoozing. As for the wine, well, she simply very much enjoys wine.

"Text me the details," she says to Keisha, then squeezes her arm in parting.

Renee makes her way across the room, choosing to avoid the coffee bar. She had an iced Americano with cold foam after spending thirty minutes on the treadmill in the hotel's gym. Any more caffeine will give her the shakes, and the last thing she wants is to give any inclination that she's nervous while in front of a (small) crowd of people. She sidesteps and grabs a bottle of ice-cold water instead.

As she approaches the door leading to the hallway, Renee stiffens. An odd sensation trips her internal wires and she hesitates before stepping into the hall. The uncanny feeling of being watched settles over her. She entertains a second of mental debate before slowly glancing over her shoulder.

The room is still buzzing with the energy of people, probably thirty of them lingering before moving on to their first conference obligations of the day. Renee scans quickly, not wanting to look as though she's looking for something... or someone. A few familiar faces register as her eyes sweep the room, but no one seems to be paying attention to her. She shakes off the strange feeling and continues out of the room.

CHAPTER FOUR

"Again, thank you all for joining us on this reflective journey through modernist literature and stream-of-consciousness," Renee says, making sure to float her gaze across the small conference room. She takes note of how many people are still paying attention—enough to satisfy the presenters to her left, she imagines. She'd prefer a more interested audience, but alas, this isn't her dog and pony show.

"If you have any lingering questions for the presenters, perhaps one you were too shy to ask in front of a room of strangers"—Renee gets a small rush from the smatter of laughter—"be sure to ask them before they run off to their next engagement."

The twenty or so people in the audience slip out of listening mode and begin talking amongst themselves. Renee looks at her watch and curses. They somehow went over their allotted time, which means she has less than ten minutes to dash across the hall and prepare herself for her own panel.

As she collects her notes and turns to pick up her bag, the odd feeling from earlier creeps over her once again. She pauses her movements, waiting to see if the feeling persists or is simply a leftover vibration. No, she's certain she's being watched. And while she isn't bothered by it, per se, she is slightly unnerved. With a deep breath, Renee slides her notes into her bag and slowly turns around, eyeing the room with veiled interest.

Again, nothing, no one. She searches the room with purpose this time, trying to seek out the offending starer. She grits her teeth as she comes up empty-handed, or rather, empty-sighted. Renee certainly doesn't *mind* the attention, but the sensation that's coming with it is… Well, it's different. She doesn't know what to make of it, and that is simply unacceptable.

One thing her determined searching does provide is an advancing man with whom she verbally sparred in the past. Not having the desire nor the time to reignite their chatty battle, Renee waves blithely in his general direction before hurrying out the door.

The room in which she'll present is a carbon copy of the one she just left. The walls are a dull cream that does not inspire creative thought, despite being bare—a prime blank slate. Renee silently counts the number of available folding chairs and sighs inwardly. She was hoping for a larger crowd, but this will do.

"You must be Renee Lawler." A striking woman with long blond hair holds out her hand. "I'm Kristina Burkhart."

The name registers as familiar, thanks to Renee having actually read the emails detailing her fellow panelists. Kristina Burkhart is a professor at Columbia, and her list of accomplishments is impressive, perhaps even a bit intimidating. Renee saw her headshot but hadn't expected Kristina to be so disarmingly beautiful in person. She never trusts photos of people, having been duped in the past.

"It's great to meet you," Renee says as she shakes Kristina's hand. "I'm sorry we didn't get to connect last night over cocktails."

Kristina laughs, a throaty sound that is incongruous with her appearance. A fan of juxtaposition, Renee likes her (and her attention-grabbing laugh) immediately. "Between you and me, I'm glad I missed it. But yes, it would have been nice to meet beforehand."

"I missed it too," Renee admits. "However, I'm being strong-armed into what I've been told is a *mandatory* happy hour this evening."

"Interesting. I didn't know they could require us to imbibe."

Renee lifts one shoulder. "The day someone forces me to drink—honestly, I don't even know how to finish that statement."

"Well, after this panel, you might need a strong drink." At Renee's raised eyebrow, Kristina hands her a slip of paper. "Turns out it's just you and me. The third panelist had a diverticulitis flare up."

Renee presses a hand against the surprise swarm of bees in her stomach. *It's no problem*, she assures herself. She can easily tack on an extra ten minutes of discussion, or even select another portion of her paper to read. As the thoughts overlap in her brain, she gives a quick nod to Kristina and gracelessly sits, flinging open her binder to prepare for the surprise bonus time.

As her painstakingly crafted sentences flurry in her vision, Renee overhears the moderator approach them and begin chatting with Kristina. She leaves the mechanics to the two of them; there's no way in hell she will begin this panel without having a clear idea of precisely what she's adding on to her finely tuned presentation.

Time ticks down far too fast, and Renee is unsettled when the moderator begins introductions. She tries steadying herself with some measured breaths. The rational side of her brain, trained for moments just like this, ably bats off the incoming thoughts: *You're not ready. You're going to screw this up. You have no idea what you're talking about.*

The last one, *You should give up before you start*, causes a flush to spread over the skin on Renee's neck. As she gives herself a moment to shut her eyes and gather herself—thankfully, the moderator is still droning on about who knows what—that damn sensation reenters her nervous system. Her eyes fly open and there, right there in the front row, is a person. A very, very good-looking person, Renee realizes. She bites the inside of her cheek as she and the mystery human lock eyes for what feels like an eternity. A crooked smile tilts the placid expression of the person, paired with the most subtle nod Renee has ever seen, and she really does pride herself on being a master of identifying body movements and language.

The internal hive swarms once more, and Renee grimaces. She blinks, still locked in a stare with this random, sudden human being, then moves her gaze to her binder, knowing the organized words will settle her.

She's moderately pissed to find they don't.

Kristina's elbow pokes into Renee's arm. "Ready?" she murmurs, and the word brings Renee back to earth with a thud.

"Always," Renee says out of the corner of her mouth, doing everything in her power to make the word true.

"Wow," Kristina says, angling her body toward Renee.

The room around them is bustling as people move in and out, talking with each other or scrolling on their phones. No one is racing toward the front of the room for autographs or further insight, so Renee lets her guard down the slightest bit and turns in her seat to face Kristina.

"That went far better than I expected," Renee says, allowing herself a relieved exhale. The two women easily sidestepped their missing panelist, their subjects and analyses coming together to incite effortless and engaging conversation with each other.

"It did, but that's not what my wow is for." Kristina reaches out and touches Renee's forearm. "Believe me, I did my research on you before driving up here, but I'm still stunned at how… how brilliant you are."

Normally, Renee basks in such idolatry, but with Kristina—who has a longer list of accomplishments and publications, plus a mannerism that is more approachable and absorbing than anyone Renee has ever met—oddly, she finds herself wanting to be the giver, not the receiver, of praise.

"Nonsense," she says quickly. "You were phenomenal. You carried the conversation. I was continually blown away."

"High praise, coming from you." Kristina smiles, revealing perfectly aligned white teeth. Renee wonders if she has any flaws, any at all, and how hard they'd be to uncover. "How about we settle for both being absolutely amazing?"

"I'd cheers to that, but I'm missing a glass of wine."

Kristina squeezes Renee's arm before moving her hand back to the table. "Wine for you, sparkling water for me. We can cheers at that so-called mandatory happy hour later on."

"You don't drink?" Not one for subtlety, Renee doesn't think twice before voicing the question.

"My wife is in recovery," Kristina says without missing a beat. "I was never much into drinking, could really take it or leave it, so when I met her, I just"—she shrugs—"left it."

Wife. She didn't expect that. Renee has never claimed to have any sort of gaydar, or even awareness of people's preferences. In the past, prior to meeting Courtney and then Kate, she tended to rely on stereotypes to help her identify and compartmentalize people. Since spending more time with her fellow professors— one of whom appears stereotypically gay but isn't (Courtney) and the other who gives no obvious outward clues to her sexual identity (Kate)—Renee has had her world and eyes opened up to the more intricate matters of gender and sexuality. She's still learning, will likely always be learning, but she is truly terrible at spotting gays out and about in the wild.

"That's admirable," Renee says.

Kristina cocks her head to the side and studies Renee. "You're not married, are you?"

"No," she says quickly. Maybe too quickly. "Never." She pauses, realizing how her emphatic responses could come across. "Marriage has never been a focused goal for me."

"I imagine not, since I have no doubt you achieve everything you set out for."

"The only reason I'm accepting your praise is because I know it's coming from your own sense of accomplishment in life."

Kristina lets loose another loud, full laugh, and Renee's shoulders relax. She'd never admit it out loud, but Kristina intimidates her, just a tiny bit, and leveling their playing field is important to her. She senses this is someone she wants to be professionally connected to.

"I had a feeling I'd like you, Renee." Kristina glances at her vibrating watch. "That's my wife. My kids are starving." She sighs as she adjusts the straps of her bag over her shoulder. "I have one adventurous eater and one who would eat macaroni and cheese for every meal if we allowed it, and my wife is vegan. Fortunately, I'm a restaurant-whisperer and find places that make everyone happy."

At the mention of children, Renee feels something tighten in her chest. Before she can lean into the feeling, Kristina is giving her a quick hug.

A hug. Short, one-armed, but a hug nonetheless.

When exactly did Renee become…huggable? She chafes against the notion but doesn't hate the burst of friendly human contact.

"Truly, Renee, this was amazing. Thank you for sharing the space with me. I'll see you later."

With that, Kristina is off, a haze of peppermint-scented air trailing in her wake. Renee rests her hand on the back of the chair, needing a grounding point. She certainly didn't come to this conference with the intention of making an actual friend, and yet that's what seems to be happening. For someone who relies largely on professional connections, Renee isn't quite sure how to navigate a long-distance friendship with a fellow academic, but she has a concrete feeling that meeting Kristina is a pivotal, purposeful event for her. If she were into things such as fate, she'd chalk it up to that, but instead, Renee settles on the simple excitement of connecting with a kindred spirit.

CHAPTER FIVE

Church Street is alive with the festivity of fall. People walk in pairs and groups, some solo like Renee, all taking in the crisp Vermont air and stunning cerulean sky. No one seems to be in a hurry as they stroll over the brick sidewalks, popping in and out of stores. The vibe is decidedly Vermont: laid-back, friendly, and welcoming.

Renee, meanwhile, is doing her best to travel over the bricks without snagging her heels between any loose offenders. She worries for a fleeting second that she looks like an intoxicated penguin but is far more concerned with the prospect of falling, so she carries on at a pace she would normally deem too slow.

As she nears Sweetwaters, the restaurant hosting the aforementioned happy hour, Renee feels a tug of nostalgia in the pit of her stomach. This particular block is very familiar to her. During her graduate program at the University of Vermont, she spent two years bartending in a basement club housed beneath a high-end restaurant. She took classes with the daughter of the restaurant's owner, and he'd taken a liking to her, eventually offering her the paid-under-the-table gig. Renee got quite the extracurricular education in that bar, and has never spoken of it after graduating from UVM. Some pages, she believes, are better left unwritten.

As she walks into Sweetwaters, Renee glances down at her outfit. Maybe she should have changed. She's planning on heading back to New Hampshire in the morning, so this is her last chance to impress the conference-goers with another stunning heel-outfit combination. The incoming brisk temperatures made the decision for her; the thought of her legs goose-pimpling when she walks back to the hotel in 45-degree air didn't sound appealing, so pants it is.

"Girl, am I glad to see you. I was beginning to think you were trying to ditch us again." Keisha swings past the entryway and grabs Renee around the waist, guiding her toward the bar, where a group of professional-looking people have spread out. "A warning," she whispers near Renee's ear. "That awful Tom person from SUNY is on the prowl and he's asked me four times whether or not you were coming."

Renee groans. She'd gone toe-to-toe with Tom at a conference years ago. It hadn't been a good ending for Tom, but the man is persistent. Or dumb. Perhaps both.

"Please tell me you've directed him to a more viable option."

Keisha laughs under her breath. "Of course I have. Two, in fact. But he is dead set on you."

"Maybe he's in the market for a verbal ass-whooping," Renee says as they approach the bar.

The noise Keisha makes in response is somewhere between a laugh and a vocal cringe. "Renee."

After ordering her wine, Renee leans against the bar and raises one corner of her mouth. "Keisha."

"He wants more than a scholarly chat," Keisha says out of the corner of her mouth, shifting her gaze to smile and wave at someone across the bar.

"And he'll never get it."

She swivels her head to study Renee intently. "Are you finally seeing someone?"

"No." Renee bites back her retort about everyone's fascination with dating and marriage. If she didn't know better, she'd think that was the focus of the conference. "You know I don't have time for that," she adds.

Keisha leans in closer. "You don't *make* time for that. Don't try to fool me, Dr. Renee Lawler. I've had your number since the first day I met you."

"Well thank God Tom doesn't."

Keisha's laugh is bitten short by the advancing man of the hour. "Damn good thing you're not wearing a skirt because the sight of your legs would knock that man dead. Okay, it's been real, goodbye and good luck!"

As Keisha vanishes, Tom takes her spot. His smile, cocky as ever, diminishes the natural handsomeness of his fifty-something face. In another lifetime, perhaps Renee would have been interested.

"You're a difficult woman to pin down."

"That's intentional," she says, turning to receive her glass of wine.

"2020 Cayuga White, straight from Shelburne Vineyard." The bartender, a woman with soft masculine features, winks at Renee. "Let me know if you need anything."

Something odd flutters where that smack of nostalgia had been only minutes ago. Wine in hand, Renee takes an inadvertent step back from the bar, nearly colliding with Tom, who must have moved closer.

She swats him away. Yes, she actually raises her free hand and flicks her wrist in a manner that clearly communicates, "Move the fuck back, buddy."

Tom, never deterred by Renee's ever-charming personality, merely increases the size of his smile.

Men, Renee thinks as she takes a sip of her wine, savoring the crisp coolness of the liquid. And people wonder why she doesn't bother with dating.

"Tom," she says evenly, figuring she should nip this in the bud. "I'm not interested in whatever you're selling."

"Selling? Renee, I assure you, there's no money involved with what I'm suggesting. I think we both could use a little fun that comes for free."

If skin could crawl, Renee knows in that exact moment that hers would be furiously climbing over her skeletal structure. She wants to gag but clears her throat instead, preparing a finely worded dismissal.

"Think about it," Tom continues, undeterred. "Oh, and I'll be sure to tell Franklin Malnor our paths crossed this weekend. I know he'll be happy to hear a full report."

The tension of the moment nearly causes Renee to forget that Tom has absolutely zero impact on her job. He can try to use Franklin as a weak dagger to thrust in his sad attempts to get Renee into his hotel bed, but she knows better.

"Sorry to interrupt, but are you drinking the Cayuga White?"

Renee, still censoring her highly unprofessional imagined retort, snaps a response at the interloper. "Yes. Clearly."

"Don't mind her," Tom interjects. "She's not known for pleasantries."

The amount of restraint that Renee exercises could fuel an entire country's electricity for a year, she is sure of it. Her vision swims black for an instant, her anger swarming, searching for a way out. Her fingertips ripple with white-hot fire from clenching the side of the bar top.

"You are a heinous representation of the male sex," Renee says, her voice low enough for only Tom to hear.

He laughs in response, seeming to rev up for a return attack—one he presumably thinks is all fun and games—until the stranger interrupts once more.

"I think you should walk away now," the voice says evenly.

Renee marvels at the crisp, cool tone. She tilts her wineglass, eyeing the pale liquid with more curiosity than is warranted.

"Oh? And who are you? One of her hopelessly devoted fans from the university?"

"I don't have fans," Renee cuts in, her words capped with ice.

Tom sighs with a dramatic flair rarely heard from anyone outside of a fourteen-year-old girl. "Don't believe her. She plays at the whole modesty thing, but this woman—"

"That's enough." That voice again. This time, Renee looks up from her wine and takes in the person standing just close enough to Tom to put the press on him.

"Oh," she murmurs as recognition dawns.

Tom looks between Renee and the other person, his eyes flitting back and forth several times before his smirk finally collapses in on itself and he steps aside. He hesitates for a moment, as if dying to jab in one last remark, but his overbearing intelligence must summon some common sense within him as he walks away without another word.

"I didn't need to be rescued," Renee says coldly, moving down several spots at the bar and sitting down. To her surprise, the person follows her, keeping a seat between them as they rest their elbows against the bar.

"Okay," they say simply.

"I've spent years dealing with his exact kind of pompous male energy." Renee puts her wineglass down a bit too forcefully. "I can handle it. On my own."

"Okay," comes the repeated, ever-calm response.

"And for the record, *I* am in charge in those situations. He never had the upper hand. I was perfectly in control the entire time, and knew precisely how that interaction would unfold." Renee straightens her posture. "I have an arsenal of comebacks in waiting. He did not stand a chance against me."

"I believe you."

Several ounces of fight leak out of Renee. "As you should."

"I do."

"Great."

"Wonderful."

Renee purses her lips. "Fantastic."

"Glorious."

"Tremendous."

"Terrific."

She turns her head slightly, seeing that her rescuer's eyes are trained forward, staring at something across the bar. "Sublime."

They nod. "Awesome."

Renee sputters. "Awesome? That's your pick?"

The person turns and faces Renee, putting their androgynous features on full, unconcealed display. Renee's hand flies to the base of her throat as her breath catches there. Never in her life has she seen brown eyes the color of cocoa powder, but there they are, locking with Renee's eyes in a way that feels both exciting and unpredictable. Those gorgeous eyes are framed by the most luscious eyelashes—unadorned by mascara, she's certain—Renee has ever seen on a man or a woman. So captivated is she by those eyes that she nearly misses the confident smile tilting lips that look supple and highly kissable.

What the fuck, Renee thinks, taken aback by her own assessment.

"I happen to like the word awesome," they say. "It has a lot of applications."

"Right," Renee replies, her voice an echo of its usual presence.

"I'm Hunter." It comes without preamble, the sudden introduction, and something about the gentle assertiveness, the assumption that Renee would even want to know this person's name, strikes her as fascinating and strangely arousing. "And I'd like to buy you another glass of wine."

CHAPTER SIX

The fresh glass of Cayuga White appears on the bar top in front of Renee despite the fact that she merely gave a half-nod in response to Hunter's stated request. *They didn't even ask*, Renee thinks as she rubs her thumb over the base of the glass. She can admit it was kind of hot, the statement in place of the question.

A flicker of curiosity rises within her. As Hunter talks with the bartender, the very one who winked at Renee earlier, she studies their body.

The facial androgyny is one thing, but the outfit is another. Hunter's clothes seem to be made for their body: navy khakis rolled once at the bottom to highlight dark-brown oxfords, a perfectly pressed white button-down shirt tucked neatly into the pants. No tie. Renee scans Hunter's hands, which look strong. She feels her neck begin to flush. Strong, but not overly masculine. Hunter's nails are neatly trimmed. No rings, no watch. And the hair—slightly tousled deep black hair, cropped very short.

As Renee continues her perusal of Hunter's body, Hunter angles a hip just so, giving a shifting view of their chest. It's then that Renee gasps, hoping to hell that the sound stayed in her throat and didn't make it out for the general population to hear.

Hunter has breasts. Literal, actual breasts. Breasts that push gently against the fabric of the button-up shirt.

Renee considers hyperventilating. How in the world did she miss *breasts*?

As Hunter exchanges a laugh with the bartender, Renee makes quick work of rearranging pronouns in her brain. Hunter. She. *She. Her.*

She'd deal with that bizarre moment of finding another woman's lips kissable later. Much later, in the dark privacy of her hotel room.

And no, not in *that* way. In a purely mental, academic, hypothetical, deconstructive way. The only way for Renee.

Those untamed thoughts are shoved to the side by her academic voice piping up about gender identity, reminding her that just because Hunter has breasts doesn't mean she identifies as female. Renee can't very well *ask*, but she doesn't want to—

"So," Hunter says, turning her attention back to Renee and cleanly interrupting her thoughts. "Is now the time where I fangirl over how phenomenal you were today?"

"You mean"—Renee gestures to the area further down the bar—"when I was eviscerating Tom back to his true subhuman nature?"

Hunter lets out a low whistle. "You really are ruthless."

"Sometimes. And sometimes not." *Do not be coy*, Renee reprimands herself. *Stop it, you fool.*

"Well, yeah. I'd imagine it would be difficult to be cutthroat all the time."

"It would be a less than happy existence." And exhausting. And alienating. Not that Renee has spent part of her life living just that way.

Hunter sits down, keeping a seat between them. "I agree. But for the record, no. I wasn't referring to the destruction of Tom. I was referring to the conference."

Renee feels her brain shift gears back to the moment she recognized Hunter. Right. She was at Kristina and Renee's session. Hunter is, in fact, the very person Renee locked eyes with before beginning the presentation. She was responsible for the bees. Renee shakes her head. What the hell is going on?

Nothing, her rational voice assures her. *Nothing is going on.*

Bolstered by her reasonable internal dialogue, Renee smiles at Hunter. "You're a fan of psychoanalyzing the role of gender in contemporary literature?" As she realizes the words that are spilling from her mouth, Renee fights the urge to hide her face in her hands.

"Are you guessing that from my appearance? Or from the fact that I voluntarily attended a discussion on that exact topic?"

Surprise shakes Renee at her core. She tries very hard not to believe herself to be superior, but she's constantly teetering off balance when someone meets her at her level. "Honestly? Both."

Hunter shrugs, putting Renee back at ease after her uncharacteristic bordering-on-vulnerable response. "I've never felt overly feminine. But I've grown to be completely comfortable in my skin, even if it confuses people." She side-eyes Renee, but there's a smile attached to the knowing look. "As for the panel discussion, I admit it wasn't an entirely voluntary attendance."

"Ah, I see. You read my bio in the program and just had to come see if the words matched the experience." *There you are,* Renee thinks. *And we're back.* She feels her confidence resume its normal status.

"You'd like it if that was my why, wouldn't you?"

The underlying coyness in Hunter's voice causes a few of Renee's neurons to trip over themselves. She rights them before they can misfire through her mouth. "Probably."

Hunter laughs, her entire face lighting up with amusement. It is, in a word, enchanting. There's something about her that feels magnetic; Renee is being pulled in, but she has no clear idea which part of her body is holding her internal magnet. A quiet, unfamiliar voice within her speaks up, alerting her that yes, this meeting of the minds feels similar to the earlier one with Kristina, but also, something is noticeably different. Renee shushes the voice before it can complete its explanation.

With a start, Renee tunes back into the conversation just as Hunter is saying, "to be supportive."

"Supportive," Renee echoes.

Hunter studies her carefully. "You weren't listening."

"I was distracted," Renee admits.

"By?"

The flush that was taking up space on her neck now threatens to consume Renee's jaw. "Thoughts," she says, hoping her voice is level.

"Thoughts," Hunter says, echoing as Renee had. "You're a tightly closed book, huh?"

"It's not the first time I've heard that." Renee takes a sip of her wine. "Though you're the first to use a literature analogy to express the thought."

"Point for me." Hunter leans back on her barstool. "As I was saying, while you were inexplicably distracted, my ex-wife presented at the conference. We're still close—just friends, she's remarried—and since Aury was on kiddo duty, I offered to step in as moral support for the day."

"Aury?"

"My ex-wife's new wife." Hunter flashes Renee the same crooked smile she sent her in the conference room. "She's great. And I'm not just saying that. I genuinely like and respect her. Plus, Kristina's happy, and so are the kids. But enough about me and my slightly messy life."

Renee perks up. "Kristina? Kristina Burkhart?"

"The one and only."

"Kristina's your ex-wife?" Renee looks around the room, expecting Kristina to pop out from behind a group of people.

Hunter nods. "She couldn't make it tonight. Aury wasn't feeling well, something about possible food poisoning."

Renee stifles a laugh, remembering Kristina's irritation with having to select lunch for the family. Perhaps she'd be off the hook from now on.

"I can't tell you how many of these conferences I've been to," Hunter continues. "Kristina had to drag me to the first few. Somewhere along the way, I started actually enjoying them. I mean, we're divorced and I still come." Hunter laughs, shaking her head slightly. "I guess I just like listening to people talk about things they're passionate about."

"So you like smart women," Renee states.

It isn't until Hunter raises her eyebrows just enough to indicate the deeper meaning behind what was mostly intended to be a fairly basic remark that Renee realizes what she said... how it sounded...and the unerring truth behind her sudden desire for Hunter to like her. Platonically. No, not even that: she just wants Hunter to *admire* her. No, not *her*. Her brain. Yes. That's it. She wants Hunter to be—Renee fights the urge to slap herself as she shuts down that unraveling trail of thought.

"I do," Hunter says. "Smart women make things happen. What's not to like?"

Renee is secretly glad for the light response. She was treading in unfamiliar waters, and while she doesn't feel at risk of drowning, she's pretty certain she had momentarily lost sight of the shore.

"Speaking of smart women..." Hunter looks over her shoulder. "Do you know Charlotte Yeastedt? Phenomenal speaker. Her presentation on the evolution of the American Dream in fiction was incredible. She's on my fangirl list and it looks like she might need a distraction right about now."

Renee follows Hunter's line of sight and cringes, seeing none other than the common Neanderthal standing with Charlotte and several other women. "I'm beginning to think Tom is the focus of your fangirl list."

"He is most definitely not on my list," Hunter says as she stands. "You, however, were."

"I see. And now you've checked me off as a completed task?" Renee tries to keep the bitterness out of her voice but she hears some of it edge through.

Hunter moves so she's leaning against the empty seat between them. She waits until Renee holds eye contact with her before she speaks.

"You, Renee Lawler, could never be described as a task to complete." Hunter holds her gaze. "And fuck anyone who has ever made you feel that way."

A short laugh bursts from Renee. As much as she doesn't want Hunter to run off and socialize, she needs to collect herself before she, too, goes off on a networking bender. "Go. Have fun."

"Meet me back here in thirty?"

The earnestness of the request touches Renee in a way she hadn't realized she could be affected. All she can do is nod in response.

Later, after a final glass of wine together—one that was crowded by several other happy hour attendees who wanted more words with Renee—Hunter nods toward the door and Renee, after saying her goodbyes, hopes to God she looks cool and collected as she follows Hunter out of the restaurant.

As they stand in front of Sweetwaters, Renee acknowledges a fleeting regret for not having changed into a skirt. She looks down at her legs as she taps one heel against the brick. Yes, it would have been good—awesome, one might say—for Hunter to have seen her toned legs.

Again, she's knocked back by her untamed thoughts. It's because of the heels, she assures herself. Her calves look so *awesome* in heels, it's really just a matter of community service that Hunter should see them in their full glory.

"This was unexpected." Hunter's voice brings her back from her legs.

"What? The change in temperature?"

"The weather predicted that. No one could predict this." Hunter gestures to the space between them.

Renee swallows. She has zero understanding of what's happening, but her confusion and worry supersede any kind of curiosity or need that may be crawling out from dark corners, knocking around in her body.

"Us meeting and hitting it off," Hunter clarifies, seeming to sense her distress.

"Right. Unpredictable." The word itself chafes against Renee. If it isn't predictable, it isn't for her. She looks up at Hunter, who she imagines would tower over her if she weren't wearing such high heels. "But awesome," she adds.

A full smile breaks out on Hunter's face. "So awesome," she says. "Dr. Renee Lawler, it has been a pleasure."

Renee takes Hunter's hand in hers and is momentarily unmoored by the softness of her skin. "An absolute pleasure."

Hunter holds on to Renee's hand for several beats longer than necessary, finally releasing it with a short squeeze. "Till we meet again," she says, then turns and starts making her way down Church Street.

A sudden chill rolls through Renee's body. She wraps her arms around her torso and takes a deep breath. Sure, the temperature has dropped, but it isn't anywhere near cold. The chill isn't coming from the dropped temperature, though. Renee looks behind her, curious to see if Hunter is still visible somewhere in the mess of people on Church Street. Seeing no sign of her, she spins back around and aims for her hotel, already fighting the urge to erase the entire night from her memory.

CHAPTER SEVEN

The drive back from Vermont is pleasantly unremarkable. Renee is ready to be home, though—ready to be safe and secure, unbothered, in her home. She likes that the conference ran at the end of the week so she's coming home on Saturday with the rest of the weekend to regroup before returning to work on Monday. She drums her fingers in anticipation as she cruises through her neighborhood. Despite her desire to hurry home so she can walk through her front door and leave the events of the weekend in the driveway, she slows down as she turns onto her block. The trees are showing off, their deep red and burnt orange leaves waving gently in the fall wind. It's a bit overcast, nothing like the crystalline sky in Vermont yesterday, but the low, pale gray clouds provide the perfect backdrop for the vibrancy of the trees.

This is Renee's favorite time of year: October's last hurrah before giving in to November. The temperatures swing recklessly back and forth between leftover summer heat and incoming winter briskness. A person has to check the weather every day, if not multiple times a day, to ensure they are properly prepared for the temperamental New England fall climate. Renee appreciates that for once, everyone has to be prepared. Not just her.

She exhales, low and slow, as she pulls into her driveway. The phrase *home, sweet home* echoes in her mind, and she accompanies it with a short laugh. She loves her house, but nothing about it has ever felt sweet. Too, she visually connects that phrase with a nice little cottage, something fitting for a lone wolf such as herself. Something quaint and low-maintenance, tucked into the idyllic border of the countryside.

The intimidating brick colonial sitting at the top of Renee's long driveway isn't exactly…quaint.

She stops the car and stares up at the house for a moment. Over the summer, she had the shutters repainted in a striking, deep black. She likes the contrast against the slightly faded red brick. The front door boasts the same paint, and while her mother had warned her the finished product would be "uninviting," Renee disagrees. The overall appearance of the century-old home is stately and mature. Renee herself gave the landscaping a refresh, and the vibrant greens, now dulled by the change in season, shine against the exterior of the home when they're in full bloom.

Stepping inside and locking the door behind her, Renee takes a deep, satisfied breath. She drops her keys in the bowl on the mission-style table in the entryway. Stylistically, it's an odd choice, but Renee's father made the table and she refuses to part with it. It may clash with the rest of the interior of the home, which is largely contemporary with a side of modernist trimmings, but the table will remain forever.

She eyes her suitcase with contempt. The urge to shower, change into comfortable clothes, and attack her work email is strong, but Renee hates an unpacked suitcase. As she grabs its handle, cursing under her breath, she hears a noise that is entirely out of place in her home.

Sniffling. Specifically, the type of sniffling that comes with tears. Crying tears, not mid-onion-slicing or post-lawn-mowing-allergy tears.

Renee's eyebrows crease. Something is amiss.

She stands, motionless, waiting to hear another sound. It's possible she imagined it; she is quite tired, and her brain has been doing all sorts of odd things since that damn Hunter person elbowed her way into that irritating, borderline inappropriate, conversation with—

There it is again. A decidedly more teary sniffle. Renee takes a step toward the stairs, wondering how desperately she needs a nap if she's having aural hallucinations.

"Renee?"

That voice. It's a surprise to hear and it stops her approach toward the stairs. Renee waits for her body to catch up to her mind, curious to see what she'll feel upon hearing that voice in person for the first time in… She stops short. How long *has* it been?

She inspects her immediate surroundings, certain she doesn't see anyone. "Where are you?"

An exasperated sigh replies before the words, "The living room."

Renee tips her head to the side. "No you're not. I'm standing right outside of the living room, and you are most definitely not in there."

"Oh, for fuck's sake." The sniffling has subsided, replaced by a very familiar, gravelly, always-tinged-with-anger voice. "What is this, then? The sitting room? The extra living room? The entertainment room? I'm in whatever is connected to the fucking kitchen. The one with the comfortable sofas."

The great room, Renee thinks. She wisely keeps that to herself as she walks through the lower level of her house, footsteps echoing on the dark hardwood floors. Before she has time to collect her thoughts and pin down precisely the last time she heard that voice, she is standing in the sprawling, window-walled great room at the back of the house.

Her eyes waste no time zeroing in on the miserable-looking lump of a human tucked into the corner of the light-gray sofa. There's a pile of used tissues on the floor, the very sight of which makes Renee grimace. She flicks her eyes to the side table, hoping to God—she holds in her angry gasp. A cup. A sweaty plastic cup.

And no coaster.

"Jessica," she says, fighting the irritation that is quickly consuming her. "Would it kill you to put a coaster under your drink?"

The noise that comes from the lump—Jessica, in a clear state of distress—is full of its own special kind of irritation. Notably, the kind that has been building for twenty-five years.

"I know you're dead inside, but you might be able to figure out that using a goddamn coaster is not exactly at the top of my list of concerns right now."

"I am not *dead inside*," Renee says, moving across the room and perching on the edge of the sofa. She keeps a safe distance between herself and Jessica, having no desire to catch whatever melancholic plague has overtaken her. "I merely like my tables to avoid being stained."

Jessica sits up and angles her body toward Renee. She pushes the hood of her sweatshirt down, revealing a haircut Renee has yet to see.

She peers at Jessica's sandy-blond hair, tilting her head to confirm that, yes, the entire bottom half of her head is shaved. The tight bun near the top of her head calls up memories of that horrible "man bun" trend, but Renee keeps that comment to herself.

"Well, that's new," she says instead, gesturing to Jessica's hair.

"I don't expect you to like it," comes the retort. Jessica stretches her legs out in front of her. Her eyes are bloodshot, and the tip of her nose rivals Rudolph's in brightness, highlighting the unusual paleness of the rest of her face.

Something tugs at Renee's heart. She bites the inside of her cheek. "So! This is a surprise."

"Renee, please."

"Well, it is! You show up without calling or emailing for the first time in how long?"

"Three years, give or take two," Jessica mumbles. She finally meets Renee's eyes, and as always, Renee is taken aback by the startling clarity, the unusual and unsettling omniscient energy emanating from that gaze.

They stay locked in that moment, their eerily similar cobalt blue eyes speaking things neither one is willing to verbalize.

"I'm...I'm going through a difficult time," Jessica finally says, looking away. "And that's all I want to say about it. I thought it was a good time for me to visit for a few days."

And there it is. Delayed, but present after all: Renee's long-buried, oft-forgotten maternal instinct. She reaches out, surprising them both, and rests her hand on Jessica's hunched shoulder. Jessica's flinch is surely nothing more than a reaction to an unexpected touch, Renee is sure of it.

Her daughter, her wickedly independent, moody, introverted, wildly secretive twenty-five-year-old daughter has finally come home. And she has come because she is struggling.

Renee certainly isn't happy to hear that—no mother, no matter how loosely the term is applied, wants their child to struggle. But a struggle means a problem. And a problem can be fixed.

Renee Lawler is nothing if not a fixer of problems.

"Great!" Renee says, standing up. "Are you hungry?"

Jessica looks at her as if she's grown a second head. "Hungry?"

"Yes, hungry. How long have you been sitting here in your little pit of misery? Surely you're hungry by now."

"Nope."

"No? Okay. Right." Renee crosses her arms over her chest. "Thirsty?"

Jessica looks pointedly at the offending un-coastered cup.

"Dammit," Renee says, stalking over to the table in three steps. She wipes up the condensation, hoping it hasn't left a permanent stain, and replaces the cup in its spot, this time on top of a marble coaster. "While you're here, I'd appreciate it if you'd respect my home."

Jessica laughs quietly, not bothering to hide her disdain. "I'll do my best."

Vexation pricks the back of Renee's neck. Were she not 50% responsible for the very DNA that made Jessica the way she is, she would be more annoyed. As it is, she can only (partially) blame herself for the snarky, thinly disrespectful mannerisms of her daughter.

"What do you need?" she asks, genuinely at a loss.

Jessica shakes her head. "I'm good. You can go do whatever you need to do. I know you just got back from Vermont."

Renee's ego swells happily. "You knew I was in Vermont? Did you hear about the conference?" She throws her shoulders back. "Would you like me to re-create the presentation that utterly wowed the—"

"No," Jessica says flatly. "I'm sure it was good."

Good. More like awesome. The last word trails into a mental image of a certain brown-eyed woman standing before her, looking at her with admiration and interest. Immediately, Renee shakes out the image, returning her brain to her daughter.

"If you change your mind…"

"I won't." Jessica flicks her wrist toward the entryway to the room. Renee smothers a laugh, her maternal pride clapping at the shared gesture, even if it was borne of agitation. "Go do whatever. I'll be here. We can get takeout later."

"Okay." Renee nods once. "Awesome plan."

An alarmed look sets in on Jessica's features. "Awesome? I have literally never heard you utter that word, Renee. What the hell kind of conference was that?"

"A very, very good one," she replies before turning and stalking back from where she came.

CHAPTER EIGHT

On Sunday night, Renee asked Jessica to give her a rating for her "motherly abilities," and was stung when she received a score of four out of ten. Renee knew she wasn't going to get a ten, or even a nine, but after spending the majority of Sunday tending to Jessica's needs, she was certain she'd at least surpassed the 70% range.

As she walks into Berringer Hall, the building that houses the English department at Pennbrook University, early Monday morning, Renee reviews everything she'd done to accommodate Jessica:

1. She did not pressure Jessica to use coasters, but did slide one under her drink several times.
2. She offered to make Jessica's favorite dinner, but Jessica claimed she wasn't hungry.
3. She didn't knock on the door to the guest room more than four times during the six hours that Jessica holed up in there on Sunday.

4. She put her phone on silent during the forty-three minutes Jessica spent with her in the great room.

5. She didn't even *check her email* during those forty-three minutes, a monumental achievement.

6. She did not pressure Jessica to talk about, well, anything. Renee accepted the silence. She hated it, it was painful, but she did it.

The only conclusion Renee can draw is that Jessica noticed that Renee was unusually distracted, which must have taken away from her nurturing capabilities. Renee isn't proud of or thrilled about how often her mind wandered to the image of Hunter (she doesn't even know the woman's last name, for God's sake) over the shortened weekend. She has convinced herself of myriad things regarding her brain's betrayal in determinedly floating back to that evening at Sweetwaters, but she was also certain that Jessica's presence would help erase Hunter from her mind—at least until Monday, when Renee's work-brain would take over, ably smashing any leftover preoccupations.

As it turns out, she was wrong on all accounts. She hates being wrong.

Renee squeezes her hands into fists before using her hip to apply just the right amount of pressure to the door to the English offices. She *will* get her mind under control. Simply being back at work, surrounded by people who need her, will shift her brain back to a place she's familiar and comfortable with. A mental place she can predict.

"Good morning, Dr. Lawler." Audrey smiles broadly from her seat behind her desk. She has proven herself a very capable secretary, if a bit on the odd side. Renee likes her mostly for her resourcefulness and organizational skills, but does wish she could improve her people skills a bit. However, the lack thereof does create some much-needed humor around the office, so it works out.

"Audrey," Renee says in greeting. She pauses at her mailbox and feels nothing but excitement for its overflowing state. "I see nothing slowed down in my absence."

"Not one bit. Have you checked your email?"

Renee sends her a look that incurs a blush and a nervous laugh.

"Of course you have," she says quickly. "I meant that as a joke. Ha ha." In true Audrey form, she doesn't actually laugh—she enunciates the sounds and makes them words.

"You've taken up humor in the last week?"

A snort sounds from nearby, letting Renee know she and Audrey aren't alone despite the relatively early hour of eight a.m. If she had to guess, she'd mark that unattractive nasal noise as belonging to Courtney.

"I just wanted to be sure you were aware of the ten o'clock meeting you have with Dr. Malnor," Audrey says, smoothly sidestepping her boss's dig.

Renee feels the confidence drain from her body. She had somehow forgotten all about that meeting. "Of course," she says, lying through her teeth. "I knew—"

"Morning, Dr. Lawler." Callie Lewes speeds through the office, waving on her way to the door. She's gone before Renee can return her greeting.

Audrey's eyes follow Callie's departing form. "She's been like that lately. Here one minute, gone the next." Something wicked gleams in Audrey's eyes, and Renee wonders what she knows.

"You'd tell me if there was something I needed to know." She drops her volume, purposely posing a statement instead of a question.

Flustered, Audrey nods. "Yes. Of course, Dr. Lawler."

Renee doesn't quite believe her. Her hackles raise, bringing with them some remaining complicated feelings connected to her conference experiences. Audrey knows better than to keep Renee out of any loop pertaining to her staff, but there's something about that look in her eyes that says otherwise.

"Why isn't my mail sorted?" With a flourish, Renee takes the two steps to the edge of Audrey's desk and drops the stack on her keyboard.

Audrey jumps back. "I—I—I'm so sorry. I overlooked that. I'll take care of it right now."

"Perhaps if you weren't so distracted with others' behaviors, you'd remember to focus your attention where it's required."

Audrey nods as she shuffles the envelopes and magazines. She won't meet Renee's eyes, and just as Renee opens her mouth to lob another cold reminder of her expectations of Audrey, there is the sound of a clearing throat behind her.

Renee whips around, ready to redirect her attack. Instead, her defense melts at the sight of Kate, who's standing with her arms crossed, looking at Renee as though she is the cruelest, meanest, most insensitive person to walk the earth.

It's a look of grave disappointment, one that wisps into Renee's bloodstream and settles in the dregs of her heart.

"Kate," Renee says, her voice still laced with agitation despite the crushing feeling in her chest.

"Renee." Kate nods toward the hallway behind her. "I was hoping to catch you before your meeting. I have some ideas about the budget."

Renee is tempted to throw a parting, icy glance at Audrey, but that damn expression on Kate's face tells her she'd live to regret it. She narrows her eyes and stalks to her office, knowing Kate will follow.

Renee throws open the door, inhaling the familiar scent of knowledge, power, and the pleasant lime-ginger scented oil diffuser she purchased on a whim at the start of the semester. The relaxing smell is juxtaposed against the other formidable energies bouncing around the small space.

"How was the conference?"

One of the things Renee likes about Kate is that she saves all her talk about feelings for her girlfriend. She sticks to the important stuff—work—with Renee. In fact, Renee can't remember Kate ever asking her the banal, "How are you?" and she isn't mad about it.

"Very good," Renee says as she moves toward the window and peers outside. She knows she was feeling compelled to avoid Kate, but she can't pinpoint the reasoning for it. "Everything went smoothly."

"That's great. Did you meet anyone?"

At that, she whips around to glare at Kate. "What? What did you hear?"

Kate, rarely shaken by Renee's sometimes mercurial moods and interactions, barely reacts to the fiery question. "I didn't hear anything. I simply wanted to know if you'd kept up your reputation as the Networking Queen."

Renee relaxes a tiny bit, enough to set the record straight. "You and I both know that you've got the magical networking skills."

"Oh, please, I—"

"No," Renee says, holding up one hand as she sits behind her desk. "You have a way with people that I lack. I can admit that. I may be good on the technical, professional end, but you...You know how to connect."

"I won't argue that."

"Because you know I'm right."

Kate nods. "You can be a little rough around the edges. For example, your interaction with Audrey just now."

Renee pulls her laptop out of her bag and powers it up, planning to ignore Kate's selected topic of discussion for as long as possible. "I saw you're on the email regarding the call for papers in classical studies. I heard U Penn is looking for Shakespeare-related work."

"I'm already working on it."

"Of course you are."

"I'm not letting you off the hook, Renee." Kate eyes her. "What was that?"

"I'd like my mail to be organized. Is that a crime?"

"It is when you speak to Audrey like she's incompetent."

Renee rolls her eyes. "First of all, she's not incompetent. Secondly, I did not speak to her like she is."

And then Kate does something that drives Renee completely insane. She goes silent.

Yes, she stands there, watching Renee carefully, not speaking a damn word. She waits Renee out. No one can wait out Renee like Kate can, and she wants to hate her for it, but has come to discover that hating Kate is impossible. She is the most likable person Renee has ever met.

So Renee does what she does best.

Ignores the problem in the room and turns her focus to something unrelated: her email.

Seconds tick into minutes as Renee keeps up the ruse. About four minutes in, she begins to squirm. She peeks at Kate, who hasn't moved an inch. The disappointed look is back. Its tendrils sneak back into Renee's chest.

Renee makes it another thirty-seven seconds before she cracks.

"Fine. My daughter came home. I wasn't expecting her, and it's an adjustment. She's only visiting, but I'm not used to having her in the house. So I suppose I'm a little distracted." Renee mentally pats herself on the back for being honest.

Surprised that Kate hasn't immediately responded with reassurance, Renee looks up and finds her staring, slack-jawed.

"What?"

Kate opens and closes her mouth several times before sputtering, "You have a *daughter*?"

Renee nods.

"I'm sorry. What? Since when do you have a daughter?"

"Since twenty-five years ago, give or take a few months."

Kate shakes her head, clearly shaken by this admission. Renee's forehead wrinkles in confusion. Why in the world is Kate so thrown by this? Surely she'd known.

"Renee. In all the conversations we've had, how is it that you've never once mentioned that you have a daughter?"

"I didn't realize I had to make an announcement."

"No," Kate says, stepping forward. "Don't do that right now."

"Do what?"

"That." Kate gestures toward Renee. "That 'you should know even if I don't tell you' defense mechanism."

Renee's chest warms, indicating an incoming blush. Or hot flash. These days, she can never be sure. Either way, she doesn't want that feeling right now.

"All right. Yes, I have a daughter. I should have explicitly told you."

Kate still looks bewildered. "Who's the father?"

"Liquid from a vial."

That one takes Kate back a step. "You...you were inseminated?"

"Yes." Renee looks down at her hands. "Kate, it's simple. I wanted to have a child, but I wasn't in a relationship at that time. I had a very clear timeline of how I wanted to complete my schooling and enter into this career." She looks back at Kate, her colleague, but also someone she considers a friend. "Jessica was planned into that timeline."

Silence sits between the two women as Kate digests the information. Renee still doesn't understand why Kate is acting like it's such a big deal, but she respects her, and therefore respects her reaction.

The only problem is that the longer Kate is silent, the more conflicted Renee starts to feel. Has she been hiding Jessica? Unintentionally, she supposes it's possible, but on the flip side, she never reveals much about her personal life. She doesn't see the appeal of mixing her work life with her non-work life.

"I'd like to meet her," Kate says, breaking into Renee's thoughts.

An unexpected flash of emotion pricks at Renee's eyes. "Oh," is all she can say.

"When you're ready," Kate hastens to add.

"Right." Renee steels herself. "I haven't been hiding her, you know."

Kate looks as though she wants to argue that but doesn't so much as move her mouth.

Suddenly needing to end this totally-unrelated-to-work conversation, Renee tightens her posture. "We can talk more later," she says quickly, not entirely meaning it. "I need to prepare for my meeting."

Kate merely nods, sending one last baffled look in Renee's direction before leaving and shutting the door behind her.

Only then does Renee relax. She slumps in her chair, dropping her head backward. She gives herself two minutes to mentally shift gears, then plummets back into her budget.

Renee makes it through her meeting with Franklin. It doesn't go well, nor does it go poorly. It just *goes*.

Armed with new department items and costs to examine with a fine-toothed comb, Renee sets off from Old Main. She finds herself walking slower than usual, timing her stroll with her colleagues' teaching schedules. She hasn't completely settled down from her conversation with Kate and is hoping to avoid any further discussion with her.

By mentally shelving that whole mess, she accidentally opens the brain portal that exposes Hunter once again. There she is, her soft, deep brown eyes dancing with amusement. Renee huffs. So the woman had nice eyes. It isn't monumental; plenty of people have nice eyes.

Not that color, her damned smitten internal voice sings out.

Kindly shut up, Renee commands the interloper.

It isn't just her eyes, though. Renee has a very clear image of Hunter's hands resting on the bar top. Her impossibly short nails, smooth skin, nary a ripped cuticle in sight. The bartender had similar hands, Renee remembers. Her eyes, though, were a very plain brown, nothing like Hunter's.

"Stop it," Renee says out loud.

She continues walking back to Berringer and is just passing the student union building when she sees a familiar form heading toward her. Renee checks her watch. Right on time.

"Time to replenish Dr. Jory's coffee?" she calls out.

Callie stops short. An amused look paints her attractive features. "Am I that obvious?"

"Only to someone who pays attention."

Callie closes the distance between them. Her honey-blond hair, still lighter around her face from the summer sun, hangs in a loose braid over her shoulder. Her dark-blue eyes—a pretty color, but nothing like Hunter's—reflect her amusement.

"I hear you presented with Kristina Burkhart at that conference." Callie sounds impressed. "I love her work."

"I did, and yes, she's spectacular. You would really enjoy the paper she shared during our presentation. I could see if she'd send me a copy for you, if you'd like."

Callie's eyes light up. "That would be amazing."

Renee shifts her bag from one shoulder to the other. "Callie, I don't think I properly thanked you for reading over my paper. I do appreciate your feedback."

"You're welcome. I was happy to help."

It had been an interesting shift, from having Callie as a student years ago, to overseeing her graduate teaching assistantship in the department while she began her PhD, to now overseeing her as an associate professor within the department. It has taken time for Callie to stop being intimidated by Renee—her words, not Renee's for once—and now they share a mutual admiration.

"Callie," Renee says suddenly. "Can I ask you something?"

"Yeah, of course." She narrows her eyes. "Unless it's about Kate. That's still off-limits."

"Yes, I know. If I want to know something about Kate, I'll go to Kate." Renee smirks. These lesbians and their hyper-protectiveness over their relationship. It's darling. "And let's not forget that if I want to know something about *you*, I'll—"

"Go to Courtney, because Kate's lips are sealed." Callie raises her eyebrows.

"You took the words right out of my mouth." Renee shifts her weight from one foot to the other. "So. My question." Callie watches her. Damn it, Kate must be teaching her The Art of Making Renee Uncomfortable. "Do I...do I, uh, throw a vibe?" Renee rushes the words, regretting them before they fully leave her mouth.

"A vibe?"

"Yes. A vibe."

Callie shrugs. "Doesn't everyone throw a vibe?"

Renee sighs. She should have asked someone outside of her department—someone who, lacking a literary brain, wouldn't overanalyze a very simple question.

"Yes, so then, do I throw a...a certain vibe?"

Callie must hear the unease in Renee's voice because her eyes widen almost comically. "Oh God. Wait. Are you...are you asking me what I think you're asking me?"

"Yes. Maybe? Probably." Renee nods, hoping she doesn't look as unhinged as she feels. "Very likely, I'd say."

"The kind of vibe I throw, for example?" Callie cringes as she says it.

"Why that face?" Renee asks, gesturing at her visible discomfort.

"Because if I'm off track, this is going to be a very awkward conversation."

"You're not." Renee infuses as much authority into the words as she can muster. "I'm asking you if I throw *that kind of vibe*."

Callie nods, but it looks reluctant. "Wait, no, I'm just nodding because I understand, not because—oh my God, why couldn't you ask Kate this?"

"You're a better resource."

"Thanks, I think?" Callie stuffs her hands into her jacket pockets. "Okay. My honest opinion?"

"Yes!" Renee resists the urge to stomp.

"No." Callie releases a loud breath. "I don't think you throw a vibe."

"I see," Renee says. She can't tell what she's feeling, if she's feeling anything at all. "None whatsoever?"

"Not of the queer variety," Callie says, finally sounding confident again. "A vibe of control and power, one that clearly says 'do not overstep your boundaries with this woman'? Definitely."

"All right." Renee thinks about Tom and how he must not have any kind of vibe-radar. Or, in all likelihood, he's just an ass. "Thank you. This was enlightening."

"Yeah," Callie says, a smile beginning to curl the edges of her lips.

"End of discussion, never to be discussed again," Renee says before Callie can ask a follow-up question. Not that she thinks she would, but she's happy to squash even the idea.

"As you wish, Dr. Lawler. Coffee?"

Renee shakes her head and carries on her original, unquestioned walk to Berringer Hall, not daring to meet Callie's eyes as she passes her.

CHAPTER NINE

Renee slides her finger over the trackpad and clicks. No harm in browsing, she tells herself as she skims Columbia University's English faculty webpage. Sometime between her run-in with Callie and the end of her unproductive workday (something she won't admit to anyone but herself), Renee realized that not only does she not know Hunter's last name, she also has absolutely no idea who she is. At all. Profession, age, marital status (that doesn't matter, of course; Renee is merely curious), hometown, current home address, all that good stuff. Just the basics.

And so, feeling like a cross between a stalker and a private investigator, when she got home from work, Renee sat down at the island in her kitchen and popped open her laptop, ready to do a little sleuthing. She began with Columbia, with Kristina Burkhart, because having watched the slow dance Kate and Callie did around each other for months, Renee knows workplace romances are a "thing" and seem to be preferable for lesbians. Granted, Kate and Callie are her only evidence supporting that theory, but she has a funny hunch that Kristina and Hunter met at Columbia.

Kristina has an entire page devoted to her on Columbia's website. Renee skims it, impressed all over again. She makes a mental note to reach out to Kristina—for the sake of getting Callie access to that stellar paper and research, of course. And to maintain a beneficial professional connection.

Alas, there is no mention of Hunter anywhere on Kristina's page, nor is she listed as a member of the English faculty at Columbia. Perhaps she'd once been a visiting professor, or a TA. Again, she thinks of Kate and Callie.

Renee prides herself on being observant. She notices things that others don't. And she often doesn't share the information she gathers from her observations; she prefers to keep it to herself and watch as the dominos fall. The instant Callie walked into her interview for the TA position, the energy in the room had changed. Renee attributed it at first to the fact that Callie and Courtney were friends, but were determined not to let anyone else know that (they failed, naturally). It wasn't until she made a point to introduce her new professor from Tennessee, Kate, to the newly appointed graduate teaching assistant, Callie, that Renee saw it.

Their attraction was palpable. She knew in that moment that they'd find their way to each other, but there was no way in hell she would have ever let them know that she saw it coming.

Honestly, it was far more entertaining to watch the two women play a darling game of cat and mouse with each other than it would have been to drop the bomb and say, "How about you two just fuck already?"

Too crass for Renee. And not nearly as gratifying.

She drums her fingertips against the bright white quartz countertop. She already searched Columbia's entire website for the name "Hunter" and the results were not promising. Sure, there were Hunters, and also hunters, but none of the result-blurbs jumped out as plausible connections to Renee's Hunter.

Her drumming stops, fingers splayed, hovering above the countertop. Her wrist is starting to ache when the slamming of the front door jolts her out of the panic of mentally referring to Hunter as *hers*.

"You're back!" Renee calls loudly, spinning around on the stool. She presses her hands against her thighs, hoping none of her limbs are shaking as badly as her insides are.

"I'm back," Jessica says without fanfare, leaning against the arch that separates the front hallway from the kitchen. "What are you doing?"

"What? Nothing." Renee spins back around and shuts her laptop, much too forcefully for someone who had been doing "nothing."

Jessica eyes her suspiciously. "Look, I know we don't see each other that often, but I gotta say, you've been extra weird since I've been here."

"I have not." Renee stands and crosses over to the stainless-steel refrigerator, pulling it open to inspect the contents she has memorized. "What would you like for dinner?"

"If there's something—if I'm, like, in the way, or—"

"You are not in the way of anything." Renee continues staring at the offending arrangement of food in the fridge. "Shall we go out? Let's go out. My treat."

"Whatever you want. Just let me change."

When she is certain Jessica is safely upstairs, Renee shuts the door and opens the freezer, waving the frigid air toward her. Heat from simple thoughts of Hunter have her off-kilter and quietly aflame. She has to get a grip. And Jessica is the perfect distraction.

After half a glass of pinot grigio—not nearly as good as that damn Cayuga White—Renee feels her internal rumbling stop. Or pause. Yes, it's probably just paused. She taps the side of her wineglass before lifting it and tipping more into her mouth. She'd much prefer a permanent stop over a flimsy pause, and if this is the key, well then so be it.

"You do realize we've been sitting here for ten minutes and you've already almost drained your glass?"

How fun, a twenty-five-year-old child monitoring her mother's alcohol intake. Simply adorable.

Renee waves off the comment. "Any interest in the burrata appetizer?"

When her question is met with prolonged silence, Renee looks up. "What is it? You don't like burrata? We can do the cheeseboard instead."

Jessica looks like she's caught between laughing and crying. "I'm lactose intolerant."

"Right. Of course." Minus one point for the mother at the table. This is off to a grand start. "Is there something nondairy that interests you?"

"The calamari sounds good."

Renee stops herself from gagging out loud. "I see you've forgotten"—she looks up at Jessica, whose cocky smile gives her away—"about my seafood allergy," Renee finishes.

"It was a joke, Renee. The prosciutto wrapped asparagus, then?"

"Perfect."

After they place their orders with a rather distracted waitress, Renee and Jessica sit across from each other in silence. It isn't the comfortable silence that develops over time between two people who are content in one another's presence. Nor is it the awkward silence that protrudes from two people finding their way back together after having burned bridges and lifelines.

It's the kind of silence that screams, *I have absolutely nothing to say to you and I'm very aware that you're experiencing the same thing but I will allow hell to freeze over before I give in first.* Jessica, unfortunately, is a Taurus. Renee should have just named her Jessica More Stubborn than an Ass's Ass Lawler.

"So," Renee says, unable to continue suffocating under that mute veil. "How long are you staying?"

"Not sure," Jessica says. "Why? Do you have me on a timeline I'm not aware of?"

"No, not at all. It was just a conversational question."

Jessica shrugs. "Since I'm able to work from your house, I don't have to rush back to Brooklyn."

Renee doesn't like the reference to "your house" instead of "home," but she also can't fault her daughter for that logic. She signals the waitress for another glass of wine and purposely avoids making eye contact with Ms. Judgy Pants across the table.

"Does Brooklyn feel like home to you?" The question slips out without permission.

If Jessica is fazed by it, she hides it well. "Sort of. As you know, I've never had a stable sense of 'home,' so I make do with what I have."

Yes, that punch lands squarely. Renee throws her shoulders back, preparing for a battle that would need to be waged rather quietly, given they are in a restaurant. "I'm sure you discuss that with your therapist."

"All that and more," Jessica says, raising her water glass in Renee's direction.

Something in Jessica's voice takes the fight right out of Renee. She can't place the emotion—admittedly, she isn't well-versed in Jessica's moods—but she understands the significance of it.

She takes a deep breath, giving silent thanks that Jessica has someone neutral to share her feelings with. Renee always knew she was missing some maternal marbles. This, though, hits differently. She's never been that person for her own daughter. She isn't sure if she could be, but she thinks maybe this is her chance to try.

"I don't want to—" Renee begins.

"There's something I need to talk to you about," Jessica interrupts.

"I'm all ears." Renee smiles, pleased that Jessica is the one closing the gap.

Jessica shifts in her chair, seeming to stall. Renee watches as her daughter's cheeks first lose their little bit of color then begin flaming as though the table before them is on fire. She may not be practiced in the art of Jessica, but Renee knows signs of distress when she sees them.

"Jessica, whatever it is, you can tell me."

Both women seem surprised at the uncharacteristically kind-hearted words. Renee sits back in her chair, letting the space between them shift.

"I know," Jessica says, then she huffs a loud breath out and puts her elbows on the table. Renee cringes. Jessica rolls her eyes. "We're not dining with the Queen of England."

Renee nods. She doesn't trust what might come out of her mouth. Luckily, their waitress chooses that moment to stop by with a fresh glass of wine and Renee takes a grateful sip.

"Okay," Jessica says slowly. She flicks her gaze to Renee, locking their carbon copy eyes together. "Here's the thing."

She's pregnant, Renee thinks suddenly. Panic thuds low in her chest. She is so not ready to be a *grandmother*. Sure, she could be the sexy, hip, somewhat young-ish grandmother, but the term in and of itself, no, that will never do. She'll have to come up with an alternate title, something easy to say but also something that doesn't scream "elderly woman." A shot of fear bolts through her. Would Jessica expect her to raise this child? That wouldn't be too surprising but, oh God, Renee doesn't—

So lost is she in her spiraling grand-maternal thoughts that she apparently misses Jessica's birth announcement, as she sees Jessica's mouth move but doesn't hear any noise. She gets the word "I'm," but whatever comes after that has too many syllables to be "pregnant."

"Say that again?"

Another huff, this one less irritated and more worried. "I'm nonbinary."

CHAPTER TEN

The word enters Renee's brain, spins around like a cat kneading for the right spot, then sinks down, each letter stepping forward then back into formation. On repeat. Spinning, stepping. In and out. Letters becoming a word becoming a person.

She blinks at Jessica, waiting for her to continue talking. She needs Jessica to keep talking.

"So…yeah. I'm nonbinary."

"Yes, I got that."

Jessica laughs, but it's empty and humorless. "I invite your questions and commentary." She pauses and a flicker of doubt passes over her otherwise neutral expression. "Come on, Renee, I know you're dying to say something."

She takes a cleansing sip of wine, savoring the coolness, the predictable moment of release and relief. She fights the urge to ask for a third glass, seeing as she's nearly emptied her second.

Before she speaks, Renee looks carefully at Jessica. She searches for something—what, she can't say, but she knows there's something she's missing. Or maybe this is it. Maybe all these years, she has been missing exactly this.

Shouldn't I have known? The thought has a vise grip on her brain. *I should have known.*

"Tell me more about how things are in Brooklyn. I haven't been there in years."

Their appetizer lands between them, a perfect interruption to highlight Renee's inability to attend the discussion Jessica is inviting her to.

To punctuate her own point, Renee grabs a neatly wrapped stalk of asparagus, admires the slight char on the prosciutto, and bites off half of it.

Jessica watches her, this time with amusement. "Is it good?"

"Very," Renee mumbles around the food. "Try one."

"I will. But just so we're clear, since I can tell you're not ready to have this full-blown conversation: I'm nonbinary, my pronouns are they/them, and please call me Jess. Just Jess."

Renee nods slowly. "All right. Jess."

"I'm still me," they offer, leaning forward slightly. "Still your pain in the ass child."

"I know that." Renee twists the napkin on her lap. "Tell me about Brooklyn," she says again.

Jess nods as they pick up a piece of asparagus. "The neighborhood stopped that whole rapid change thing that was happening for a while. It feels like things have calmed down." They shrug and take a bite. "Wow, that's really good. So, there's a new coffee shop on the corner of my block, and…"

Renee slips into the cadence of her daug—her child's voice. That's going to take some adjusting, she muses. As it has recently become evident to her, she doesn't spend much time announcing the fact that she has a daug—*child*—in the first place, but now she will need to rearrange how she speaks about her. *Them*, she reprimands herself.

The concept of nonbinarism is not new to Renee. Given her profession and the population of Pennbrook University, it couldn't be. For God's sake, she just gave an entire presentation to a room full of literati about the very construct of gender in Jeanette Winterson's writing. Yes, Renee is liberal. Aware. Evolved. Woke AF!

But this…this is different. She continues watching Jess talk, smiling as they become more animated. Jess isn't a passing student in the hallway, or even one in Renee's classroom. She isn't a character in a book Renee is teaching, nor is she the genderless narrator in *Written on the Body*, a book Renee has analyzed to its near papery death. A book, she now thinks, she should give to Jess.

Jess is hers. She carried Jess in her womb. She gave them her DNA, brought them into this world. When Jess announced their bisexuality in high school, Renee barely blinked. Despite her usual inability to spot a gay, she'd seen that one coming from two football fields away. Frankly, she'd been expecting that Jess would proclaim to be a lesbian, so the inclusion of men in their sexual attraction had been a bit of a surprise, but Renee took it in stride. She'd even bought Jess a bisexual flag and hung it in their room as a surprise. Yes, she still pats herself on the back for that one.

Renee didn't see this coming, not from a single football field away, nor a trip around the world. It's fine, absolutely fine. It just requires some adjustment.

Renee can adjust. Absolutely.

She brings herself back to the table just as Jess is wrapping up a monologue about the subway system.

"And are you still seeing Flint?" Renee is *pretty* sure Jess didn't mention his name in the last five minutes.

Jess's hand stops dead on its way to their water glass. After a beat, they say, "Yup."

Renee tucks that bold-ass lie in her back pocket for another time. "I'm not ignoring your…change." She knows that isn't right, and tries again. "Announcement?"

Finally, Jess smiles and it isn't tinged with a negative emotion. "We can go with announcement. And I know you're not ignoring it. Or me. I know you need time to process." They tuck a stray piece of hair, having fallen from the knot on top of their head, behind their ear. "I know you better than you think, Renee."

Their entrees appear before them. Renee sneaks glances at the plate in front of Jess. They selected the short ribs, which came with cauliflower grits, mushroom gravy with roasted shallots, and steamed green beans. It looks exquisite.

"Eye for an eye?" Jess asks, arching one eyebrow, a trick their grandfather taught them.

Renee laughs. She takes in the feeling of relief and familiarity that sweeps through her. Whenever she took Jess out to eat when they were younger, Renee became, without fail, jealous of Jess's order. She was always happy with her own order, it was just that the tempting meal across the table always looked better. She'd taught Jess to share, using the phrase "eye for an eye," so they could swap bites of each other's meals without someone's hand getting defensively stabbed by a fork. Neither Jess nor Renee was particularly good at sharing.

"Eye for an eye," Renee agrees, cutting into her bone-in pork chop. She drags her fork through the sweet corn puree, loading a delicate bite into her mouth before returning to the fingerling potatoes topped with chopped bacon and arugula.

Jess swipes a piece of pork from her plate and Renee swings right over and snags a forkful of short rib.

"The grits," Jess says around their bite of pork. "Do not sleep on these grits."

Once they've eaten their fill and Renee has ordered a final half-glass of wine, the two settle back in their chairs and enjoy a new kind of silence. Renee has to admit that Jess seems lighter post-announcement. They had seemed unusually burdened since they'd shown up at Renee's house, but now, Jess's cheeks are flushed with life.

"I do have a question," Renee starts.

Jess snorts. "I've been waiting."

"The pronouns," she says, making sure her voice doesn't give anything away. "I may make errors."

Jess waits, but when it becomes clear that's all Renee had to say, they reply, "That wasn't a question."

"There's one coming." She inclines her head. "What happens when I make a pronoun error?"

Jess shrugs. "It's not the end of the world. I know you like to be A-plus perfect in everything you do, but this is an area where you'll probably mess up. I know that. I won't be mad about it, as long as I can, like, tell you're trying, you know?"

"I will try." Renee nods once. "Are you going to tell your grandmother?"

"Eventually."

Renee stifles a laugh. That conversation is one she'll need to witness. Her mother is not the most progressive person on the planet. She does, however, have a massive soft spot for Jess, and Renee has often wondered if her own lifelong ability to do no right was illuminated when Jess arrived and could do no wrong.

"And Flint knows?"

Jess sighs heavily. "Of course Flint knows. He was the first person I told."

While it makes sense that Jess told their partner before their mother, it still stings in a way Renee wasn't expecting. "He's accepting?"

"Yup." That same noncommittal response.

Renee's motherly instincts raise their hackles. "Back to the pronouns," she says without preamble.

"You're really stuck on that," Jess says through a laugh.

Renee throws up her hands. "Can you blame me? I've spent my entire life ensuring words are correct, that they line up appropriately, and pronouns, in particular, are assigned correctly. And yes, Jessica—Jess—it has been in a very binary manner." Renee drops her hands to her lap when Jess swats at them, a clear signal that Renee has swerved into her classroom habit of professorial gesticulation. "The amount of times I've corrected the use of plural pronouns in reference to a singular object or person—you'd be stunned."

"You and your red pen."

"Yes, well, my pen and I have had to adjust. And so we have." She pauses, weighing her next move. "But that's not my question."

"Yeah, I realized that when all your words lacked the use of a question mark."

Renee wants to roll her eyes, she really does, but she recalls too well the fact that she had inadvertently taught Jess to roll their eyes when they were a mere three years old, which set off an avalanche of teacher and administrator complaints about Jess's "incurable attitude." Preferring to be a model of appropriate behavior, Renee still tries to avoid rolling her eyes in front of her impressionable child.

"Is it customary for everyone to state their pronouns upon meeting someone new?"

Jess closes their eyes, seeming to fight off a burst of laughter.

"You find that funny?"

"No, no. Just sometimes, when you speak, I think you think you're standing in front of an audience." Jess opens their eyes. "It's just me, Renee. You don't have to be so formal."

"I know." And she does. But she's comfortable with it, and so it continues. "So? My question?"

"Didn't you change your email signature?"

She had, adding "she/her" below her name, and she'd encouraged her staff to do so as well. They are a united pronoun-addressing front, that English department. Renee nods.

"Then doesn't that answer your question?"

"Not exactly," Renee says carefully. "I'm talking about meeting someone in person. And they state their name. You can, uh"—she swallows hard, hoping to avoid stumbling over her words—"tell they have a female body. Which I know doesn't mean they identify as female," she hurries to add. "I guess I'm wondering, if they don't come right out with it, how are you supposed to know?"

The look on Jess's face is a mash-up of amusement and pride. "You know what? You're actually doing really well with the pronouns."

Renee smiles, pleased with herself. She remembers, too, how quickly her brain had adjusted pronouns once she'd realized Hunter had breasts. Now she's on another tailspin, wondering if she shouldn't be using female pronouns for Hunter after all.

"Answer the question, Jess."

Jess laughs, again leaning their damn elbows on the damn table. Renee bristles. Has she taught this child no manners?

"I can't. Not really, anyway. It's different for everyone. Is this about someone in particular?" There goes that damn eyebrow again.

"No," Renee says, too quickly. "Just a nonspecific inquiry."

"Okay." Renee can tell Jess doesn't believe her. "I would wait until this nonspecific person says something. In my experience, people will tell you what pronouns they use if it's important to them. I have a friend who will answer to any pronoun."

Renee shakes her head, and a piece of her hair dislodges from her low ponytail. "What? How? No. What?"

Jess laughs, clearly enjoying their mother's elitist English language crisis. "You'd have to meet them to understand."

Later, on the drive home, Renee's mind floats back to Hunter. She's certain there is a possibility that Hunter identifies as nonbinary, but is flustered by the fact that she doesn't—can't—know for certain. The fact that everything in her daily life is circling back to Hunter is another complex situation she'll need to tend to, but that can wait.

"Jess," Renee says, seconds before she pulls into her driveway. "Do you have any tips for finding someone on the Internet?"

"Hmm. Depends. Is this a nonspecific question regarding a nonspecific person?"

Renee glares at her child. "Sometimes I regret that you contain fifty percent of my DNA."

Jess goes wide-eyed, then bursts into laughter. It's the most genuine sound they've emitted since showing up on Renee's couch a week ago.

"Holy shit," they say between breaths. "Man, I love when you let your guard down. You're actually pretty funny, Renee."

Renee waves her off but enjoys the new feeling of pride—acceptance?—that hits her square in the chest. "Tips?"

"Details?"

Renee squeezes the steering wheel. "I know a first name, no last name. But I do know the full name of…their ex-spouse." *Well done*, she thinks. Nice and obtuse.

"Easy. Use their first name, then a plus sign, and the ex's full name. You should hit on at least some kind of wedding announcement. That should get you a last name. From there"—Jess spreads their hands wide—"the Internet is your oyster."

"I'm allergic," Renee mutters, which sends Jess off on another run of laughter.

She smiles as she parks and follows Jess into the house, feeling every single emotion the night has delivered.

CHAPTER ELEVEN

Renee skims the website, her finger hovering over the trackpad. A few days have passed since Jess told her they identify as nonbinary, and what Renee has slowly come to realize is that she isn't as informed as she thought she was. While she knows the technical definition of the term and how it could be applied, there are missing pieces when it comes to the person and the term. Jess is her daughter. *No*, her brain interjects. *No more gender-identifying child terminology.*

But that's it, the problem—the mountain Renee is struggling to scale. She has spent twenty-five years having a daughter, and now, suddenly, she no longer has a daughter.

"She is still Jess," she says quietly, then immediately sighs. "They. They are still Jess."

A frustrated grumble surges from her gut and she switches tabs to clear her mind. Unfortunately, she clicks right onto her other search of the morning, the one pertaining to a nonspecific person who is unnervingly specific.

Jess's search tip of combining Hunter's name with Kristina's full name did the trick. Renee now knows a last name (Ciccone) and that Hunter and Kristina used to live in Brooklyn. Presumably, Kristina still does, but Hunter's current job or whereabouts aren't jumping off the page with confetti.

Renee opens a new tab, types in *Hunter Ciccone address*, then repeatedly jabs her backspace button until the letters disappear. Horrified with her newly acquired interest in stalking, she shuts her laptop and stares at it as though it's the perpetrator instead of her own brain's command to her fingers.

"Stop it," she says aloud. Aware that these admonishments are becoming a daily event, she shakes her head while exhaling every bit of breath from her lungs. She releases the energy with the air, hoping for some kind of cleansing or erasure on the inhale.

If only she could do the same with her brain.

Muffled voices from the hallway become louder and then they reach a right-outside-the-door volume. It's Courtney and Kate, and Renee picks up on what sounds like good-natured argumentative tones. She crosses the room and yanks open her door with a flourish.

"And what do we have here?" she asks the two startled faces that blink back at her.

Courtney gestures to Kate, who throws a hand against her hip. "This one still thinks she has more of a right to a TA than I do."

"No, Courtney, I never said it's a *right*. It's a need."

"Seniority!" Courtney shouts.

Both Kate and Renee reel back, and Renee is certain the look on her face mirrors the shocked one on Kate's.

"Did she just yell?" Kate says out of the corner of her mouth.

"More like bark," Renee replies. "Ferociously."

"No," Courtney says, waving a finger between Kate and Renee. "There will be no ganging up on me. I will—I'll leave."

Neither woman responds. Courtney's eyes dart between them. Renee assesses her, noting a tense wildness that wasn't visible earlier in the week. Poor thing. Maybe she really does need a TA.

"Perhaps," Renee begins, resting her hand on Kate's forearm, prepping her for the incoming blow, "you and Kate can work out a way to share her TA."

Kate gasps loudly. Her hand flies to her chest and grasps at the lapel of her navy-blue blazer. Courtney gawks, her eyes so wide they nearly pop right out onto the speckled beige floor, which desperately needs a mopping.

Renee wonders how she ended up with the world's most dramatic professors.

"I'm sure Callie would be happy to help both of you," Renee continues. "It's not that big of a deal, really. You can all work it out."

Now Kate and Courtney seem to have formed a renewed alliance as both are staring at Renee as though she's sprouted a second head, which maybe wouldn't be terrible; that new, pristine brain could come in handy.

"What's the problem?" Renee folds her arms over her chest. She loves her idea. Why these two are reacting so absurdly to it, she really doesn't know.

"Callie?" Courtney finally says, eyeing Renee suspiciously. "As in, Callie Lewes?"

"Obviously."

Kate remains silent while Courtney sputters, "Renee. Are you concussed?"

Renee twirls her finger in a rapid circle. "I don't have time for your little head games. Pun intended. What's the problem?"

"Callie's not my TA," Kate says. Her tone is gentle, but her smile shows confusion. "She was, kind of, but that was two years ago."

"Callie is a professor. You hired her," Courtney adds.

"I know that." Renee does know that. Obviously, she knows that. "What's your TA's name? Allie? Calia? It's close to Callie. I just mixed it up."

Kate's nose wrinkles a bit. "My TA's name is Victor."

Renee runs her hands down the front of her neatly pressed white silk shirt. She knows she can't recover from this extremely uncharacteristic snafu. She also can't leave these two by themselves, lest they have a meeting of the minds about her odd behavior.

"Right. Victor, lovely young man. Courtney, walk with me to Old Main. I have some ideas."

Without waiting for a response, Renee stalks back into her office. She grabs her jacket, stuffs her laptop into her bag, and stalks right back into the hallway, where Courtney is waiting. Kate, smartly, has disappeared.

Given that Courtney towers over Renee, it's difficult to keep up with her long strides. Today, however, she's grateful for the physical challenge. She's not quiet because she's out of breath, for the record. She's thinking. About halfway through their trek across campus, Courtney breaks the awkward ice.

"Is, um, something going on? With you?"

Renee shakes her head, but not too hard because she needs to make sure her hair stays neatly tied into the low chignon she worked it into early this morning. "I'm perfectly fine."

"Look. I know we don't talk like you and Kate talk, but"— Courtney stuffs her hands into the pockets of her leather jacket—"if there's something you want to talk about, I'll listen."

"No need," Renee says brusquely. "Now, about your workload dilemma."

"Okay, it's probably not as bad as I'm making it seem."

"That's a quick turnaround." Renee glances at Courtney, a little disappointed she's not giving more pushback.

Courtney blows out an exasperated breath. "I've been informed by two colleagues that I'm assigning too much work. And that's why I'm feeling overwhelmed with grading."

Renee stays silent, letting Courtney work through her mini therapy session. She could have gladly told her the same thing, but she has no doubt it's Kate, and maybe even Callie, who beat her to it. Some things just sound better coming from colleagues as opposed to bosses.

"I'm looking into ways to scale back for the rest of the semester. And yes, I'll run everything by you before I put any change into effect. I just"—another loud exhale—"I don't want to not do enough. I know you understand that."

She does, maybe too well. Renee is very aware of the reputations that precede both Courtney and her: hard-asses who demand a lot of thinking and a lot of written product. She and Courtney suffer from the same ailment of Doing Too Much, which spreads neatly into the highly contagious student plague of Needing to Do Too Much.

"I do," she assures Courtney. "Perhaps we should chip in for a group therapy session."

Courtney laughs, then stops suddenly when she sees Renee's expression. "Oh, shit. I thought that was a joke."

"It is."

"You're not laughing."

Renee shrugs. "Hence the need for group therapy."

Courtney snorts and they fall back into silence as they climb the steps leading up to Old Main. The sight of the building always gives Renee a renewed sense of purpose. The ancient brick that wraps around the exterior of the wide building, the creaky hardwood floors that hold the footsteps of an inestimable number of students and professors alike. The doors in this building are far less temperamental than those in Berringer Hall, as is the heating and cooling system, but the air itself is grandiose and breathes nothing but pure academia.

Renee inhales deeply as they make their way to the third floor. When she stops outside the door leading to the dean's secretary and Franklin's inner annex, Courtney holds up her hand.

"I'm just here for the walk." She shakes her head like a stubborn child. "I am not going in there."

"I don't need you to," Renee says airily. "You can sit and chat with Donna or go back to Berringer."

"You don't need a bodyguard?"

Renee shoots Courtney a murderous look as she pushes open the office door. "When have I ever?"

Courtney leans against the doorframe, holding the door open with her foot, and waves at Donna, Franklin's overbearingly kind secretary. "I seem to remember a time or two when you drank—"

"Donna!" Renee exclaims. "So lovely to see you, and oh! Look at that gorgeous new top!" She turns slightly and sends Courtney a second homicidal glance, this one hurling knives from her eyes. "Is Franklin running late again?"

Donna shimmies her yoga-toned seventy-year-old shoulders in Renee's direction. "I thought you'd like this, dear. And he'll be ready for you shortly."

Renee glares at Courtney. "You can leave now."

"I was just about to, but first—"

Courtney is unceremoniously cut off by Franklin's door opening and two people emerging from his office. Renee, still eyeing Courtney with complex desires of extermination, sees the shift in her expression. Whoever is with Franklin must be someone Courtney doesn't know, which is odd. She's as familiar with the staff at Pennbrook as Renee is, if not more so since she tends to be social with other departments. Curious, Renee turns to identify the stranger.

She staggers a bit when she comes face-to-face with Hunter, who does a double take, then points at Renee.

"Renee Lawler," she says, voice smooth and revealing zero connection to the surprise shining in those mesmerizing brown eyes.

"Ah," Renee manages. She tries to quell the panicked mixture of feelings rising within her. "Yes."

Hunter smiles, the surprise ebbing away as it's replaced with an expression Renee can't define. "I wondered if I'd run into you."

At that, Renee feels the betrayal of a blush storming her cheeks. "Well. Here I am."

"You two know each other?" This comes from Franklin, who's leaning against Donna's desk, watching the awkward interaction with amusement.

Naturally, just as Renee steadily proclaims, "No," Hunter responds, "A bit." They stare at each other. Just the sight of Hunter is enough to take Renee right back to Vermont, to watching her flawless, strong hands pass Renee a glass of wine. It takes a monumental amount of control to avoid looking at Hunter's hands right now.

"It's nice to see you," Renee says, her voice clipped. She registers her mistake immediately and takes a few quick steps toward Franklin's office. "Franklin, let's get started. I have a class in two hours."

She stops in the doorway, waiting for Franklin to follow her. Instead, she hears Hunter amiably introducing herself to Courtney, who supplies all the natural confidence and kindness that evaporated from Renee the moment she locked eyes with Hunter. Discomfort rages within her and she impatiently taps her foot—snug in a four-inch fuchsia high heel that balances out the boring navy blue of her skirt—as she registers Franklin discussing something with Donna. Renee has half a mind to walk into that office and sit herself down without another word to any of the four people in the outer office, but that would be outlandishly rude, even for her.

Finally, Franklin brushes past Renee, beckoning her into his office, but she hesitates. Without permission, her neck swivels enough to catch Hunter's eye. A tiny thrill ripples through her when she realizes Hunter was waiting for her to turn around.

"I'll see you around," Hunter says. With a parting smile that could melt any glacier rooted in the newly tempestuous seas of Renee's body, she leaves, waving goodbye to Donna.

"Renee? I thought you were in a hurry," Franklin says.

"No—yes. I am." She takes one last look at the door Hunter disappeared behind before stepping further into Franklin's office to discuss that damn budget yet again.

CHAPTER TWELVE

There's an unmistakable comfort in the sound of a classroom, post-lecture, mid-student application. The murmurs, the smatters of "Oh!" and "Wait a minute" and "What about this?" that punctuate moments of connection. Scribbles of pens and pencils over notebook paper (Renee respectfully bans laptops from her classes, having suffered through far too many distracting incidents with them), crinkling pages, a screech of a highlighter marking up a text that can no longer be returned for full price.

It's a very specific type of Eden, and Renee stands before it, eyes bright as the sun, taking in the lush garden of growing knowledge before her. She's extra proud of this class, a group of mostly juniors and seniors, many of whom she's instructed previously. They're in the thick of applying their prior knowledge of literary theory and criticism. Under Renee's guidance, they've taken off their gardening gloves and are elbow-deep in the weeds, tugging strands of Creeping Charlie to redistribute the soil of their thinking patterns. Their arms are scraped by clusters of thistle, fingernails caked with dirt. She's taught them to bypass the threads of poison ivy and stop aiming for the roses. The overgrowth has been neatly trimmed back, allowing more space for the sun and rain to seep in.

Renee rests her hand on the top of her lecture podium. The garden isn't perfect, not yet, but there are far more flowers than weeds blooming in these young adult brains.

While she loves that this group competently works independently of her, she doesn't love the time it leaves her to let her own brain get clogged up by errant brambles. She just can't seem to get herself back to the version of Dr. Renee Lawler she was prior to going to that godforsaken conference in Vermont. This alone—the hyperfocus on one event—is unlike her. The mismatch between how she feels and how she'd like to feel hangs heavily over her, like an overcast sky threatening to dump a storm that she is wholly unprepared for.

Hunter. What in the entire fuck of all fucks is Hunter Ciccone doing here, at Pennbrook, on *Renee's* turf? She hasn't been able to get answers (not that she's asked, because how could she pass that off as being casual and nonspecific?), and the mere sight of Hunter was enough to throw Renee so far off her usual tracks that she hasn't even been able to continue her Internet searching.

After meeting with Franklin yesterday, Renee hustled back to Berringer with her head down. She ignored Audrey, ignored Kate, slammed her office door, and sat, frozen, at her desk for twenty-two minutes. Then, on a will of their own, her hands typed out a terse email, hit send, and picked up all her things.

She was home, newly frozen on the edge of her bed, within ten minutes.

It was the second time in all of Pennbrook history that Dr. Renee Lawler had *canceled a class*.

She spent her time at home staring at the walls, eyeing the ceilings suspiciously. Every so often she leered at her reflection in a mirror, searching for whatever had gone wrong. Each time, she came up empty, perplexed, and annoyed. If Jess were there, they'd tell Renee to "get a grip," but Jess was in Brooklyn. Renee didn't miss them, exactly, but she wouldn't have minded a dose of the "get your shit together" attitude only Jess could supply.

Alas, Renee had gotten her shit together by boldly ignoring the quietly raging sea of confusion inside her. She anxiety-cleaned the kitchen then let herself be distracted by a documentary she'd been meaning to watch. This morning she'd gotten up earlier than usual, gone for a brisk walk around the neighborhood, and landed in her office before seven a.m. She was a professional at feelings-avoidance and now was her time to shine.

"Dr. Lawler?"

The student's voice brings Renee back from her seesaw thoughts. She glances around the room, noticing that everyone is packing up.

She looks at the student before her. JT. Bright, bright kid with absolutely terrible fashion sense. Then again, it was possible the terrible fashion sense was…fashionable. Renee shudders.

"Yes, JT?"

"Do you have a minute?"

Ah yes, this was probably about JT's last essay, which had earned them a B+ instead of an A. It just wasn't up to par.

"Yes. Would you like to chat here or in my office?" The rest of the class has left, calling back goodbyes, thank-yous, and well-wishes for the weekend.

"Oh. Here's fine. It's quick." JT runs their hand through a mess of platinum blond hair. "I just wanted to thank you."

Renee involuntarily steps back. Maybe this isn't about the essay.

"You're the first professor I've had who hasn't misgendered me," JT says in a rush. "I get that it can be, like, weird or whatever. Confusing? I don't know." They exhale loudly, their apple cheeks puffing out dramatically. "My generation gets it, mostly, but my professors aren't in my generation? So it's different?"

Renee nods sagely, forgiving the statements posing as questions in JT's nervous speech. "The age gap has become a chasm."

"Yes! Exactly."

"Are you inferring that I'm old?"

"Wait, no. No! Not at all, no, I'm so sorry."

Renee smiles. "It was a joke."

"Oh. Right." JT wrinkles their nose. "You don't joke a lot."

Echoes of her recent conversations with Jess and Courtney sift through Renee's head. Should she joke more? She'll consider it.

"Anyway," JT says, clearly nervous about the joke statement. "Thank you. I should go."

"Wait." Renee pauses, wanting to be sure she gets this right. "You don't need to thank me. It's important to me that I honor my students' identities. I should be thanking you for giving me the opportunity to do so."

The expression on JT's face is one Renee has never before seen on a student, and likely never will again. Even JT seems to realize they are on the receiving end of an extremely rare version of Renee, one not many people can claim to have witnessed.

"Okay." JT nods. "You're welcome. And also thank you."

"Have a good weekend, JT."

Renee's phone buzzes with a text as JT waves and exits the classroom. It's Audrey, asking her when she's coming back, because someone's there to inspect the wiring in her office. As Renee packs up and walks back to her office, she remembers Courtney saying something about how Pennbrook is finally updating all things technology. It's been a long time coming but Renee is going to freak out if someone forces her to stop asking for paper copies of essays.

The English offices are unusually loud for a Friday afternoon. Normally people have started leaving for the weekend by this time, but there are three professors clustered around Audrey's desk. They don't give her a second glance as she passes them and Audrey nods toward Renee's office, giving her the go-ahead.

"No," she says as she rounds the corner and looks at the space in front of her closed office door.

The spoken word was an accident. She believes it's also an accident that Hunter Ciccone is standing in front of her office.

With all the noise behind her, it's impossible that anyone, including Hunter, heard the slipped word. But Hunter looks up, a smile spreading evenly across her face as she looks at Renee, who has taken up human ice sculpture once again and is frozen in place at the start of the hallway leading to her office.

"Dr. Lawler," Hunter says in greeting. "I hope I'm not inconveniencing you."

CHAPTER THIRTEEN

It takes Renee several seconds to melt her limbs enough to move toward her office. Part of her doesn't care if Hunter thinks she's walking strangely, what with blocks of ice encasing her quads, but a larger part of her is screaming, *Of course she notices, get your shit together!*

There's another small voice edging into the internal conversation. This one has many opinions about Renee's outfit, and the excellent choice of matte black heels that are simple enough to allow her stellar calves to steal the show.

Also, there's the part about the pale-gray skirt currently hugging her hips being an inch shorter than the majority of her skirts.

Renee brushes past Hunter, careful not to touch her, but Hunter steps aside before the opportunity presents itself. Chafed, and irritated that she feels that way, Renee opens her office door with more force than required.

"Does this one stick like the one out there?" Hunter asks, hovering in the doorway.

"No," Renee says, the word encompassing her available lexicon.

"Huh. Are you always that rough with it?"

Renee, her back to Hunter, swallows what feels like an entire packet of Pop Rocks. "No," she repeats.

Hunter pulls a Kate and waits Renee out. She does it just as casually, even more patiently. Renee busies herself with unloading her bag, pushing her desk chair back and forth, staring out the window, tapping her feet. She glares at a bookshelf, wondering if it needs to be emptied, dusted, and reorganized. Probably, but she'd need spray and a dust rag for that, which means she'd have to pass by Hunter and go all the way to Audrey's desk—it's not her greatest avoidant idea, so she dismisses it.

Biting the inside of her cheek doesn't help, so Renee turns to face the present problem. Hunter hasn't moved from the doorway.

No, she's standing there, every bit as *Hunter* as Renee's memory recalls. If she's not mistaken, Hunter's wearing the same perfectly fitting navy khakis coupled with dark-brown oxfords. The white button-down is gone, replaced by an oatmeal-colored fisherman's sweater that hugs Hunter's frame without being tight or form-fitting. Renee avoids looking at anything from the neck up. Locking eyes with Hunter from ten feet away in the hallway was more than enough for one day.

"Rough day?"

"No."

Hunter shakes her head. "All right. I don't want to be in your way, so I'll get to work and get out of here as soon as I can."

Renee watches as Hunter unpacks several items from her backpack. She has no idea what any of them are for, but Hunter clearly has a practiced method with the objects.

"Oh," Renee says, slow awareness finally dawning on her. "You're here to check my wiring."

It sounds like Hunter stifles a laugh before she turns her head to Renee and says, "Yep."

Several moments pass before Renee feels her entire body flame with a feeling somewhere between embarrassment and arousal. Recognizing the latter feeling, dormant as it's been, only increases the former. She's certain she'll burn to ash within minutes.

She hears Jess's bossy voice in her head, commanding her to get a fucking grip.

The problem is that she can't quite get that grip when she's around Hunter. The very thing—person—causing her to lose her steadfast grasp on her perfectly ordered life and internal universe is now kneeling on the floor of her office, arranging a magical set of tools.

"This will only take me a few minutes," Hunter says, standing up but keeping her back to Renee. "Your secretary gave me a full list of dead spots in other offices and that one weird spot in the conference room. She didn't know anything about your office, though."

Renee bites the tip of her tongue. In other words, this experience could have been avoided if Renee had only been more forthcoming about the fact that she gets very poor Internet connection near her window. Convenient.

"The window," Renee says, welcoming new words into her vocabulary. "There's a dead spot there."

Hunter nods and does whatever it is she does with her tools, walking slowly around the office, taking extra time near the window.

"You seem really thrown by me being here." The words are casual, the tone even more so, and Renee feels a surge of violence.

"Of course I am," she snaps. "I was perfectly fine with knowing I'd never see you again, and suddenly here you are, all over my campus."

Hunter doesn't say anything. She continues using her special little tools, making insipid little notes in a shiny little Moleskine notebook she's pulled from her back pocket that perfectly hugs a rather nice—*no*.

Finally, Renee hears her say, "Go on."

So, tearing her eyes from Hunter's lovely back pockets, she does.

"What are you even doing here, Hunter? Of all the places you could go, or work, if that's what you're doing, you had to come *here*? Did you know I was here? Is that why you came here?" Renee picks up a magazine and fans herself, thankful that Hunter isn't looking at her to see how vibrantly red her face must be. "If I find out the reason you're here is because of me, I—I'll do something about that."

No response, then, "Keep going."

Renee throws up her hands, the magazine flying, hitting the wall before sliding into the garbage can by her office door. To her horror, she realizes her door is open. She stomps the two steps to it and slams it.

"You can't be here. You have to leave."

"Well, the thing is, Renee, I can be here." Hunter turns around then, looking Renee straight in the eye. "And my company signed a contract, so I have to be here."

"Your company," she repeats.

"TruSystems." Hunter gestures with one of her tools. "We do everything: wiring, systems, maintenance. We have a couple branches."

"*Your* company." Back to the limited vocabulary, apparently.

Hunter nods. "I co-own it with my brother."

"You co-own a company with your brother." Okay, perhaps she's become a parrot.

"Yes. Renzo. He takes care of the background stuff, sends me out to be the face of the work." Hunter wiggles her eyebrows. "I'm the better-looking child."

"And you know about wiring."

"I have a degree in electrical engineering, and one in computer science. I do it all."

The final phrase sends a shiver through Renee's body, which has apparently decided to shift out of the wildfire warning zone. The abrupt change in temperature leaves her mute.

Hunter watches her, keeping her distance as though she's observing a wild animal that's been removed from its natural habitat. The analogy, Renee has to admit, isn't too far off. She's not clear where she is or what's happening to her.

"We can..." Hunter trails off, still watching Renee carefully. "Do you want to talk about this?" she finishes, her voice so low Renee has to strain to hear her.

"Wires?"

Hunter cocks her head to the side, a move Renee's seen hundreds of people do over the span of her forty-seven years, but never before has the motion struck such a tender chord inside her. "I mean, sure, we can talk about my job. But that's not what I meant. And I'm pretty sure you know what I meant."

Renee stiffens and backs against the closed door. She's barely managing the internal war her body is waging, and Hunter wants to *talk*? Can't she see that Renee is six words away from self-combustion?

"I don't think that's necessary," she gets out. She winces, realizing the doorknob is viciously pressing into her lower back.

"Okay," Hunter says easily, moving back to her backpack. As she methodically returns her tools to her bag, she adds, "If you change your mind, you know where to find me."

"No, I don't," Renee says. She doesn't know why she says it. There's absolutely no reason for her to say it.

"Your secretary has my card." Hunter slings her bag over her shoulder. Renee allows herself 2.7 seconds to bask in the warm cocoa glow of Hunter's eyes. She doesn't understand how there's warmth coming from her; by Renee's rationale, Hunter should be cold and done with her. "Your office is in good shape, by the way. Just that one spot by the window, like you said."

"Can you fix it?"

"The new wiring coupled with the system overhaul that we're doing should take care of all the dead spots, but I'll be sure to double-check this one for you."

"Thank you." Renee straightens her shoulders, and the doorknob takes the opportunity to thrust into her once again.

"You're welcome, Renee." Hunter stands in front of her. She seems to be waiting for something, but Renee has no brain power left to figure out what she wants.

"What?" she asks.

Hunter smiles and gestures to the door, which, yes that's right, is blocked by Renee's terrified body. "I know you want me out of here, but you're going to have to move in order for that to happen."

Renee quickly steps aside. Hunter steps forward, reaches for the doorknob, and pauses. She waits for Renee to meet her eyes.

"I promise I won't make this difficult for you," she says, her voice just above a whisper. And before Renee can summon up a response, Hunter has once again disappeared behind a closed door.

The ice shatters, leaving Renee with a sheer frost covering her body, ghostly cold shivering her most sensitive stretches of skin.

The problem is, the Hunter of her memory and the Hunter of her very recent present are one and the same. Renee had nearly tricked herself into believing it was all a fluke, that there wasn't a pull where there is usually a push. That she isn't curious—a baseline word that can't contain the true breadth of what Renee is thinking and feeling. Her shoulders tense and she internally curses Hunter for showing up in her world and messing up all her neatly ordered thoughts by simply existing.

Hunter Ciccone. Here, at Pennbrook, for what seems to be an undetermined amount of time.

In all her wild, jagged thoughts, Renee hadn't imagined that. Having no choice but to accept it, she decides right then and there that the next time she encounters Hunter, neither will wonder which one of them is in control of this situation.

CHAPTER FOURTEEN

The wine is fighting back. There was a feisty war on Friday night, and Renee thought she'd won the upper hand fair and square, but now, in the blinking late autumn sunlight of Saturday morning, she admits there's a chance she was wrong.

It's Courtney's fault, really. After Hunter left Berringer Hall, Renee locked herself in her office and paced a worn trail of distress into the already distressed hardwood floor. Layer upon layer of thought and internal dialogue consumed her until Courtney nearly broke down the door with her impassioned knocking. Renee tried to put on a good front but failed spectacularly; however, Courtney seemed oblivious to Hunter's visit and assumed Renee was deep-diving into some kind of work-related crisis. It was so much easier to flow with that assumption, and Renee had soon found herself at Fiona's, the poorly lit, heavily poured bar several blocks from campus.

The fact that Renee can't remember how many glasses of wine she had is Courtney's fault, too. She sits up with a start, cursing the steady drumbeat in her head. She'll need to take a walk of shame to retrieve her car from campus. Courtney's gem of a husband, Nick, had gleefully dropped Renee off before ferrying his irritated wife home.

Renee rubs her temples. That's right. Courtney had been in a terrible mood. She wishes she could remember the cause of that foul mood, but nothing other than a fog of alcohol is coming to mind.

Her feet hit the plush off-white carpet of her bedroom. She tentatively wiggles her toes, hoping for the best. The room isn't spinning, which is a good sign, but Renee feels as though she's been hit by a truck that reversed over her a second time, just to make sure she was down for the count.

She makes it to her en suite bathroom without incident. It's the reflection in the mirror that caps off the rising terrible feeling. Renee peers at herself, her pointer finger prodding the bags under her dull blue eyes. She's never seen this shade of pale on her own face before, and she doesn't like it.

"Enough," she says quietly, as much to herself as to her reflection.

It's no secret to anyone that Renee likes wine. She really, truly likes it: the taste, the flavor, the sensation, the release. She can acknowledge there have been several times when she's had too much to drink. But never has it seemed like a problem, per se. A crutch? Sometimes. An escape? Yes. A liquid eraser? Absolutely.

But Renee has lived enough life and drank enough wine to understand she can't rely on it forever…nor as much as she has in recent years. So while she'd love to blame her current state of affairs on Courtney, she can admit she's the only person deserving of blame.

After showering, Renee eyes her reflection once more, hoping for a change. Some color has returned to her cheeks, but her eyes maintain a lifelessness that she does not care for one bit. Hoping it's not too cold outside, she dresses in leggings and an oversized sweatshirt. A brisk walk should help blow away the rest of her brain fog.

She trails her fingertips over the banister as she descends the stairs leading to the kitchen. She prefers the main staircase, the one at the front of the house, because of the landing that sits midway on the descent. It's a regal entrance into the foyer, but since Renee is currently feeling more like hired help than a princess, she slinks down the back stairs, leaving the light off.

She regrets this choice when something brushes against her ankles, leaving her no choice but to shriek and flatten herself against the wall. If she had any trace of a hangover, it's gone now, thanks to the shot of adrenaline.

Heart pounding, Renee fumbles her way down the rest of the stairs sideways, never detaching her back from the wall. When she reaches the kitchen, she flips the light switch and peers at the stairs.

"Don't be so dramatic," Jess says, coming into the kitchen. "You'll scare him."

Renee's eyes dart from the staircase to Jess, then back to the staircase. "Who is 'him'? And when did you get here?"

Jess gives her a strange look. "Uh, yesterday afternoon? You said hello to me when you came home, reeking like a vineyard."

It's a nice punch of self-awareness and self-loathing straight to Renee's gut, which is already tender from the previous night's events. "Right. Of course." Renee points a shaky finger toward the stairs. "And what is that?"

"Oh my God, seriously, Renee," Jess mutters before jogging up to the top of the stairs. They come back down with a purring, creamsicle-colored mass in their arms. "This is Mr. Purrington."

"A cat?"

"Obviously." Jess picks up one of Mr. Purrington's paws and waves it at Renee. "This is your grandmother," they coo sweetly into the cat's ear. "You can't trip her on the stairs, tempting as it may be."

Renee moves around the kitchen, not because she's not interested in meeting her grandchild, but because she desperately needs a glass of lemonade. As she pours it, she listens to Jess baby-talk the cat, who actually is quite darling.

The full glass disappears in three large swallows. Thankfully, it does its sugary, acidic trick, and Renee instantly feels more alert.

"Jess," she says, smoothing her hair into a damp ponytail. "Why is your cat here?"

Jess nuzzles his bright pink nose before gently placing him on the floor. "Where I go, he goes."

Renee gasps a bit as she watches Mr. Purrington sashay toward the inviting sofa in the great room. "That cat is massive."

"He's a Maine coon, or at least, like, ninety percent." Jess has a very proud parental expression on their face. "I've had him since he was a kitten. He has a really cool personality, kind of dog-like, so don't worry. You'll like him."

"I have nothing against cats," Renee says, watching to make sure Mr. Purrington doesn't raise his claws to her pristine furniture. "But I'm not understanding why he's here."

Jess is silent, fidgeting with the strings of their hoodie. Renee inspects their face, looking for clues. Like a zap of lightning, a memory from last night flashes in her mind: Nick dropping her off in the driveway where Jess's car was parked, and there was Jess, two duffel bags hanging from their shoulders. Renee *had* said hello to them before breezing into the house and going straight to her bedroom.

But on the way, she passed the guest room. The memory of the image flickers into Renee's mind. The door was open, and the ceiling light was on. The room, previously cleaned from Jess's last visit, was already in a slight disarray—a pile of boxes in the corner, a cat carrier just inside the door, and a giant blue suitcase at the foot of the bed.

"Oh dear," Renee says now, widening her eyes. "You're actually moving in."

"It's temporary," Jess says immediately. "I just need some time away from the city."

"But why? I thought everything was going well."

"Well, it's not." Jess slumps onto a stool at the island.

Renee waits, trying to summon Kate and her infallible patience, but she can't. Patience has never been her forte.

"Jessica, it's perfectly fine that you stay for a while." Renee tests the truth of her statement and finds it's not a complete lie, but she's also not sure how she feels about the undetermined length of the visit. She notices Jess is shooting her a look and she reels back a step, hoping to God the child can't read her mind. She quickly realizes her mistake. "Sorry. Jess." Satisfied,

Jess slumps back over. "It's fine," Renee repeats. "I just…Well. Right. I hope that…If you want to…"

Seemingly amused by Renee's inability to make a full statement, Jess perks up and smiles. "Are you trying to be a caring, interested mother right now?"

Renee scoffs. "I'm trying to say that if you want to talk about what's going on, I'm happy to listen." She narrows her eyes. "But not if you're going to be an ungrateful brat about it."

"I'm so proud of you." Jess laughs. "Who knew you had it in you, Renee?"

Considering her overall state of mind, a casual ribbing from Jess is not what Renee needs right now. She reaches for her phone then remembers it's still upstairs (well, she *thinks* it's upstairs; she hasn't actually seen it since sitting in a dark corner of Fiona's last night). Fine. She doesn't need the distraction of a podcast. She only needs fresh air and physical movement, and she needs it now.

"Where are you going?" Jess asks as Renee walks toward the hallway leading to the front door.

"Oh no," Renee says, turning to face Jess. Her misguided, angered confusion comes out in a rush. "You don't get to be my babysitter. Under no circumstances do I need to report to you or tell you where I'm going. This is my house, Jess. Mine. We are both grown wom—adults. For as long as you stay here, I will treat you as such and expect you to do the same for me."

"It was a simple question, Renee." Jess shrugs. "You don't have to be manic about it."

Resuming her walk to the front door, Renee snaps, "Who raised you?"

"Not you!" Jess calls to Renee's retreating form.

When she hits the front porch and the door is shut firmly behind her, Renee raises her hand to her mouth. She wasn't expecting the sting of tears in her eyes, or the thud of emptiness in her gut.

She wasn't expecting Jess, or Mr. Purrington.

She never expected Hunter Ciccone, the first time or the second.

And above all else, she never expected to watch herself fast-forward, no seat belt, into a crisis she cannot name.

Three quick, chilly miles later, a winding route that eventually led her to her car, Renee slips through the front door and pads down the hallway toward the great room. She's sweaty and unkempt, but she needs to talk to Jess.

Not finding them lounging on the couch, Renee peeks into the other rooms before she marches upstairs. She can hear the low beat of music coming from the closed door to the guest room—or what she now supposes is Jess's room.

Renee knocks hard, twice, and Jess opens the door almost immediately. Mr. Purrington follows them, sniffing Renee's socks before winding himself around her legs.

Jess smiles down at the cat. "I knew he'd like you."

The simple turn of phrase turns Renee's confidence into something mushy. *How?* she wants to ask. *How did you know he'd like me? What do you know about me that would make you think that?*

Renee clears her throat against the swell of emotion threatening to spill out. She does not care for emotions, especially when others can see them. She'll let them out in a hot shower in fifteen minutes.

"Jess," she begins. "I have a question for you."

Jess straightens their posture and looks at her. There's a veil over their eyes and Renee wishes it wasn't there…but she understands why it is. "Okay. You can ask, but I may not be ready to answer it."

Renee nods as though she was expecting that response, which she somewhat was. Jess, after all, is made of her DNA. "Your cat's name is Mr. Purrington." She waits for Jess's nod. "I'm wondering how you know he's a mister. I mean, certainly the veterinarian can verify he has male genitalia, but has Purrington himself communicated to you that he identifies as male?"

Jess's eye roll hits the stratosphere before their shining blue eyes circle back to Earth and settle on their mother. A genuine smile tugs at their lips. "Are you hungry? I was about to make BLTs for lunch."

"I'd love a BLT. Let me shower and change and I'll help you."

Jess waves her off. "I can handle it. Come down when you're ready."

The two part ways, Jess heading downstairs and Renee continuing to her bedroom with Mr. Purrington trotting beside her. She glances down at the fluffy orange and white cat, then kneels before her bedroom door and offers him her hand for a sniffing. He does a thorough inspection, complete with little huffs and a tentative lick of Renee's knuckle, before butting his head against her hand. She strokes his fur, surprised at how unbearably soft it is. The purrs she receives in return nearly shake the floor beneath them.

"I think you like me," she whispers. "I think I might like you, too."

CHAPTER FIFTEEN

"I know it's not my best work. I know that you know I can do much better. I'm not asking for a rewrite, or even an opportunity to resubmit the same paper after fixing those embarrassing errors."

Renee taps her pen on her desk as she takes in the student before her. Viola Kensington, a graduate student who has done nothing but impress Renee for years, is nearly in tears. She's right: Her latest essay is below her caliber of achievement. Renee was floored when she read it, certain that the wrong name had somehow affixed itself to the front page.

"Then what are you asking?"

Viola shows no indication that she's thrown by Renee being unmoved by her emotional state. She presses her hands into her knees and takes a shaky breath. "For compassion."

Renee balks, then gawks, then laughs. Viola's head dips lower.

"I didn't mean to laugh," Renee says. "It's just that no one has ever asked me for that. Not so boldly, anyway."

"Well," Viola mumbles, "there's a first time for everything."

The two sit in an impasse of stubborn silence. Renee's certain Viola is waiting for her to ask why, exactly, she's in need of compassion. But that would require a foray into the emotional dregs of a young woman's life, and Renee isn't willing to go there.

A knock on Renee's office door adds to the building pressure in the room, and hoping an ajar door will help decompress the thick air, Renee calls out, "Come in!"

She doesn't miss the incredulous look Viola shoots her.

Callie Lewes leans into the doorway, takes one look at Viola, and immediately backs into the hallway, calling, "Sorry! I can wait!"

"No, no, it's fine," Renee says. "Viola and I were just wrapping up."

Callie returns to the doorframe and looks directly at Renee. Aha. There's something going on in that look, Renee realizes. She glances at Viola and wonders when the young woman began shrinking down into the seat of the hard wooden chair.

"Professor Lewes," Renee says calmly. "How can I help you?"

A sheet of paper appears in front of Callie's face. "When you have a moment, I'd like your input on this list."

"What is"—Renee gestures with her non-pen-tapping hand—"the list?"

"Poems." Callie peeks over the top of the paper. "For the APIDA heritage celebration."

Renee's pen lands hard on her desk. "That's in May. Isn't it still autumn?"

The paper shakes once, equally hard. "We're trying to stay ahead of the game."

A quick look at Viola confirms Renee's suspicions. She's gone a ghostly shade of white and appears to have marbleized into a statue. Renee's not sure if she's even breathing.

Renee stands and walks to the door, taking the paper from Callie. "I'll look it over and get back to you by the end of the week."

A quick nod and Callie's gone, fleeing from the scene of a crime Renee is slowly beginning to solve.

"Viola," she says, placing the list on her desk. "Come walk with me."

The walk to the campus library is long enough for one of Renee's practiced metaphorical chats about focusing on academics instead of personal connections and short enough to spare Viola any embarrassment at having to confirm or deny Renee's oblique insinuations. By the time they reach the sprawling stairs leading to the library, Viola's breathing has returned to normal, and her cheeks are rosy both with the cold and with understanding. She thanks Renee and disappears into the slow packs of students cruising the campus.

Renee watches her go. She ignores the tug of protection she feels for the young woman and, satisfied her one-sided discussion soothed Viola's wounded ego, walks into the library.

She breathes deeply, taking in the intoxicating scent of a well-loved building full of books and knowledge. The quiet murmur that accompanies the scent is Renee's favorite kind of ASMR. It's loud enough to dull her own thinking, but overlaps and threads in a way that makes it impossible to know what anyone is actually saying.

As she walks through the entryway, Renee waves to the hipster-looking young man at the information desk. He salutes her—probably a former student—and she carries on, making her way past the clusters of tables until she reaches the reference collection.

Some professors in her department prefer to have TAs or favorite students run library errands for them, but Renee never misses an opportunity to lose herself in the stacks. It's the one place where she feels at peace. The books exist. They don't talk to her, don't ask questions that don't have clear answers. They simply sit, willing to be perused. Willing to be safely explored.

Idly, she walks, trailing her fingers over the diverse textures of the language and linguistics book spines. She doesn't have a specific errand today, but she did need a quick walk to get her brain ready for her evening graduate-level class. It's her first time teaching the Race and Religion in Early Modern Literature course, and though she exemplifies confidence in the classroom, she worries she's not doing the material justice. Thankfully, the class is composed of a stellar group of academically-focused students who keep Renee on her toes while providing valuable, positive feedback.

Renee pauses at the floor-to-ceiling window at the end of the row. She'll have to talk to Callie about what appears to be a misdirected crush on Viola's end. She has no doubt that Callie—

The sentence piles up on itself, a single car crash in Renee's brain. She blinks away the haze of burning rubber and steps quickly to the side so that she's hidden behind the tall bookshelf as the voices swoop nearer.

"And over here, too. The students complain that this study area has a weak signal."

There's no response to the sentence. Renee bites her lip.

"See that table there?" A brief pause indicating a nod. "That's the worst of it."

"Wow, yeah, this is a dead zone." Renee tastes blood and releases her lip, unwillingly leaning toward the sound of Hunter's voice. "Good, this helps." There's a shuffle of noise, a zipper unzipping. An unbridled shiver rips through Renee's body. "Let me jot down some info."

The original voice picks up the conversation. It sounds like Heidi Baker-Kent, the librarian who specializes in all things STEM. Despite that smear of character, Renee quite likes her.

She's also very, very attractive, donning large glasses that only add to her sex appeal, and typically wearing very, very high heels.

Renee drops her eyes down to her feet and flexes one foot. Sexy footwear: check. She's certain Heidi's heels can't compare with this pair of maroon leather four inchers.

She strains to hear whatever Heidi is droning on about. Instead, a flirty giggle floats over to Renee's ears. Her mouth gapes. Heidi is—no, Heidi is *married*. To a man! But that— Renee gasps. A second coquettish giggle, bookended by soft murmurs, has zoomed around the stacks and hit her square in the face.

Heidi Baker-Kent, STEM librarian, is flirting with Hunter. *The nerve of that bespectacled heterosexual hussy.* Renee's spine goes rigid. She has to see it to believe it, as if the fucking giggles aren't enough evidence.

She arches onto her tiptoes—why, she has no idea, because the floor is carpeted and will mask anything outside of stomping—and takes one perilous step to her right. She grips the side of the steel shelf and leans her body just enough to catch a glimpse of Hunter leaning over a table, writing something down in her perfect little Moleskine notebook. And yes, there's fucking Heidi Baker-Kent, doing her own leaning—palms pressed on the table, arms squeezed to her sides just so, giving Hunter a straight shot of busty cleavage. Renee cannot compete with that cleavage. It's pale, almost milky-white, downright satiny from this angle. Softness exudes from the tops of Heidi's breasts, the tantalizing shadowed line between them begging—

A slam of blush hits Renee hard, yanking a full breath out of her. She's always noticed Heidi Baker-Kent's cleavage—it's impossible not to—but never before has she, well, *looked* at it.

Another giggle erupts from the table and, struck by that and her own breast-epiphany, Renee takes a poorly decided step backward, loses her balance, and grasps wildly at the bookshelf. Her finger catches the edge of a Chomsky text and it drops to the ground, a sad line of its brethren following suit.

She'd like very much to hiss a string of expletives, but mortification takes over and she practically jumps around the shelf, hoping against hope that no one noticed the sudden and invisibly caused parade of falling books.

"Is your library haunted?" Hunter asks.

Renee, already dying a slow death of humiliation, feels her life shorten even more when Heidi's cheeky laugh swarms over her like a thick fog.

"I had no idea!" Renee hears the carpet-muffled sound of Heidi tip-tapping toward her. "I'm so glad you were here to witness that! No one would believe me."

Knowing her hiding spot is in dire threat of being exposed, Renee gets back on her tiptoes and scurries to the opposite end of the stacks. She can't bear to be discovered any more than she can stand to hear Heidi Baker-Kent and her breasts continue to charm the theoretical pants off of Hunter.

It's a risk and Renee knows it, but when she reaches the end of the row, she dashes backward in the open aisle. She detours to the opposite side of the reference area, finding herself in the religion section. Great, she could use a little Jesus right now. She takes a few seconds to get air into her lungs, then a few more seconds to settle her somersaulting mind.

She has to get out of this library before Hunter sees her. Renee weighs her options. Thankfully, she knows the library like the back of her hand, but unfortunately, there's only one exit in this area, and to get to it, she has to pass the spot where she last saw Hunter and Heidi.

"Okay," she says, a bit louder than intended. She adjusts her skirt—it was fine—and pats down her hair—also fine. Shoulders back, regular-sized chest out (damn Heidi and her inviting cleavage), Renee nods once before stepping back into the aisle.

The moment her entire body rounds the corner, she hears "Dr. Lawler!" from behind her.

Renee closes her eyes, bidding farewell to her undetected escape. She turns around. "JT," she says, hoping her voice isn't shaking. "What are you doing here?"

"Research," they respond happily. Sure enough, they're holding a stack of books. Of course they are, because they're standing in the damn library. Renee sighs internally. "Our last class inspired me to dig deeper into Critical Race Theory. I think I'm going to use it as my focus for my final paper."

"Wonderful." Renee nods. "Great."

JT grins. "Yeah, honestly, the book on top here is awesome. Okay if I bring it by your office sometime?"

Awesome. Renee would like to weep into the pages of that awesome book, knowing she absolutely will not leave this library without having to face Hunter "Awesome" Ciccone.

"I'd like that," she tells JT. "If you'll excuse me, I have a meeting to get to."

JT attempts to wave with a hand that's holding that wobbly stack of books. Renee leaves them in the middle of the aisle and resumes her new walk of shame.

She holds her breath as she approaches the end of the stacks. She waits to hear her name called again, but there's no sound. Two more steps confirm that the table where Heidi Baker-Kent had so boldly presented her expertly packaged breasts to Hunter is empty.

Renee heaves a glorious sigh of relief and, high on her unexpected clandestine exit, picks up her pace as she exits the reference collection area and spins a quick turn into the awkward space that houses bathrooms and a water fountain before—

"Whoa," Hunter says, grabbing Renee's arms. "Easy."

Renee emits a sound that crosses between a grunt and a moan. She was *so close*. She can see the grand double doors that signal her exit from this cursed library.

It takes her a moment to realize Hunter's still holding her arms because she's unsteady. Apparently that's what happens when one speed walks into another human being.

"I'm sorry," Renee says, manners eclipsing her current state of mind.

"It's okay," Hunter says, loosening her grip but not letting go. "You're in a rush."

"Yes. I have—a class."

Hunter nods, finally releasing Renee's arms. She misses the touch immediately, almost craves its return. In defiance of her traitorous feelings, Renee crosses her arms tightly over her chest.

On second thought, she slides her arms so that they slip under her breasts and arches her back just so, hoping to give Heidi Baker-Kent a cleaved run for her money.

Why not, she thinks. *Two can play.*

"I'm not a professional in this area," Hunter begins, "but I don't think you're wearing the best footwear for speed walking."

Renee opens her mouth, ready to challenge the statement, but pauses when she realizes the truth behind it. Satisfied, she adjusts her arms, smooshing her meager cleavage into something she hopes is tantalizing. Shoes: noticed. Cleavage: in progress.

"You'd be surprised what I can do in these heels." Confidence: double check.

Hunter's expression does not hide a damn thing, and Renee awards herself the Library Flirt Win of the Day. Fuck Heidi Baker-Kent and her sexy oversized glasses and impressive cleavage.

"For example," Renee says, awareness of her flirtation dive-bombing into the confusion that always seems to accompany it, "walk quickly back to Berringer Hall. Nice to see you, Hunter."

She makes it ten steps before Hunter calls after her, and despite the fact that Renee wants nothing more than to own this moment and ignore her, she finds she can't. When she turns to face Hunter, there is no mistaking that grin on her handsome face.

"I think you forgot something." Hunter holds up *On Language*, the very Chomsky book that took the first fall before signaling its friends to join it on the floor.

Renee isn't sure what shade of red her face turns, but she feels every flame of heat from her scalp to her toes as she turns and books it out of the library.

CHAPTER SIXTEEN

The noise of the restaurant sifts in and out of Renee's ears, not distracting enough for her liking. She glides one finger down the side of her water glass. She'd like something stronger but has decided to put a new rule into practice: No alcoholic drinks while sitting alone. It puts a cramp on one of her favorite weekend activities—finding a moody bar to disappear into, a gregarious bartender to observe—but something nameless has shifted inside her. She loves wine, really and truly does, but lately, she's wanted to feel sharper. More aware. And less unprepared.

She smiles down at the table. The thought of being unprepared is foreign. Renee can't recall a time when she was unprepared to the point of being in disarray. Her smile slips when she thinks about recent events, recent people. She's not in disarray and refuses to unravel to that point...but she's past the point of pretending the ground beneath her hasn't begun to quiver with incoming change.

"Sorry we're late," Courtney says. Renee jerks her head up. "This one"—she nods at Kate, who's standing next to her and looking apologetic—"had to explain something to Audrey fifteen different ways before it clicked."

"It's my fault." Kate nods as they sit down with Renee. "I thought she understood that you can't add a PDF directly into a Google doc."

"In her defense, that is one of the more annoying challenges of a Google doc," Courtney says.

Kate readily agrees and Renee listens as the two women launch into a discussion about the pros and cons of Google applications. She watches them as they talk, feeling an unusual moment of gratitude for the presence of these two people in her life. Courtney, much to her own and Renee's chagrin, has been in Renee's life for decades. Over the years, Renee swears nothing has changed about Dr. Courtney Wincheck-Rodriguez. She's just as tall and admirably in shape as she was when Renee met her twenty years ago. The amount of time Courtney's spent playing or coaching basketball is rivaled only by the amount of time she spends grading essays. As always, her plain brown hair is pulled back into a tight, no-nonsense bun. Renee has always liked that there's nothing remarkable about Courtney's appearance. She's so effortlessly real, such a "what you see is what you get" person. That type of personality is exactly what Renee has needed to balance her out, professionally, for all her time spent at Pennbrook University.

And then there's Dr. Kate Jory. The opposite side of the scale, Kate has the uncanny ability to stabilize Renee's unspoken personal needs. It's a cop-out to say there's just *something* about Kate's personality, but it's the best Renee can do. She knew the moment she met Kate that she needed this woman in her life. Never mind her utter brilliance in the classroom and with the written word, there's something beyond that, something intangible but always present. The very vision of Kate is comforting to Renee, though she'd never tell her that. Her cropped dark hair and pale skin illuminate her warm but intense hazel eyes. She's on the shorter side—a juxtaposed visual with Courtney that Renee adores—and curvaceous. Callie, Kate's girlfriend, still claims that Kate is an enigma, and Renee agrees.

She can come across as cold and unfeeling, but when she feels safe with someone, Kate is a ring of warmth and open adoration.

Renee doesn't get swept into that ring very often, but knowing that it's possible is generally enough for her.

It takes her a moment to realize the Google-related debate has stopped and both Courtney and Kate are eyeing her with concerned curiosity.

"Did you solve all of Google's problems?" Renee deflects, not liking those expressions.

Kate and Courtney exchange a loaded glance. "Renee," Kate starts. "Can we cut to the chase?"

"Don't we always?"

Courtney clears her throat. "If you have bad news, just tell us now, okay?"

Renee shakes her head once. "Why would I have bad news?"

Another loaded glance transpires between them. "You summoned us," Kate says gently, "to meet you for dinner."

"You didn't ask," Courtney chimes in. "And that's fine! Perfectly fine. But you kind of…ordered us here."

"Which can only mean that there's something you need to tell us, and since we're here and not at work, we're assuming it's not good news," Kate finishes.

Renee looks back and forth between the two women—her colleagues, primarily, but also two people she considers friends. She wants to laugh but knows it could come across as insulting.

"I don't have any news," she says, breaking the worried tension. "I simply wanted to have a nonwork evening with two good people."

Courtney looks at Kate, but her gaze is settled on Renee. "You're sure?"

"Very." Not at all, but that's beside the point. "Shall we have some drinks?"

This must convince Courtney that all is well because she relaxes immediately and reaches for the drink menu. Kate, however, ever the perceptive one, continues watching Renee until she predictably breaks under Kate's silent spell.

"Jess moved home," Renee blurts out. Damn Kate and her magical ways of getting Renee to be very un-Renee.

"Oh," Kate says, blinking. "Wow, Renee."

Courtney peels her eyes from the drink menu. "What's happening? Who's Jess?"

Kate busies herself with her napkin, abandoning Renee on a deflating raft of avoidance. She glares at her water glass, wishing it were wine. As if summoned by Renee's wishes, the waitress appears to take their drink orders. Once she's gone, however, two pairs of eyes lock on Renee. Kate must have slid Courtney the golden nugget of silent patience, instructing her to use it when she needs Renee to open up.

It's not the first time these two have ganged up on her and she's sure it won't be the last. Honestly, she doesn't even mind; it shows they care.

"Jess is," Renee begins, dropping her eyes to her hands, which are knotted together on her lap. "Jess is my daughter." She shakes her head. "My child."

Courtney looks rightfully confused but Kate's stoic expression doesn't change. Courtney stares down Renee for a few beats, then looks over at Kate. "Wait. Why don't you look surprised, Jory?"

"I told her a bit ago," Renee admits. "It…Well, it just sort of came out." A nervous laugh slips through her lips. "Ironically, so did Jess. As nonbinary."

"Wait. Wait wait wait." Courtney presses both hands against the table. "You have a *child*? As in, one you birthed?" She shakes her head, bun tight and unmoving. "No. You adopted. Right? You definitely adopted. But…what? When? Is this…" She looks back at Kate. "Are you two fucking with me right now?"

"No," Renee says.

Kate shakes her head.

Courtney laughs loudly, but it's a laugh of disbelief, not humor. "I've known you for nearly twenty years, Renee, and not once in that span of time did you feel the need to tell me you have a real, actual child roaming the earth? I thought we—I thought we were friends."

"Courtney," Kate says gently, laying a hand on Courtney's arm. "Don't be harsh."

"I'm not! But can you understand why I'm shocked?"

"Yes, absolutely, but I don't understand why you're angry." Kate's voice is the epitome of calm, something Renee knows will only further irritate Courtney.

Red rims Courtney's cheekbones. "Because! This isn't like having a bad hangnail and not telling me about it in a text message." She looks back at Renee. "Why didn't you tell me about this?"

Renee weighs her responses before opening her mouth. "Probably because Jess has never been a very big part of my life."

Courtney inhales sharply. "Keep talking."

Their drinks arrive and Renee takes a greedy sip of her wine. She promised herself just one glass, but the way this conversation is going, she may need a second. But that's it. No more than two. Another new rule. She should maybe write them down.

"You realize this is the most vulnerable you'll ever see me, correct?"

The two precious puppets across from her nod in unison. There's something in Kate's expression that Renee sees but doesn't understand. She'll ask about it later.

"I don't hide the fact that I have a child." Courtney balks and Renee holds up her hand. "I don't. Like I told Kate, I don't hide Jess. But I also don't advertise the fact that she—they exist." She shakes her head. "The pronouns are an adjustment, as you can imagine, after having a daughter for twenty-five years and suddenly having a child who doesn't identify as male or female."

Courtney's expression softens. "So Jess has just reappeared and come out? At the same time?"

"Somewhat. Jess has always been in my life, but I suppose you'd say they've been on the periphery. We lead very different lives, and we always have. Truthfully, we've never spent much time living under the same roof, which was a choice I made. And to be clear, I thought I was doing the right thing."

Finding she has a rapt audience now, plunging into the truth feels easier. "I had Jess when I was twenty-two, via artificial insemination. I always knew I wanted to be a mother." Renee swallows against a gentle surge of emotion. That much, she knows, is true. "And I love Jess dearly. They certainly got my fair share of DNA." She smiles. "But I've always been so career-minded. I knew I couldn't juggle my studies with raising a child, so I leaned on my parents. A lot. Maybe too much."

Renee breaks to take a sip of wine. "Looking back, I could have waited. Twenty-two was awfully young to suddenly have a baby, and not have a co-parent, especially when I was so wrapped up in acquiring degrees. But here we are. I got my career, and Jess turned out pretty damn well."

There's more, of course. There's so much more Renee could spill out on the table before Courtney and Kate. But she holds back, not wanting to open her own floodgates any more than she wants their sympathy, or their condemnation.

"I can't believe you have a kid," Courtney mutters. "No offense, Renee, but you're not exactly...maternal."

"Mmm, yes, please know that Jess would certainly agree with you."

"And," Kate says, her voice warm, "Jess is now living with you?"

Renee nods. "Quite suddenly, yes. Jess and Mr. Purrington, their cat. They're staying—living—with me until Jess figures out their next move."

"Ah," Courtney says sympathetically. "Job issues?"

"Oh, no. Jess works from home. They're quite brilliant with a computer." Renee feels herself straighten in her chair, proud to have a piece of maternal-sounding information. "It took some cajoling, but I finally got Jess to tell me that their relationship ended. Abruptly, it seems, and they couldn't find a new place in Brooklyn, so they came to my house." Renee catches herself. "Home. They came home. Anyway, Flint, their boyfriend, couldn't handle Jess being nonbinary. He said something about his manhood feeling threatened."

"Well, that's pathetic," Courtney says. "Jess is better off without him."

"How are things going with Jess being home?" Kate asks.

Renee brightens. "I think they're going well. We're both on a learning curve, but we'll get there. It's—I like having Jess around," she admits.

"Why don't you invite Jess to come see Pennbrook?" Kate suggests. "It could be a great opportunity for them to see you in a different light."

"Wait," Courtney says. "Do you honestly think Renee stops being so, you know, so *Renee* just because she's not at work?"

"Oh, not for one second."

"Excuse me," Renee says dryly. "I'm right here with very capable ears."

Kate rests her cheek on her hand and gives Renee one of her sweeter smiles. "Think about it. I told you before and I still feel the same way. I'd really love to meet Jess."

"Me too," Courtney says. "I'm intrigued. Hey, you know what else is intriguing?"

Renee sits back, glad that Courtney is taking the conversation in a new direction. "Tell us."

It's Courtney's turn to rest her cheek on her hand, but the look on her face is feigned innocence, a far cry from Kate's genuine kindness. "You fighting with the electrical engineer in your office."

Renee feels the color leak from her face. *Fuck.* In the week that's passed since the…heated discussion, she's been walking carefully in and around her office. She thought she was in the clear, especially after she and Courtney had too much to drink last week and she never so much as asked what was bothering Renee. Goddamn Courtney, with the ears of a bat. Renee squints at her. Come to think of it, her features are somewhat Chiroptera-esque.

"That's a loose interpretation of the truth." Renee throws back a large sip of wine. "But I'll tell you what *is* intriguing." She points at Kate with her free hand. "Someone's professor-girlfriend continuing to break the delicate hearts of graduate students."

"Oh, God," Kate groans. "Viola."

"You're not off the hook," Courtney says to Renee before turning to Kate. "She told you?"

"Of course she told me. We tell each other everything." A faint blush warms Kate's cheeks, only adding to her delicate beauty.

"Isn't that romantic." Courtney rolls her eyes. "Did she show you the video?"

"There's video?" Renee interjects. "Good God, of what?"

Kate shakes her head. "Not whatever you're thinking, I assure you that. It was a project. A project that went awry."

Courtney throws her head back and laughs. "That's putting it lightly, Jory."

"As head of this department, I'm going to need to see that video."

"I'll have Callie send it to you, but really, Renee, it's not nearly as tawdry as this one is making it seem."

Courtney shrugs. "Look, I've never had students fawn all over me the way that Callie does. It's fascinating. But mostly entertaining."

"Speaking of," Kate begins. "Last night, Callie and I—"

"Wait. No. Excuse me, no," Courtney frantically interrupts. "When did we become talk-about-sex friends? To be clear, we are *not* talk-about-sex friends."

Renee, who was leaning in to make sure she heard every word, jolts back into perfect posture during Courtney's tantrum.

Kate, looking a mix between entertained and horrified, says, "I was referring to a documentary that we watched about cultivating safe relationships in the classroom, but since you brought it up, please know that I have no complaints."

"No. Stop." Courtney strokes her chin. "But that does begin to explain why the graduate students are throwing themselves at her."

"This conversation has gone completely off the rails." Renee signals the waitress. "Let's order food. I'm starving."

"And then we can get back to your heated dispute with the electrical engineer," Courtney says casually as she picks up her menu.

"What in the world are you talking about?" Kate asks.

"She knows." Courtney jerks her head toward Renee. "Sounds like some wires were crossing in a dangerous way in Renee's office."

A large, wordless feeling sinks through Renee's body. She reminds herself that Courtney is not a mind reader, so there is no possible way she could know what Renee's been thinking. But the mere fact that she knows Hunter exists is not ideal. The reality that Courtney overheard at least some of the interaction in Renee's office is less than ideal.

As Renee searches for a way to escape this conversation, Kate jumps back in. "You know, Courtney, Callie knows a little something about—"

"Do not finish that sentence, Jory. I mean it."

As Courtney dives into a monologue about her long-term friendship with Callie and the explicit boundaries they have enforced, Kate turns her attention to Renee. There's no mistaking that look on her face. Renee wants to squirm but instead she submits to feeling swaddled in a bubble of safety.

Kate knows. Exactly how much she knows, Renee isn't sure, but she isn't in any rush to find out.

CHAPTER SEVENTEEN

"Okay!" Renee's voice is deceptively jaunty, but it does the job of masking her jittery insides. "Do you have everything you need? Laptop? Water? Snacks?"

"You act like it's my first time hanging out on a college campus." Jess checks their reflection in the hallway mirror. "Or are you trying to make up for lost time and pretend it's my first day of—"

"I just want you to be prepared," Renee says. She stands behind Jess and checks her own reflection. The contrast in mother-child appearance always surprises her. When she was pregnant, she imagined she'd give birth to her carbon copy. Instead, while they're both around the same average height, Renee's body curves with feminine proportions that Jess's flatlines almost in a boyish way. They have a stockiness to their form that's foreign to Renee, something that must have come from the donor's DNA. Jess's sandy-blond hair is a bit coarse, nothing like Renee's thick but soft chestnut brown hair. Both have opted for updos today. The man bun has made a sad return on Jess's head and Renee has swept her hair into a bun that's looser than Courtney's but still very, very neat.

The one constant between mother and child is the exact same cobalt blue eyes. Same shape, same size, same lashes. Same intensity that alternately strikes then submits. Jess blinks at their reflections and Renee smiles, placing a tentative hand on Jess's shoulder.

"You're welcome," she says gallantly before turning to pick up her bag.

"For what, exactly?"

"Gifting you those gorgeous eyes."

Jess snorts as they follow their mother to the car. "The last thing I want to do is inflate your already oversized ego," they say as they shut the car door, "but thanks. I get a lot of compliments on them."

"As you should."

After a few blocks of silence, Jess looks over at Renee. "Do you?"

"Do I what?"

"Get compliments. On your eyes."

Her grip tightens on the steering wheel. "What does that matter?"

"I'm curious," Jess says simply. "Flint"—their voice wavers before regaining strength—"uh, he always said it was his favorite part of me. I guess that should have been a red flag. I mean, my eyes? Yeah, they're nice, but, like, maybe he could have liked my heart more? Or my kindness?" Jess burrows into the seat. "Never mind. I don't want to talk about that."

"You can," Renee says quickly. "I'll listen."

"I know." After a pause, Jess picks up their earlier line of questioning. "So, do people compliment your eyes? Maybe people that you, you know, date?"

"I do not date." The clipped tone would be enough to shut Courtney up, maybe even Kate, but Jess, limited in their interactions with Renee, doesn't heed the warning.

"Seriously? Not at all?"

"No."

Jess waits, incorrectly assuming Renee will elaborate. When she doesn't, they press. "Why not?"

"Why should I?" It's not what Renee intended to say, but it's too late.

"Companionship? Fun? Connection? Sex?"

Stopped at a red light, Renee whips a fierce look toward her passenger. "That is something we do not ever need to discuss."

"What?" Jess asks, the lilt in their voice confirming that they know precisely what.

"My sex life," Renee says loudly. Perhaps some reverse psychology will do the trick. "Can you honestly say you want to know anything about me as a sexual being? I'm your mother, Jess."

"Yeah but you're not, like, a mom."

A small fire burns right below Renee's heart, incited by the flaming arrow of those words. She can't bring herself to sputter any kind of retort.

Jess sighs. "I didn't mean that the way it came out."

"I believe you did."

"No, Renee, I—"

Renee holds up one hand. "Stop. Please stop. I'm going to work, and you're coming with me because my nosy colleagues are dying to meet you. If you're uncomfortable right now, and feel the need to shoot fiery arrows into my sensitive spots, imagine how I feel." She takes a breath but Jess interrupts before she can continue.

"I'm sorry. That was shitty. But tell me the truth. Are you only taking me because your friends want to meet me? Or do you actually want me to be there?"

Renee slides the car into her parking spot and turns the ignition. She looks over at Jess, seeing a familiar look in their penetrative eyes. "I do want you here, Jess."

Jess waits, then nods, seeming to believe her. "Then let's do this thing."

Renee was half expecting a welcoming committee, maybe a small parade with confetti, to greet them as they walked into the offices. Instead, there's Audrey, talking on the phone and looking flustered. And that's it.

Jess looks around with a faint smile on her face. "This place could use some updating." They jerk their finger behind them. "Step one, that door."

"It's on the list," Renee says. She hesitates at the hallway leading to her office, unsure if she should present Jess like an interesting gift to Courtney and Kate, or let them find Jess in her office.

Callie bops down the hall, clearly having come from Kate's office. There's no mistaking that sappy smile on her face.

"Morning, Dr. Lawler." She stops and looks at Jess. "And hello, Jess. I'm Callie. It's great to meet you."

Jess shakes Callie's hand while Renee tries to keep from showing surprise on her face. Then it clicks, Kate's words from the other night: She and Callie tell each other everything.

Renee flashes back to the look on Kate's face at dinner and her own awareness that Kate certainly knows more than Renee thinks she does. She hasn't had a chance to work that out, but now that the other memories are falling into place, she remembers something with a jolt.

The vibes. The day she had the audacity to ask Callie if she, Renee, gives off any non-heterosexual vibes.

And Kate and Callie tell each other everything.

Renee looks at the floor, wondering if a trapdoor is lurking beneath the shabby hardwood. Now would be a lovely time for it to magically appear.

She looks up to find Jess watching her. Callie's gone.

"You good?"

"Of course," Renee says, nearly snapping but catching herself just in time to neutralize her tone. "My office is just down here."

She leads Jess into her space, motioning toward the more comfortable chair opposite her desk. "Make yourself at home."

Jess drops into the chair. "So what's on the agenda?"

"Well," Renee begins, checking her desk calendar. "I imagine the two office busybodies will be in here momentarily, now that Callie's alerted them to your presence. After they finish their interrogation, we can—"

A knock interrupts Renee. She and Jess both look up to see Hunter standing in the doorway.

"Good morning," she says, her voice an unexpected salve to Renee's nerves. "I can come back if I'm interrupting."

"No," Renee says quickly and accidentally loudly. "You're not interrupting. Is this about my wires?"

Out of the corner of her eye, Renee sees the weird look Jess sends her, but she's too focused on Hunter to address it. In the days since the Chomsky incident, Renee has given herself many pep talks, all leading to the same conclusion: She must stay in control when she and Hunter are breathing the same air. Easy. Totally easy. Control is her forte, after all.

"You're with a student," Hunter says, but Renee waves her off as she steps back around her desk and leans against it. She's quite pleased with her outfit choice—a sleek black pencil skirt with a tempting slit up the right thigh, a sapphire blue silk camisole beneath a deeply cut black blazer that hits just at her hips, and of course, delicate matte black heels that give her calves extra oomph. If she angles her left leg in just the right way, that slit over her right thigh will split perfectly. Glancing down, she sees she's nailed it.

"No, actually, this is my daugh—my child. My Jess." Renee smiles through the panic, perfect slit momentarily forgotten. "My offspring."

A look of mortification flashes over Jess's face. "Renee. Don't be weird."

"My spawn," Renee clarifies, her pervasive love of language having shoved the panic away.

"Oh for God's sake. You went too far." Jess stands and extends a hand to Hunter. "Hi, I'm Jess Lawler."

Renee is certain that Hunter has noticed her skirt's slit and the skin beneath it, but she swiftly turns her focus to Jess. "Hunter Ciccone. Great to meet you."

"Are you one of Renee's nosy colleagues?"

Hunter grins. "Nosy, sure. Colleague? Not quite. My company is doing an overhaul of the wiring and computer systems, so it's a temporary professional relationship."

"Oh, right on. I do tech support management for a medical transcription company."

Renee watches, momentarily stunned, as Hunter and Jess lapse into an easy conversation that makes it sound as though they've known each other for years. And here she is, unable to act like a normal human being around Hunter.

The two nerds appear to be enjoying each other so much that they've forgotten that Renee is in the room. With a huff, Renee returns to her desk chair and opens her laptop. *Control*, she repeats. *You have it. Now keep it.* A fine form of control is ignoring, and she does just that, letting the two geek it out over geeky computer geekery.

"Knock knock."

Renee rolls her eyes without looking up from her computer. Much like Audrey, Courtney possesses the gene to speak instead of act. "Come in," she says. "We're having a party."

Courtney looks at Jess and Hunter, then glances over at Renee. "Interesting guest list." Her voice is low enough that only Renee hears it, and she has to physically restrain herself from launching over the desk like a panther and attacking her.

"Jess," Renee says loudly. "Sorry to interrupt. This is Courtney Wincheck-Rodriguez, one of those nosy colleagues I told you about."

"Oh, hey, it's good to meet you."

Courtney stares at Jess. "You really do exist. And those eyes. My God, you're really hers."

"I hired you," Renee says airily, still not looking up from her laptop. "And I can just as easily fire you."

"You'd never." Courtney nods at Hunter. "Hunter, right? I think we met over in Old Main."

"That's me." Hunter glances over at Renee. Not that she can see it because she's still hyperfocused on her fascinating laptop, but oh can she sense it. "Jess, it was great talking with you. I'll let you all get back to work."

Before anyone can object or agree, yet another body appears in Renee's doorway. Callie, back from wherever she'd run off to. "Oh, good, you're still here, Jess. I found that website. Can you come look at it?"

"Yeah, sure." Jess excuses themself and Courtney trails after them, making some lame excuse about needing to see the website, too, but Renee knows she's caught up in curiosity.

With a start, Renee realizes she and Hunter are alone in her office. Again. After repeating her control mantra one more time, she dares to look up and finds Hunter standing in front of her desk, arms crossed casually over her chest.

"You have a child." Hunter's voice holds a note of fascination.

"As do you. Two, correct?"

"Good memory." Hunter leans her hip against the side of Renee's desk, forcing Renee's eyes to linger at the point of contact. "I didn't peg you for a parent."

"Not many do."

Hunter watches Renee carefully. "I'm willing to bet there's a lot about you that most people wouldn't guess or expect to be true."

The words have their desired effect, hitting parts of Renee that are rarely seen, let alone acknowledged. She feels it acutely, the slip-slide of wonder tumbling into her unlit corners, her body reacting far too strongly, far too quickly.

No. She bites the inside of her cheek. This woman possesses too much power over Renee's finely honed system of control. She has to get the upper hand back. Immediately.

Renee slowly leans back in her chair, watching Hunter's eyes drop from her face to her torso to her legs. Once she's satisfied Hunter's gaze is where she wants it, she eases her right leg over her left, crossing her legs and exposing that slit once more.

There's but a handful of silent seconds before Hunter says, "Have a drink with me."

"I thought you were here about my wires."

Hunter grins, a wicked tilt to her lips that Renee is shocked to discover she'd like to lick right off of her. "We can discuss all things electrical engineering over a glass of wine."

"I don't want to talk about electrical engineering," Renee says flatly.

"I know." Hunter stands up to her full height. "I have to admit, Renee, I'm not sure what you do want to talk about, but I know you want to talk. To me."

Arousal clings to Renee's most delicate body parts. She curses her body for being so weak. "You're awfully confident."

"No, I'm just really good at reading people." Hunter takes a few steps backward until she's nearly at Renee's door. "There's no harm in a drink or two. We've already done it once, so let's do it again."

"Okay. Yes." Renee grips the edge of her desk, shocked at her tongue's betrayal.

"Good." Hunter gestures toward Renee's desk. "I see you have my card. Text me. I'm free Thursday evening."

The moment Hunter disappears from Renee's line of sight, she blindly grabs at the damn business card lying innocently on top of her calendar. She'd taken it from Audrey nearly a week ago and has been staring at it since then.

She lets loose a string of whispered expletives and holds the card over the trash can. Seven seconds later, she slips it into the side pocket of her bag and zips it up tight.

"So," Jess says. It's nearing five o'clock and they're walking to Renee's car after having made a stop in the student union building. Renee side-eyes Jess, waiting for the question she's certain is coming. "Who's Hunter?"

"Hunter told you who Hunter is."

"Yeah, but who's Hunter to you?"

Renee presses the tip of her car key into her palm. "Just… Hunter." In an effort to build a more open relationship with her child, Renee adds, "It's complicated."

Jess bursts out laughing. "That's what all the lesbians say."

Renee stares at her. "I'm not—I am not a lesbian."

"Maybe not, but—"

"Again, Jess. My sex life is not up for discussion."

"Fine. I really don't want to hear about it, anyway. But Hunter," Jess says pointedly. "I think Hunter should be up for discussion."

Instead of an answer, because she has none, Renee flicks her wrist, tossing the conversation to the side. "Are you hungry? We can stop for takeout on the way home."

"Is that Italian place on Broad Street still open?"

"Fiamma? Yes." Renee drives off campus and heads for Broad Street.

"I like your colleagues," Jess says after a moment. "Courtney and Callie are really cool, very funny. And Kate."

"And Kate what?"

Jess shrugs. "I'm not sure how to explain it. There's just something about her, you know?"

Renee nods. "Sometimes I think I'd be lost without Kate." The weight coupled with the truth of the statement hits Renee square in the chest. "She and Callie have a lovely relationship," she hastens to add.

"Mmhmm," Jess murmurs. "And you say you're not a lesbian."

"What do you mean by that?" Renee's words are capped with ice, emerging from the glacier of her most guarded spots.

"Renee," Jess says softly. "I never saw you date a single man when I was growing up. I know I've missed a lot because I'm not always around, but…I don't know. The way you look at Kate isn't how you look at other people. And honestly, there's major energy vibing between you and Hunter. Don't you think, maybe, you might be interested in women?"

"I'm not interested in anyone." And for forty-seven and a quarter years, it was true. Renee feels akin to a baby deer, just learning how to walk on brand-new, shaky legs. "I adore Kate. I know that, and I tell her that. It's not romantic."

"Okay," Jess says easily. "But Hunter."

"But Hunter nothing. We're having drinks, all right? That's all. And we—we've already had drinks. In Vermont." Renee grits her teeth. "So this is simply another round of drinks. We're friendly. That's all."

She catches Jess's shit-eating grin out of the corner of her eye.

"It doesn't mean I'm a lesbian," Renee adds.

"I know. You can be whatever you want to be. I'm just saying, I wouldn't hate having Hunter as a stepmother."

"That's quite enough," Renee says, her voice arching toward an unfortunately high decibel. "I'm never taking you to Pennbrook again," she mumbles.

Jess dissolves into laughter and Renee can't help but to smile, the weight she's forcing herself to carry lightened by the sound of her child's amusement…even if it is at her expense.

CHAPTER EIGHTEEN

In five minutes, it will be 7:00 p.m., and Hunter should appear. At least that's what her apology text said at 6:00 p.m.

Good evening. I'm so sorry, but can we meet at 7:00 instead of 6:30? I had an unexpected system issue come up and need to resolve it before quitting for the night.

Renee had scribbled her finger over the screen, frustrated and unsure of how to respond when she first read the text. She'd already been waiting in her office since her last class ended at 4:00. She had plenty of department chair things to do, and she completed her task list with efficiency. Too much efficiency, maybe, because by 5:15 she found herself with nothing to do but watch the clock and wait for 6:30.

Having to wait until 7:00 only gave Renee more time to get lost in attempting to sort through her thoughts regarding Hunter. She started at the top: Why in the world had she agreed to have a drink with her? Her agreement made sense only in an oblique way. She was…curious. Dodgy as she is about her own feelings, even Renee can't avoid the naked truth of that reality.

Curiosity pocketed, Renee bypassed several treacherous rungs on her ladder of Hunter-thoughts, stepping directly onto the one labeled "You think she's attractive." Well. No avoiding that one, either. As an evolved, mature, intuitive woman, Renee can absolutely admit to herself that yes, she finds Hunter attractive. She has from the moment she saw her, truthfully. But it's not an earth-shattering revelation. Renee finds plenty of people attractive. Men. Women. She doesn't discriminate; anyone can be attractive!

Much to Renee's dismay, the ladder only gets longer and begins to disappear into a thick puff of fog, making it ridiculously difficult to see where her thoughts are descending to. By 6:59, she's feeling almost agitated at the prospect of Hunter walking into the now deserted English offices.

On cue, her phone buzzes with a text.

I'm in the parking lot. Ready?

With a huff, Renee stands and yanks on her coat. Not that this is a date, because it is most definitely nothing of the sort, but really? Hunter wants to meet *in the parking lot*? She fights the urge to stomp all the way downstairs and out the door, but resists only because she doesn't want to compromise her favorite pair of deep-chocolate-colored heels.

Renee gasps when her skin collides with the outside air. It must be twenty degrees warmer now than it was this morning. She shakes her head. New England falls have a magical, trickster way of luring their inhabitants into false hope. Honestly, it'll probably snow tomorrow.

"When was the last time you stepped outside?"

Renee turns to the sound of Hunter's voice, finding her leaning casually against the nearly empty bike rack. Her arms are crossed over her chest, causing the top buttons of her button-down chambray shirt to pull teasingly apart. Renee averts her eyes as quickly as she can.

"This morning," she admits, taking a step closer to Hunter. "It was a busy day."

"I don't know about you, but I love these fake-out days." Hunter stands up and Renee takes her in. Golden brown khakis kiss every inch of her long legs. Her shirt sleeves are rolled up to her elbows. It's not warm enough for that, and Hunter seems to silently agree as she pulls on a dark-green field jacket while continuing to talk about the temperatures. The overall look is masculine and strong. Confident. Very attractive.

Renee bites the inside of her cheek. *Enough with the attractive bullshit*, she commands herself. Within seconds, her internal voice replies, *Stop fighting it, you idiot.*

She barely stops herself from gasping out loud, horrified that her internal monologue has turned against her in such a bold manner. At a loss, Renee stares at Hunter, waiting for her to give some kind of cue that Renee can follow since apparently she can no longer rely on her own instincts.

Hunter looks at her carefully, those soft but deep brown eyes searching Renee's. "Are you okay?"

"Of course." Renee shakes herself back into control mode. Fuck her disloyal inner monologue. She doesn't need that disruptive little bitch. "Where to? I'm assuming we'll walk somewhere."

"Actually," Hunter says, gesturing to a car. "I'm driving us somewhere. Come on."

Renee knows, she *knows*, she would have been salty had Hunter not opened the passenger door for her, but she's ill prepared for the trickle of sensations that accompany the image of Hunter holding the door open, waiting for her to settle in, and smiling at her before gently shutting the door.

"Nice car," she murmurs when Hunter slides into the driver's seat.

"Oh, yeah. Thanks. I don't care much about cars. I just liked this one."

Renee is certainly not an automobile aficionado, but even she knows that a Range Rover is most definitely a status symbol. She lets it slide, though, not wanting to burst Hunter's darling little bubble.

"Where are we headed?" Renee asks as Hunter drives them off campus.

"It's a surprise." Hunter glances over at her. "I have a feeling you don't like surprises, but I have another feeling that if I told you where we're going, you'd balk, so sit back and enjoy the short ride. And try to trust me."

Renee wants to scoff, she truly does, but she knows better than to give in to that urge. Instead, she listens to Hunter ramble about how nice Chestnut Hill is, what a great mixture of quaint and modern its buildings are. It's a factual observation and something Renee loves about her town. Chestnut Hill has a way of blending historicism with the ever-changing tide of times; nothing feels too old, and nothing feels too new, though there are certainly buildings that are both.

"It's a lovely place to live," she says during a break in Hunter's mostly one-sided conversation.

"Have you lived here your whole life?"

"More or less." Renee shifts in her seat to look at Hunter. "I was born here and grew up here, but I left for college. My father grew up here and he was very attached to the area."

"How's your relationship with your parents? Must be good since you've stayed here."

Frost invades the car. Hunter must feel it because she nods once before saying, "Too soon?"

"Much."

"Can't blame me for trying." In the darkness of the car, Renee can just see the corner of Hunter's lips lift in a smile. "Good timing. We're here."

Renee looks out the window. She looks back at Hunter as she turns the ignition and the car settles into silence. The dark quiet envelopes them until Hunter opens her door.

"Hunter."

Hunter shakes her head as she shuts the driver's door and opens the door to the back seat. "Nope. Just trust me, Renee."

Renee turns forward and stares out the windshield. She knows exactly where they are but has nothing but confusion as to *why* they are where they are.

Hunter continues bustling about, opening and closing doors as she removes items from the car and walks them to a place in the darkness that Renee can't make out. She waits—for what, she doesn't know. Part of her wonders if this is some weird trick Hunter's playing on her. She begins working up the nerve to ask Hunter directly if she's trying to—

The passenger door swings open and there Hunter stands, a soft but confident smile lighting up her face in the glow of the car's overhead lights.

"Were you really waiting for me to escort you out of the car?" She holds out her hand and Renee stares at it.

"Of course not," she says, continuing to stare at Hunter's hand as she slides out of the seat and definitely does not use Hunter's hand for assistance.

Hunter shuts the door behind Renee, pulling them both into a meek darkness. They stand for a moment, removed from the noise of traffic. Just as Renee's eyes begin to adjust, she feels Hunter's hand on the small of her back and she blinks rapidly, trying to bring something, anything, into perspective.

"Can you trust me?" Hunter's voice is low, close to Renee's ear.

She refuses to shiver, imagining that's precisely the reaction Hunter is going for. Instead, Renee straightens her shoulders and nods curtly.

Hunter takes her hand and Renee nearly does shiver at the smooth skin wrapping around her fingers. Cautiously, as her heels are not the ideal footwear for their current location, Renee lets Hunter lead her away from the car.

CHAPTER NINETEEN

A few slow steps later, Renee's eyes adjust to the darkness, and she sees the area Hunter has set up for them. There, in the middle of a dry field, sit two camping chairs. Between them is a low table with a silver bucket on top. As they get closer to the spot, Renee realizes there's also a camping lantern on the table, sending a pale yellow glow over the grass.

"Had I known this was where you were taking me, I would have dressed more appropriately." Renee gestures toward her feet.

Hunter's eyes scale her body up and down, landing on her heels, which probably have mud and grass stuck to them. "I like you just as you are."

A miniature thrill runs through Renee. She brushes it off as quickly as it comes and sits down. She has zero camping experience and is relieved to discover the chair is surprisingly comfortable. She wiggles until she finds the perfect spot, then throws one leg over the other, crossing her legs neatly and swinging her foot to a beat only she can hear.

The world is silent as Hunter stares at her moving foot. Renee can practically feel the heat coming off Hunter, and as she watches Hunter's eyes track the movement of her foot, a single drop of sweat slides its way between her breasts.

She presses her hand against her chest, certain she's blushing and irritated about it. This body-betrayal bullshit needs to stop.

Hunter clears her throat as she moves toward the table. "Thirsty?"

"Yes," Renee says, horrified to hear the desire in her raspy voice.

"Me too," Hunter murmurs. She reaches into the bucket and pulls out a bottle of wine, turning it to show Renee the label. "Care for a glass?"

Eyes wide, Renee looks up to meet Hunter's eyes. "Where did you find this?"

Hunter grins as she pulls out a corkscrew and goes to work. "A friend of mine was driving through the area, and I asked him to bring me a couple bottles." Seconds later, a cold glass of Shelburne Vineyard's Cayuga White is in Renee's hand.

She doesn't ask, instead rolling the thoughts in her head where it's safe. Hunter remembered the wine they had the night they met. Hunter arranged to have someone bring her more of the wine. A couple bottles, she said. Renee nearly chokes on her first sip, understanding the implications of that.

"Is it as good as you remembered?"

Renee nods, swirling the wine in her stemless glass. "I'm impressed that your camping gear includes actual glasses and not the plastic kind."

Hunter's quiet, and when Renee looks over at her, her eyes are trained on something in the distance. Renee watches her, taking in the sharp lines of her profile. Hunter's jawline is a thing of beauty, angular and pronounced. Her cheekbones are softer but still bold. In the dim glow of the camping lantern, Renee can barely make out the long, dark lashes that frame her captivating brown eyes.

"Get ready," Hunter says suddenly, knocking Renee out of her close study of Hunter's face.

"For what?"

Hunter merely points straight ahead, and Renee's eyes follow her finger.

Within seconds, their quiet surroundings thunder into roaring noise. White lights blink ahead of them before lifting and soaring above them. The dry weeds around them shiver and shake as the air charges with the movement of a gigantic plane lifting and creeping through the sky, seemingly inches from the tops of their heads. Renee grips her wineglass and the arm of her camping chair, caught between absolute fear and awe.

As quickly as it came, the noise leaves, shrouding Hunter and Renee in a new silence, the kind with sparking edges and live wires to trip over.

"Holy shit," Renee breathes.

"Incredible, isn't it?" Hunter's smile is contagious. "Sometimes I need a reminder of how small I am, but also how confounding it is that something so heavy can become weightless."

"I'm afraid of flying." The admission slips out easily.

"Really? I gotta admit, Renee, you don't strike me as someone who's afraid of much."

"There are a few things," she says, not meaning to be coy but nowhere near ready to be open. "Is that why you brought me here? To dig up my hidden fears?"

Hunter laughs. "No, but if that's the end result of this date, I think we'll both be better off for it."

There it is. The word. Renee takes a swig of her wine, wondering which one of them will address it first.

"I don't date," Renee says. She wonders if she can drown in the inch of wine still in her glass.

"And yet, here you are."

The blush returns, as does the terrible trickle of cleavage sweat. "Wouldn't you rather be here with Heidi Baker-Kent? She certainly seemed up for a date with you."

There's silence for a split second before Hunter bursts into laughter. "Wait. Wait a minute. Are you honestly jealous of that librarian?"

"No. I don't do jealousy."

"Oh, Renee, I think you do." Hunter angles her body to face Renee, who steadfastly ignores her attempt to make eye contact. "I mean, I'll admit that Heidi has some nice assets, but for one, she's married."

"And for two?"

"For two," Hunter says, "she's not you."

A rush of nervous energy slithers through Renee's body. She grips the arm of the chair with her free hand and rests her head against the back of the chair. "She flirted with you."

"She did. Boldly."

"She nearly pushed her breasts into your face."

Hunter laughs. "Like I said, boldly. So bold it made you run away and hide."

Now she really can't meet Hunter's eyes. "Did you know I was there?"

"Not at first. But then Chomsky took a tumble and I saw a flash of a woman sprinting through the stacks."

Renee finally looks over at Hunter, but only to roll her eyes. "I did not sprint."

"Close enough." Hunter leans closer to Renee but there remains the table, a stoic boundary between them. Renee has never loved squat, unattractive camping tables more. "You flirt with me too, you know."

"I absolutely do not."

"Oh, please, Renee." Hunter grins at her, seeming to be thoroughly enjoying herself. "The skirt with the slit? In your office? That's flirting, and your every move said it was intentional."

Normally, Renee would jump right into a contrarian back-and-forth about said skirt, but she can't. While she wouldn't call it flirting, she can't deny—

"Do you just want the attention?" Hunter asks, seeming to read Renee's mind. "If so, say the word. I'll adjust accordingly."

Renee opens her mouth to respond but no words arrive on her tongue. Fortunately, a familiar sonorous noise lures both women's attention away from the conversation.

Moments later, Renee shuts her eyes, letting the sound consume her. Her body aches with the pull of the plane, its forceful but languid gravity-defying artistry quieting her brain.

Eyes still shut, Renee breaks the silence. "I may flirt with you."

"So it's not just about the attention?"

"I don't know, Hunter." She can't bring herself to open her eyes. The darkness of her eyelids is the only safe place in this conversation. "I told you, I don't do this. I don't do people. I don't date."

"Why not?"

"I can't even begin to answer that." Renee feels the open curtains beginning to slide shut. "It's just who I am."

"And yet, you flirt with me."

"I find you attractive. I don't think that's a crime."

"Hardly," Hunter says, her voice calm with a teasing lilt. "I'm just wondering what's behind the flirting."

Renee opens her eyes and stares up into the endless black sky. She'd love for another plane to come through, maybe several in succession. None arrive, and Hunter seems to take her silence as an answer.

"More wine?"

Renee holds out her glass. "Just a bit. You have friends in Vermont?"

"I live in Vermont." Hunter tops off her own glass. "Moved there after Kristina and I got divorced."

"Isn't that far from your children?"

"It is, but JetBlue makes it easy for us. Luckily, my kids love to fly." Hunter cocks her head toward Renee. "I've been meaning to tell you, one of my kids is nonbinary."

"Oh," Renee says. She nods. "We have that in common, then."

"We do. Tegan is a lot younger than Jess, but they put a lot of thought and therapy into their identity."

"How did you handle it? When Tegan came out?"

Hunter shrugs. She rubs the tip of her thumb over the edge of her glass. "I wasn't surprised. Tegan came out of the womb very opinionated. They're definitely Kristina's kid." Her smile is faraway. "I think having lesbian parents, one of whom is a little gender-nonconforming, helped to show Tegan they could be whoever they wanted to be. They came out when they were nine. They're twelve now."

"Nine!" Renee exclaims. "How in the world does a nine-year-old even know the term nonbinary?"

Hunter raises her eyebrows. "You've met my ex-wife."

Renee laughs, surprising herself. "I have. Right."

"Who knows what Tegan will discover about themself as they mature. That kid"—Hunter shakes her head—"is giving us a run for our parenting skills. But they're a great kid. Ash is too. He's ten."

"How long have you been divorced?"

"Three years, almost four. We were married for fifteen. And yes, we married pretty young. We were twenty-four."

Renee remembers being twenty-four. Jess was two and Renee was away at UVM, working on her Masters. Marriage wasn't on her mind then, not that it ever has been.

"I'm lucky," Hunter continues. "Kristina and I function very well as co-parents. It helps that her wife, Aury, is supportive and generally a very cool person."

"I'm Jess's only parent," Renee says, again surprising herself. Damn Hunter for being so easy to talk to. "Sometimes I worry that I wasn't enough, that they should have had a father."

"Does Jess know their father?"

"No. I don't either." Renee smirks when she sees the quick look of panic that flickers over Hunter's face. "I had Jess on my own via a donor."

"So you wanted to be a parent."

"Yes." Renee swallows, not liking the direction of this conversation. "I've been meaning to ask you something."

"Okay," Hunter says easily. Renee marvels at what it must be like to have no skeletons in your closet, to be so casual with sudden changes in conversation that could knock on doors you haven't opened in decades.

"When we…when I—in Vermont." She fumbles for the right wording. "Where you *live*. But when we parted ways, you said 'Till we meet again.'"

Hunter nods, watching Renee. "I did."

"And then you showed up at Pennbrook." Renee puts her empty glass on the camping table. "Did you know I was there? Did you know you were coming there? Is that why you said that?"

"Yes, I knew you were there. Your bio from the conference told me so."

Renee exhales. "Right. Of course."

"But no, I didn't know I was going to be there. Renzo had someone lined up for the job, but he wasn't able to do it at the last minute. So I stepped up."

Renee takes in the information. It still doesn't add up.

"So when you said that, about meeting again?"

"Yes?"

She scratches the fabric of her skirt. "What did you mean?"

Hunter is quiet for a moment, forcing Renee to look over at her. "I meant what I said but had no idea if it would be true. But I wanted it to be true." The intensity of Hunter's gaze reaches through the space between them and caresses Renee. "The moment I saw you, I knew I wanted to see you again. To know you."

With a low startle, Renee realizes no one has ever said anything like that to her. More accurately, she's never allowed anyone to feel that way about her—or, at least, given them the stage on which to speak the words.

"What do you want, Hunter?"

Hunter coughs out a short laugh. "You know, you have a knack for being incredibly bold while simultaneously doing your best to reveal nothing."

She's right, and Renee hates it. She waits.

"Okay. Fine. What do I want? I want to see you again, Renee."

She waits again. Then, "Is that it?"

"That's it."

Renee gives herself a moment to drown in Hunter's eyes. Then she yanks herself back to the surface and nods. "Fine."

"Fine." Hunter laughs. "Well, fine is better than no, I guess."

Renee pulls her coat tighter around her torso. "I think fall is returning."

"Wait," Hunter says suddenly, twisting in her chair. "Just one more."

Seemingly out of nowhere, a plane appears above them, this one preparing to land. The world around them shudders with intensity. Renee reaches through the space between them, jerking her hand back before it hits the arm of Hunter's chair. She's not fast enough, though, and finds Hunter's hand wrapped around hers for the second time that night.

The rush of the airborne plane dissolves as it hits the runway but the rush of excitement taking up space in Renee's body has only just begun its journey home.

Hunter squeezes her fingers before letting them go. She begins to pack up their little campsite and Renee helps by folding up her chair. Together, they cart the items back to Hunter's car. The silence between them is careful but tender.

"Renee," Hunter says quietly after she's opened the door and Renee has settled in the passenger seat. "Thank you for trusting me tonight."

Renee nods, struck mute by the sincerity of Hunter's words and the depth of their meaning. She spends the ride back to campus staring out the window, lost in her thoughts.

CHAPTER TWENTY

Renee stands in front of her bedroom mirror watching her hands go through the motions of slipping her teardrop earrings from her ears. Her fingers gently place the earrings, a gift from her father many years ago, in her jewelry box. She strokes a fingertip over a pair of diamond studs that she never wears, saving them for something special. Romantic, maybe. She shakes her head, soft locks of her hair brushing her cheeks.

For someone who has read plenty of romantic plots in a wide array of genres, Renee has little understanding of what romance is. To that end, she's not well versed in love, either. Intimacy. Connection. It's all so gray to her, and she prefers black and white. She likes concrete, definable. Soft, blurry emotions chafe against her firmly rooted, orderly system of beliefs. The two clash, and the latter is so powerful that the former has never been able to penetrate the boundaries created specifically to keep them out.

There has never been room for both to coexist. But more than that, there's never been anyone to make her see that they *can* coexist.

Renee stares at her reflection in the mirror. She blinks several times. She can't see the evidence on her face, but she can feel her internal boundaries shifting, relaying lines and staking out new territory while abandoning some of the old. The ache, low in her chest, is nothing she's felt before.

Her rumination is interrupted by the sound of something heavy colliding with something firm. She gives her reflection a final pass over, still certain she can't see what she feels is changing, before walking down the hallway and pausing outside of Jess's closed door.

"Jess?" she calls, knocking lightly. "Everything okay in there?"

A second thump greets her right there at the door and Renee jumps back. She presses her hand against the door, hoping that whatever Jess is throwing at it isn't leaving marks.

"Jess?" she calls a second time.

"Fuck!" comes the reply, a throaty screech.

Renee nods once, throws her shoulders back, and activates Mom Mode. It's been a long time since she's used this part of her personality and she hopes against all hope that she pressed the right button.

With a flourish akin to a new superhero arriving on the scene and dying to make a good impression so she can join the popular superhero gang, Renee throws open the door and struts into the bedroom. As she walks in, a flash of orange and white fur bolts through her legs.

As she suspected, the place is a mess. She had no idea Jess had so much clothing with them and suddenly it's all there, strewn on every available surface. Renee cringes. She should really take Jess shopping; some of these outfits look downright—

Not now, that annoying little voice pipes up. Right. Renee searches the room for Jess, finding the top of their head skimming the top of the far side of the bed. She tiptoes through the chaos and stands before her child.

"What's going on?"

Jess laughs, a humorless noise that sounds more like a strangled sob. "Flint."

Renee puts her hands on her hips. She was waiting for this, the moment when Jess's ex reared his terrible, horrible head. She's ready.

"That bastard," Renee announces.

Another laugh comes from Jess, this one almost convincingly humored. "I don't want to talk about it." Their eyes flash as they look up at Renee. "How was your date?"

"No," Renee says immediately. "We're not discussing that. And it wasn't a date."

Jess snorts as they pull themself onto the bed. "Well, I don't want to talk about Flint. So distract me and tell me about Hunter, please and thank you."

Renee glares at her child, again wishing Jess hadn't absorbed so much of her personality. "Hunter is perfectly fine."

"Well, yeah. Duh. She's hot."

"Oh, no. No. We're not doing that."

Jess grins. "Doing what, exactly?"

"Discussing Hunter's level of attraction." Renee bites the inside of her cheek. "It's irrelevant."

"Just keep telling yourself that." Jess pats the bed. "Sit down, talk to me. I know you're probably freaking out."

Renee shifts her eyes between the bed and Jess. "I don't know how to talk about Hunter," she says quietly, still standing.

"Oh, I know. I can read it all over your stoic face." They hit the bed again, more forcefully this time. "Sit down, Renee."

She obliges, more out of fear that Jess will grab her and yank her down if she continues to resist, and Jess is frighteningly strong. Renee would prefer to avoid that kind of embarrassment.

"So," Jess says, drawing out the "o" for a full, obnoxious two seconds. "Give me all the deets."

Renee sighs heavily. "Would it kill you not to sound like a preteen?"

"Probably. Come on. Give me something to be happy about, would ya?"

"You know I've never done this before."

"Opened up to me?" Jess tilts their head to the side. "I wouldn't say never. We've had some conversations over the years."

"No, not that," Renee says, waving them off but secretly thrilled Jess feels that way. It's true, they have talked candidly but neither one has ever... Renee looks at Jess with renewed horror. "Oh, God."

"What?" Jess makes a perfect replica of what Renee knows her face looks like.

"Have I made you emotionally incompetent?"

Jess laughs heartily. "I mean, that is one of the insults Flint threw while dumping me, so, maybe?"

"I'm so sorry," Renee murmurs, placing a hand on Jess's leg. "I just realized we never talk about feelings or emotions. I never wanted my incompetency to rub off on you, but I think I've allowed just that to happen."

"You're not emotionally incompetent. More like... emotionally challenged." Jess smiles at Renee's sigh. "No, that's a good thing! Room for improvement and whatnot."

"This conversation is not making me feel better."

"Wait. Do you feel bad about something?"

Renee hesitates. The true and difficult answer is a resounding yes, but she doesn't have the emotional capacity to go there with Jess right now. So she diverts.

"Hunter asked me if I flirt with her for the attention."

"Ooh." Jess cringes. "Do you?"

"No. Yes? Sometimes, I suppose." Renee rolls her lips in, pressing them together. "I never gave myself the opportunity to explore attraction. You know I was always so focused on my career—and you—so dating was never in the picture. And now, here I am, finding myself wearing a specific skirt just in case I run into a woman I met once, at a bar nonetheless, who then plants herself on my campus, and suddenly I'm wanting her to see me in that skirt. Wanting her to—" Renee cuts herself off.

"You want her to want you," Jess supplies.

Renee straightens. "No." She makes the word as emphatic as possible but is aware that her attempt falls flat.

"Renee. It's okay. It's totally natural to want people to want us. It's, like, human. We want others to find us attractive."

"But a woman, Jess? Since when do I want a *woman* to find me attractive?"

"Um, since you met Hunter?"

Renee's shoulders sag. "It doesn't make any sense," she mumbles into her chest.

"Sure it does." Jess scoots closer and pats her on the back. "You just said that you never gave yourself time or opportunity to explore attraction. You never went on a single date when I was growing up. You're basically twenty again, opening yourself up to possibility."

"I had this idea," Renee begins, "that love was a waste of time. It could never be permanent, or at least it never stayed in one place. It shifts and changes and"—she takes a deep breath— "I don't like that."

"Because it's not predictable."

"Because it's not predictable," Renee echoes, closing her eyes for a moment.

"Nothing is truly predictable. Stop lying to yourself." Jess dodges an incoming swat to the shoulder. "And maybe Hunter showed up when she did because your little internal walls are finally ready to crumble."

"I'm not good at relationships." Renee mutters a curse. "And what's happened to my ability to censor my words before they come flying out of my mouth without permission?"

"Is this…um, is this menopause-related?" Jess whispers.

This time Renee's hand makes solid contact with Jess's firm shoulder, and Jess laughs. "I'm just saying. Something to consider."

"I don't think it's that, but thank you for the not so subtle reminder of my ever-increasing age." Renee turns so she can face Jess. "You realize that you are the greatest relationship of my life."

"Me?" Jess squeaks. "Seriously? You shipped me off to my grandparents for the majority of my formative years. I called grandma 'mom' until she finally explained that she was my grandmother and you were the one who actually gave birth to me. I mean, shit. My bedroom at their house was full of my clothes and toys. I'm pretty sure I didn't see you for a full year at one point."

Renee picks at the sharp edge of her nail. "But do you understand now why I did what I did?"

"Do I understand that you wanted to get a bunch of degrees and make a name for yourself in academia? Yeah, I understand that. But do *you* understand how that complicated our relationship?"

"Actually, yes. I do."

Jess nods slowly, holding eye contact. "Okay. Now. I'll admit that I think things between us have improved."

Renee smiles fully, nodding. "I do too."

"But I can't be your only great relationship, Renee. I'm still not sold on the word 'great,' by the way, but I'm humoring you." Jess leans closer. "You owe yourself more than just a job and a pretty cool kid."

"A job?" Renee asks incredulously. "Surely you understand that I've achieved far more than simply acquiring a *job*."

"Yeah, yeah. I know. You're hot shit in academia, okay? I'm very impressed with your achievements. Yay, you. Don't avoid the real topic here."

"The fact that I may or may not be a lesbian and am just realizing that possibility at the age of forty-seven?"

Jess busts out in laughter. "That's one way of saying it. How about we don't worry about the label part for now? Just, you know, let yourself explore attraction." Jess wiggles their eyebrows. "And by attraction, I mean Hunter."

"Hunter," Renee repeats, feeling every letter shape itself in her mouth.

"I kinda don't want to say this, but I think it might help you. What if you approached this whole thing with Hunter like a research project? Don't think of it as dating. Use that nerd brain of yours for something other than books and shit."

"Oh," Renee says loudly, perking up. "Yes. I like that idea. I can do research."

Jess groans. "I'm already regretting that suggestion."

Later, after convincing Jess to talk about Flint for five minutes, Renee retreats to her room and flops down on her bed.

A pitiful meow replies to her weight hitting the bed and she gasps and turns her head to meet a pile of orange fur.

She stares at Mr. Purrington, his eyes half shut with confident malaise, admiring the smugness it requires to lounge in such a way that your comparatively small feline body somehow overtakes more than half the king-sized bed.

Renee strokes his fur, feeling the vibrations of his throaty purr. Ah yes, now the name makes sense. This cat could wake anyone within a mile of his purrs.

She blinks in the darkness of her bedroom, wondering which is more likely to keep her awake tonight: Mr. Purrington's content vocalizations, or Hunter Ciccone's persistent knocking on the highest of her walls.

CHAPTER TWENTY-ONE

The shift in energy on campus is palpable, one Renee loves and welcomes with open arms. Yes, the Everybody Panic, the Semester Is Nearly Over tension is alive and well across Pennbrook's rolling lawns and sturdy, if outdated, buildings. It's a special kind of energy that swoops in following Thanksgiving break. Today, the first day back after that all too short vacation, is hands down the worst day to call a faculty meeting.

Naturally, Renee sends an email at 8:01 a.m. letting her department know that their presence is required at a 4:00 meeting that afternoon. She can practically hear the passionate swears and groans through her closed office door.

Little do they know that Renee, invigorated from a lovely holiday break spent mostly with Jess and Mr. Purrington, has big, big plans for this surprise meeting.

The day swims by with little splashes of disruption, nothing Renee can't manage with ease. She even finds time to drop in and visit Courtney during her freshmen Composition 101 class.

She can't quite tell if that was a look of excitement or panic on Courtney's face, but the students seemed to enjoy her little interruption.

Whatever the case, her visit helped distract her from her impending research project on Hunter. She has a plan for that, too, but is nervous to begin.

By 3:50, Renee has set up camp in the conference room she uses for faculty meetings. Pennbrook isn't a large university, and despite having hired three new professors in the last two years, she can still fit her entire department in this room. Comfortably. For the most part. Inevitably, someone (i.e., Courtney) will complain about having to sit too close to someone else.

"Hey, Dr. Lawler." Callie waves as she walks into the room and sits down as close to the door as possible.

"Callie! It's so lovely to see you."

Callie gives a quick look over each of her shoulders, confusion obvious on her face. "Uh. You...too?"

Renee spreads her arms out as though to hug the entire room. "What do you think about the decorations?"

She watches Callie look around the room. Renee worked very hard to hang the new diversity posters. She especially likes the one that shows all the different colored flags, each one representing identities that fall under the LGBTQ+ umbrella. Jess declined Renee's offer to buy them a nonbinary flag to hang on their door at Renee's house, but Renee's pretty sure she'll get one for Jess anyway.

"Oh. Wow." Callie swivels her neck to take in the whole room. "This is very nice. Very, uh, colorful."

Renee beams. "Does it feel inclusive?"

"Exceptionally," Callie says, nodding emphatically. "You've really outdone yourself."

The rest of the English department begins filtering into the room, cleanly cutting off the conversation. Renee stands before her colleagues, greeting them as they sit down. She gets more than five strange looks, the worst of the lot coming from Courtney, who's apparently still irked about Renee's surprise visit earlier.

"Colleagues! Hello, it's so wonderful to see you all! It looks like everyone had a refreshing Thanksgiving break!"

Out of the corner of her eye, Renee sees Kate send Courtney a look. Courtney nods, then looks at Renee. Slowly, she raises her hand and draws an exclamation point in the air.

Okay. Fine. Too much passion.

"Let's get started." Renee claps her hands once. "And let's get the business out of the way so we can have time to bond."

She pointedly ignores the way Courtney's head nearly spins right off her neck as she twists to shoot Kate a look of confoundment.

Renee hurries through the usual updates, checking in for curricular updates and issues regarding plagiarism. She works through an issue concerning two of her male professors and their enlarged egos.

"As for the budget," she says, making eye contact with each tenured professor in the room. "It's still a work in progress, but I'm confident Dr. Malnor and I will come to a mutually beneficial agreement soon."

"How many TAs will we have for next year?" Courtney asks.

"Enough," Renee says curtly. "Not to worry. Callie? Progress on the APIDA heritage celebration?"

Callie taps the paper in front of her. "We're good with the Agha Shadid Ali piece, and the Garrett Hongo piece. Oh, and Victoria Chang's. Waiting for your feedback on a few others."

"I'll have that to you shortly." Satisfied with her progress through the agenda, Renee pulls out a chair and joins her colleagues. They stare back at her.

"Now! I'd like to go around in a circle and have each of us share something positive that's happened this semester. Work-related topics are preferred, but we would all love to cheer on personal successes as well!"

The room goes silent as heads turn and mouths move without words spoken. Renee smiles proudly.

"Who would like to start? Kate?"

Kate snaps to attention, having been whispering something to Imani Frances, the newest hire. "Me? I didn't volunteer."

"Oh, I know." Renee flicks her wrist. "I'm sure you have something wonderful right on the tip of your tongue."

There's a choking sound from Renee's right. She's certain it's Courtney, having some sort of conniption about Renee's choice of words. Oh, the urge to flip her off. But no! This is a safe, positive space.

"I can start," Imani says, smiling at Kate before turning her deep brown eyes back to Renee. She gathers her vibrantly colored braids and pushes them over her shoulder. "My first semester here at Pennbrook has been excellent. I've felt so welcomed by the staff and the students. Specifically, I've loved teaching the freshman comp class." She laughs along with the majority of the room. "I know, I know. It sounds crazy. But it's honestly my favorite."

"You're welcome to take my section," Courtney says.

"That class keeps you humble," Renee says. "I won't let you give it up."

"Fine," Courtney scoffs. "I'll go. The highlight of my semester was Imani offering to take my freshman comp class."

Renee presses her palms against her thighs. Just as she's about to tell Courtney something that would disrupt the safety and positivity of this room, Callie interjects with a positive experience and gets the ball rolling once more.

Miraculously, the ball keeps rolling and everyone participates. Some more enthusiastically than others, but as it's the first time she's tried something like this, Renee is satisfied. Like Jess said, there's room for improvement. She clears her throat as she stands and prepares to wrap up the meeting.

"You may have noticed some decorative enhancements in the conference room." She gestures toward the walls. "It's very important to me that everyone feels safe and included in our classrooms, and that starts with our own feelings and behaviors. I recently had a student confide that many of their professors disregard their pronouns." Renee pauses, glancing at the ceiling before continuing, "I would like us to be very conscious of how our words and behaviors impact others, especially our students."

There are murmurs around the room, but with them comes an overall feeling of approval and, dare she think it, admiration.

"Thank you all for your attention during our meeting. As always, if you need anything, please let Audrey know." Renee panics. "Wait. If my door is open, come on in! I'd love to chat."

"And if it's closed?" Courtney asks, snark in her tone.

"Well, then, talk to Audrey." Renee smiles grandly. "Have a lovely evening. Go, gays!" Renee doesn't miss the horrified look Callie sends to Kate, who merely shakes her head. "And everyone else under the umbrella," Renee hastily adds.

Kate presses her hand to her forehead and a gleeful expression takes over Callie's face.

Part of the method to Renee's madness of scheduling a faculty meeting at that exact time on that exact day is the fact that Kate has an evening class. So, following the meeting and tending to various emails, Renee packs up her things and walks directly to Kate's office, knowing she's likely elbow-deep in some book.

Bingo. Renee raps on the doorframe and Kate's head jolts up. She waves Renee in, and Renee settles into the luxurious leather chair in the corner of Kate's office.

Time for Phase I of her research project.

"What did you think about today's meeting?"

Kate slides a bookmark between the pages and closes her book. "It was certainly unusual."

"But a good unusual?"

"Some might say so, yes." Kate rests her chin on her fist. "That's not why you're here."

"Not exactly," Renee admits. "I'm working on a project and you're the perfect person to chat with about it."

"Is this a work project?"

"Somewhat." Renee makes sure to keep her expression as neutral as possible. "It's regarding attraction. Human attraction."

Kate studies Renee, a completely passive look on her fine features. She's ready to start squirming when Kate finally speaks.

"Does this have to do with you asking Callie if you, and I quote, 'throw a vibe'?"

Some indefinable feeling spits through Renee's veins. Oh, she just *knew* Callie said something to Kate. That little shit.

And yet, Renee has to admit that Callie's big mouth has made this conversation a bit easier to slide into.

"In a roundabout way, perhaps. Kate, how did you know that you were attracted to women?"

If Kate is taken aback by the directness of Renee's question, she doesn't show it. She merely leans back in her chair and interlocks her fingers on her lap.

"I didn't know it. I felt it."

Renee loathes the simplicity of Kate's answer. She should have expected it.

"There has to be more to it than that," Renee says, louder than she intended.

"Not really. Attraction can be cerebral, but it's also emotional. It's a feeling, Renee. A desire."

"Yes, so it *can* be known."

Kate sighs heavily. "If you want to get down to the basics of human attraction, you have to stop relying on your brain." She leans forward suddenly. "And I know, Renee. I know you love your brain, and you depend on it. You have a great brain. We can all admit that. But at some point in your life, you're going to have to let yourself feel something." Kate pauses. "If you want to know about attraction, that is."

"But isn't it possible to be attracted to someone mentally? Sort of like a meeting of the minds?" Renee hops on her rickety little wooden roller coaster of thought and rides it toward the sunset. "That's possible. I know it is. Look at you and Callie, for God's sake. When you two met, it was so obvious that you wanted her brain."

Kate blinks. "The first time I set my eyes on Callie, Renee, I wanted much more than her brain. I didn't even know how smart she was. I only knew that she was beautiful, and I felt pulled to her in a way I could not ignore."

"But your brains," Renee protests. The weathered, splintered tracks of her roller coaster shake.

"Yes, we have an amazing mental connection." Kate nods. "Absolutely. But we are also wildly attracted to each other. Physically, that is."

Roller coaster neatly derailed, Renee shakes her head. "Too much."

"You asked."

"Not exactly."

Kate smiles, resting her elbows on her desk. "I had a girlfriend before Callie, you know. And that relationship was purely based on physical attraction. That's all we had. I kept hoping that other parts of our bodies would line up and connect, but it didn't happen. With Callie, I have everything. It started with a physical attraction, but the more I got to know her, the more I became attracted to her as an entire person. Mentally, emotionally. It's all there."

Renee nods, captivated. When she realizes Kate's finished talking, she pulls herself back into the present, away from the smoky tendrils of everything Kate didn't say.

"All right. Thank you. This has been helpful."

"Has it?"

"Yes." Renee stands up and gathers her things. "Would you be willing to continue helping me with this project?"

"Of course." Kate's tone is gentle, and Renee is thankful for it. And her. "But, Renee?" *Dammit.*

Renee turns slowly and faces her friend, the impressive professor she poached from a college in Tennessee and has grown to adore.

"Some of this you'll have to do on your own, and for that, you really need to stop thinking and start feeling." Kate smiles warmly. "I'm always here for you. And your research."

CHAPTER TWENTY-TWO

All Kate's talk about loosening her grip on her brain has made Renee anxious and irritated. Kate's right—Renee does love her brain. It's gotten her where she is today, and it's opened doors for her that were previously idle daydreams. Professionally, yes, her brain is her biggest asset, seconded only by her always-at-the-top-of-her-game personality.

Personally? Well, her brain has let her down there, she supposes. There's been no one. Romantically, that is. The bedside table drawer of previous romantic entanglements is plain and empty. Renee has always told herself that that's just her place in life, to be void of passion for anything other than the written word. Books are easier than people; she can pick them up and put them down at her leisure with not a care for the books' needs, because last time she checked, inanimate objects don't have needs.

But people, people have needs. Even Renee has needs, some of which she has tangentially filled over the years. Others haven't spoken up or tugged themselves out of the dust. It's possible, too, she's been purposely blind to them.

With lightning strikes of clarity, Renee is beginning to realize that she's been existing, but she hasn't been living. She's not entirely sure she understands the concept of living, because she has a nagging thought that living involves feeling—*all* the feeling—and her tightly organized life has had no room for feeling of any sort.

Renee stands next to her desk, pressing her fingertips into the marred wooden surface. She can feel that, the pressure and pulse of soft skin against black walnut wood. Okay, good. Great. She's not completely devoid of sensation.

With a deep, steadying breath, she inches her fingers across her desk until they meet the cool plastic side of her phone case. *Research*, she tells herself.

My Internet is acting up.

The five words shoot from her fingers into the nebulous text messaging atmosphere before she can think to stop herself.

The response comes much faster than Renee anticipated, its buzz sending a thrilling shiver through her body.

Makes sense, we're doing some updates today. How bad is it?

Renee drums her fingers on her desk, eyeing Hunter's response. For research purposes only, she settles on: *Bad enough to cause me a rather significant inconvenience with my work.*

She nods after hitting send. That should do it.

A handful of minutes pass before her phone buzzes yet again. *Well, we can't have that.*

A smile threatens the corners of Renee's lips. She's sure Kate's theories about brains vs. feelings have merit, but the vaguely flirtatious repartee with Hunter is the sexiest thing about their connection. Witty words and thinly veiled subtext are the way to a lexicon-lover's heart, after all.

Renee's phoneless hand flies to her throat, touching the heated skin at her clavicle. *Oh yeah you did*, her annoying internal fact-checker whispers. *You finally admitted something here is sexy.*

A knock at her office door catches Renee totally off guard, and she nearly trips over her moderately high heels as she tries to get into her desk chair before acknowledging the knocker.

"Yes," she calls, then immediately clears her throat of the arousal lurking there.

The door swings open to reveal Hunter, looking unfairly dapper in stone-colored khakis, a navy V-neck sweater, and dark-brown boots. Her short black hair looks recently trimmed and is tousled in a nonchalant way that only enhances the perfection of the tousle. Renee's breath catches in her throat as Hunter steps into her office, sending her a smile that can only be described as endearingly coy.

"Just here to test the strength of your connection," she says, taking another step into the room.

Renee laughs, too loudly and somewhat awkwardly. "You got here quickly," she hurries to say, trying to cover up her nerves.

Hunter points to the floor. "I've been downstairs all morning. I'm not surprised you're having connection issues, but I was hoping they would be resolved before really interfering with your work."

In a panic, Renee shuts her laptop, knowing full well that there is absolutely nothing wrong with her Internet connection. Hunter shifts her gaze to Renee's laptop, then reaches into her back pocket and pulls out some contraption.

"I don't need your laptop," she says easily. "This'll tell me everything I need to know."

"Oh." Renee clenches her teeth. She glances down at her skirt, wondering if it's short enough to distract Hunter from this ridiculous business about Internet connectivity. *Worth a shot*, she thinks, and stands up, rounds her desk, and leans against the front of it.

Hunter nods at her, just once, her eyes glued to Renee's legs. "You're doing that thing again."

"What thing?"

"That thing we talked about the other night." Hunter's eyes scan up and down, seeming to take in every centimeter of Renee's lower body. "You know exactly what you're doing," she says, her voice low and threaded with something that sounds like desire.

Renee swallows hard, feeling as though there's an earthquake sending warning trembles to the most sensitive parts of her body. Her mouth drops open the slightest bit as she realizes exactly what spot the strongest tremble has set its sights on.

She squeezes her thighs together. Hunter's eyes don't stray from their path but her body shifts, fingers loosening their grip on her special Internet tool, feet steady as hips turn and angle toward Renee, creating a straight, unencumbered path between the two women.

With agonizing slowness, Hunter finally draws her eyes up Renee's torso, lingering near her now flushed chest, before stopping once more on her lips, then climbing onward to lock into a stare that is producing undeniable heat.

Renee feels her lips part again, and with a confidence generally reserved for the classroom, she pushes herself off the edge of her desk and closes the distance, stopping inches from Hunter.

A clatter in her brain does little to detract Renee from her sole focus in this moment, and she shakes her shoulders once, twice, before erasing the remaining space between them. She shuts her eyes before bringing her mouth to Hunter's and is too shocked to be embarrassed when she realizes there's no mouth meeting hers.

"Renee." Hunter's voice is soft, permeable. "Not here."

Her voice yanks Renee back down to earth, but the firm, assured ground she left feels devastatingly shaky upon her return.

"Right, of course." She spins to return to the safety of her desk—oh God, she nearly *kissed* Hunter—but her arm is caught in a gentle grip, halting her movement.

"No," Hunter says. The warmth of her voice nearly settles Renee's panic but not quite. "Don't run from me."

"I'm just going to my desk," she manages, her words coming out in sputters.

"Not until you look at me. Okay? That's all, Renee. Just look at me."

Renee focuses on the floor. Hunter maintains her grip, the touch both secure and arousing. Renee cannot think. She absolutely cannot put together thoughts in her brain, her trusty, connect-all-the-dots brain. She realizes with a burst of stinging clarity that she has no choice but to meet Hunter's eyes right now.

And so she does, turning and steeling herself against the openly passionate expression on Hunter's face. Her brown eyes, ringed with a dark glow, and the faint blush spread across her cheeks only enhance her attractiveness.

"That was not a rejection." Her voice is clear, firm, a punctuated bell ringing through the fog of Renee's thoughts. "I want you to know that. And believe that."

"Fine."

Hunter tilts her head to the side, an amused smile taking over her full lips. "Fine? Come on, you know that's code for anything but fine."

Renee concentrates on the way her arm feels in Hunter's grasp. She wonders why Hunter hasn't let go, or why she hasn't tried to slip her arm from Hunter's hold. She wishes, fleetingly, that she didn't have on a long-sleeved blouse, so she could feel Hunter's fingers on her skin—

"Really," Renee rushes to say. "I understand."

"I don't completely believe you." Hunter squeezes her arm before dropping it. "But I'm going to trust you."

The words swing back and forth on a clothesline in Renee's head. "No. Those phrases"—she points at Hunter—"are contradictory. Try again."

Hunter laughs, the sound making waves low in Renee's belly. "You can sit here and analyze them, but unfortunately, I have to go." She gestures again to the floor. "I am working, you know."

"Right, of course. Yes." Renee runs her fingers around the waist of her skirt, making sure her shirt is still tucked in. She does not miss the way Hunter's eyes travel along with her motions.

"I'd like to take you out this weekend."

Renee nods. "Yes."

Hunter grins. "You know, you really are impossible to predict. Every time I think you're going to fight me on something, you become this agreeable person."

Confidence restored, Renee smiles broadly. "I like to maintain a bit of mystery."

"Noted," Hunter says, her voice tinged with desire once again. "I'll be in touch."

Touch. Renee hears only that word, and it sails over the tempestuous ocean in her gut, dipping and gliding.

As Hunter grips the doorknob, she turns to look at Renee, a cocky grin lighting up her face. "Seems like your connection is restored."

Alone in her office, Renee collapses into her chair. Split down the middle, she wants Hunter to come back immediately, and she never wants to see Hunter again. The reverberations from their almost-kiss are still coursing through her, knocking against her internal safeguards. She's nearly breathless when she remembers the way Hunter held her arm so gently, lightly, but with command.

Research, she assures herself. *It was just research.*

The internal trembling from earlier kicks up with a passionate vengeance. Renee presses her fist against her stomach, sliding her hand down as her body tilts back in her chair. She gasps, pressing harder.

Perhaps not the kind of data she was intending to unearth, but that's the risk one takes when collecting research.

CHAPTER TWENTY-THREE

Jess, in their young adulthood, has perfected a low whistle of disdain. It's a talent Renee never acquired, so she's certain she didn't provide Jess with this skill. In fact, Renee can't whistle at all. She admires Jess's special gift, wishes she had it, and nearly asks Jess to teach her how to do it, but after hearing the sound upward of five times in a matter of six minutes, Renee is beginning to loathe the noise.

After tossing yet another losing outfit onto her bed, she's ready this time, and the moment Jess purses their lips, Renee pounces. "If you whistle one more time, I'm going to smack your lips right off your face."

Jess, pre-whistle lips unpursed and mouth gaping, stares at Renee before breaking into laughter. "You still can't whistle," they say between wheezes. They then whistle, a short, purposeful burst.

"That is entirely beside the point." Renee opts not to follow through on her threat and throws a hanger at Jess's shins instead. "Your noisemaking isn't helping the task at hand." She glances at the clock, nerves rising as she sees how quickly time is ticking down.

"Let me see the text again." Renee hands her phone to Jess, who skims the text on the screen. "Okay, casual. Specifically, Hunter says, 'no heels, though I do—'"

Renee grabs her phone back. "I'm quite aware of the rest of that sentence, and you do not need to be."

Jess cringes, then flops dramatically onto the bed. "Sadly, I now am, and I wish I weren't."

Renee claps loudly. "Jessica! Focus, please!"

She hears the name echoing in her brain. It takes Renee a moment to realize why it sounds wrong. The room falls silent as Jess props themself up on one elbow and studies Renee.

"I'm sorry," she says immediately.

"It's okay." Jess sits up fully and rakes their fingers through their hair. "Honestly, you're doing way better with this whole thing than I thought you would."

"I'm trying." The sincerity in Renee's voice takes them both by surprise.

"I know, Renee."

She bristles. For years, Jess has called her Renee; in fact, she can't remember the last time she heard Jess use the word "mom." It's never bothered her much, likely because their relationship has often seemed more businesslike, a means to an end, than a cozy mother-child lovefest. But the changes over the past couple months have shifted more than just the landscape of Renee's home.

"Jess," she begins, striding back to her closet, keeping her back to her child. "Since I'm making an effort to call you by your requested name, perhaps you could do the same. For me."

She's met with silence, but considering her head is between two piles of sweaters, she may have missed Jess's reply. Renee backs out of the closet and looks at Jess, who is sitting on the edge of the bed, one eyebrow raised the tiniest bit.

"Did you say something?" Renee asks.

"Nope." Jess kicks their heels against the bed frame. "I heard you, though."

Renee gestures toward Jess, annoyance flaring. Her damn stubborn child. "And?"

"And I heard you," they repeat. With a smile, Jess looks at Renee. "Jeans. No sweater. Do you have a casual but sexy button-up shirt?"

Renee huffs as she returns to her closet. After rooting around, she emerges with the suggested items of clothing. At Jess's nod, she enters her en suite bathroom and makes quick work of changing her clothes.

"That's it," Jess says gleefully when Renee walks back into the bedroom. "Love the half-tuck on the shirt. I didn't know you had style in you, Mom."

The pleased feeling that washes through Renee matches the feeling she gets when she looks at Jess and sees the impressed approval on their face. With a surge of confidence, Renee flicks open the top two buttons on her shirt. Jess's hands fly to their eyes.

"Save that for later, thank you very much. Now, shoes."

Fifteen minutes later, Jess pronounces Renee officially ready for her first official date with a woman. According to Jess, who apparently Knows Everything About Dating, the airport-wine evening did not count as an actual date. This one, however: This one is real.

"I love that she keeps not giving you specifics about plans," Jess remarks as they walk downstairs together. "It's like she knows exactly how to get under your skin."

"She's had a knack for that since the moment I met her." Renee pushes coats aside, searching for her brown leather jacket. She has a feeling Hunter will like it. Not that that matters, of course. She's just being considerate.

"Huh."

Annoyed with the lack of follow-up, Renee spins on the low heel of her ankle boot. "What's that supposed to mean?"

Jess shrugs, leaning against the foyer wall. "I think that's something you need to figure out for yourself."

Renee throws her hands down to her sides. "Jess! That"— she lifts one hand and furiously spins her pointer finger in a circle—"is precisely the problem. I can't figure it out. I can't figure any of this out, and I don't know how."

"You do," they say. "You're just not letting yourself figure it out." Jess raps their knuckles against their head. "You keep letting this thing get in your way."

"Oh, for fuck's sake," Renee says loudly. "Do you and Kate have some secret friendship that I'm not aware of? You sound exactly alike. And suddenly everyone has a problem with my brain."

Jess giggles. "No, *you* have a problem with your brain and letting it dominate everything you do. Give it a rest tonight. See what happens."

"Yes, all right, wonderful advice. Any other wisdom you'd like to impart upon me before I leave?"

"Actually," Jess says, drawing out the word. "Yes. Don't drink too much."

Renee wants to glare but nods instead. "I've been cutting back."

"I noticed. And I admit, I'm surprised. Normally, when someone's figuring themselves out like you are, the drinking increases."

"I prefer clear-headed clarity," Renee announces. "The wine gets in the way of that."

Jess shakes their head, a proud smile illuminating their face. "Look at you, all grown up. I'm so proud."

Renee pulls on her jacket. She checks her reflection in the mirror and smiles slightly. She meets Jess's eyes in the mirror. "Anything else?"

"Yes. Have fun." Jess holds up one hand. "No, *let* yourself have fun."

At the door, Renee hesitates, staring at the keys in her hand. "I was looking for other pieces of advice," she says quietly, half hoping Jess doesn't hear her.

"Um," Jess says, moving closer. "Can you be more specific?"

The highlighted list of specific questions and concerns residing in Renee's brain lights up. The damn thing has spotlights shining on it. But the words are blurred, letters running into each other in a harried frenzy of unknowns. It's so messy, so thick with overlapping lines that Renee can't select a single thought from the list.

"Oh," Jess says. "It's the whole date-with-a-woman thing, isn't it?"

Renee nods once.

"It's just like any other date," Jess assures her. "Except for what's under Hunter's clothes, of course. But on that note, try to avoid having sex on the first date. Hunter seems really chill, but you don't want to—"

"I don't need that kind of advice," Renee says quickly. *Not yet.* She feels her cheeks flush. "Just tell me that Hunter is like any other person, female or not."

"I can't do that." Jess grins. "She is so clearly not like any other person, Mom. If she were, would you be going out with her?"

There's no need to answer, as they both know what Renee would say. Instead, Renee picks up her purse and bids Jess a good night, hurrying to her car as Jess reminds her to have safe sex, but not have sex, but if she does—

Renee slams her car door to cut off that last bit. In the quiet of her car, she exhales slowly. Hunter is definitely not like anyone Renee has ever met, and the weight of that truth is keeping her steady in this moment, hushing her nerves and turning the ignition.

CHAPTER TWENTY-FOUR

As she pushes open the door to Harpy, Renee remembers something she wanted to ask Jess: Are lesbians against picking up their dates? Hunter didn't even ask if Renee wanted her to pick her up; she merely told her to meet her at Harpy at six thirty. There's something about this that bothers Renee, something she can't put her finger on just yet. But on the flip side, she appreciates the autonomy the gesture gives her.

There's a good-sized crowd in the bar, not surprising for a Saturday evening. Renee has had to listen to Courtney and Callie talk endlessly about how much they love the beers that Harpy brews and serves, but she has never considered herself much of a beer drinker. She dabbled in college, of course, but spent more time with her books than with kegs. Courtney has told her several times that Renee has never allowed herself to develop a taste for good beer.

The memory of those conversations prickles the back of Renee's neck. What is it with all these people in her life telling her she doesn't allow herself to do virtually anything? How is it that they feel they know her so damn well? And beyond that, why are they annoyingly correct?

The brown leather jacket suddenly feels more like a straightjacket. Renee tugs at her sleeves. Another invasive thought zigzags through her brain: How long exactly has she been holding herself back from life outside of academia?

"Renee."

She hears her name, feeling a light and pleasant shiver when she recognizes the voice. There's Hunter, just off to her right, at a high-top table. Perfect. Being near Hunter will absolutely put a stop to her very loud thoughts.

Renee makes it to the table, a short journey, and realizes immediately that being near Hunter will only increase her obnoxious, boisterous thoughts. Because Hunter? Hunter could not look any sexier (yes, she admits it) than she does in this moment.

Perched on a stool, both feet resting on a rung, one arm lazily lying on the table perpendicular to her body, the other bent (Renee is graciously overlooking the way Hunter's elbows are *both* on the table) toward her, fist propped against her chin. Hunter's eyes never leave Renee as they track her movements across the room and she's smiling in a way that screams "I've been waiting for you and now you're here and I can't stop smiling." Never mind the casually sexy (oh God, there it is again; now that she's let the beast out of the cage, she'll never rein it back in) outfit of jeans and a moss-green Henley sweatshirt that seems to irradiate Hunter's olive-toned skin.

Renee clutches her purse to her chest. She is utterly fucked, and she knows it.

"Are you okay?" The question is paired with a wider smile and a slight raise of the eyebrows.

"Of course," Renee says quickly, taking the additional steps to the stool opposite Hunter. "I was just wondering why you didn't offer to pick me up." The comment shoots from her mouth, leaving Renee embarrassed and irritated with herself. She pauses before she sits. *That's ridiculous.* She has no reason to feel embarrassed or irritated, and the reminder of this truth bolsters her confidence.

Hunter, to her credit, appears slightly taken aback. She shakes it off quickly. After all, she's had enough experience with Renee at this point to not be shocked by her bluntness.

"I would have gladly picked you up," she says, crossing her arms on the table. "But you strike me as someone who prides herself on her independence, and I didn't want to assume that you'd prefer to be picked up."

"You could have asked," Renee points out as she sits down.

Hunter grins, her eyes lighting up with amusement. "You're right. Next time, I'll ask." She gestures to the menu on the round table. "I'm very curious to see what you order."

Renee picks up the menu and studies it. "And I'm very curious as to why you brought me to a brewery instead of a wine bar."

When Hunter doesn't respond immediately, Renee peers over the top of the menu and finds her smiling in a way that can only be described as cocky, but not haughty cocky. More like… sexy I-did-this-intentionally cocky.

"If you haven't noticed," Hunter says softly, so soft that Renee has to lean in to be able to hear her, "I like taking you out of your neatly formed comfort zones."

"Ah." Renee nods, pursing her lips slightly. "You're trying to further develop my character."

"No." Hunter props her chin on her fist again, a move that is both endearing and excruciatingly attractive. "Your character is very developed. I'm more interested in opening your eyes to new things, things you would have never considered on your own."

The seed of arousal deep in Renee's belly sprouts, blooms, blossoms, nearly explodes. She presses her tailbone into the chair, trying to alleviate some of the wild sensations ripping through her. For a moment, she feels drunk and the room seems like it's tipping.

"Your eyes, Renee." Hunter's voice rights the tilting room and Renee focuses on her, sensing the rest of the room fade into the background. "Something about that bright white shirt is making your eyes insanely blue." She exhales a short laugh. "I—I can't stop looking at them. At you."

The pulsing arousal certainly does not calm down after that admission, but Renee feels some level of control returning to her. Donning her number-one power color wasn't a conscious move, but she's very, very pleased with the consequences of her decision.

So pleased that a rush of truth decides it's time to spurt forth.

"Hunter, you do realize I've never…" Renee pauses, wanting to be sure she gets the phrasing right and avoids assumption. "I don't date."

"You told me that already."

"I know. But I don't think you read between the lines."

Hunter smirks. "Your lines are very tightly drawn, in case you weren't aware."

Renee rolls her eyes. This woman agitates her, oh she truly does, and yet she has a way of pulling Renee toward something she never imagined.

Never allowed *yourself to imagine*, the little voice corrects.

"Fine," she says aloud, then flushes. That word was supposed to stay inside. "You're a woman," she blurts.

Hunter looks down at herself. "You're not just realizing that, are you?"

"No. No, of course not." How is she supposed to say this? It may very well ruin everything—and she's not even certain what "everything" currently is or could be.

"You've never dated a woman," Hunter says easily. "And I'm guessing you've never even admitted to yourself that you're attracted to women."

The *audacity*! "Bold assumptions," Renee manages. She's too shocked by Hunter's dauntless and true statements to work any ice into her tone.

"But am I wrong?"

"No," Renee says, mustering some crisp edges into her voice. "You know you're not wrong." Her hackles begin to raise as she weighs her options for the next bullet she can fire across the table.

"Okay." Hunter leans back, adding inches of space between them. "I didn't think you'd react so strongly. I'm sorry."

How unsettling it is for Renee to register that Hunter can read her expression. A silent storm of emotion brews inside of her, torrents of rain paving the way for thunderous bolts. She mumbles an "excuse me" and darts to the bathroom on the opposite side of the bar.

Several handfuls of cold water splashed onto her face help bring her back down to a functioning level. Her hands are shaking, and she presses them, and her weight, against the edge of the sink. She can't meet her own reflection. She doesn't want to, or need to. She knows exactly what she'll see: fear.

Something crumbles inside of her, a loose brick in a long-ago mortared wall. It's not that Renee wasn't expecting this, it's that she wasn't expecting it *now*. It feels too soon, too preemptive, not at all predictable. She can't plan this, whatever "this" is. There's no checklist, no guidelines. Everything is unfettered. Everything is happening. Everything is now.

A shaky breath gives way to a steady exhale. Slowly, Renee feels her body returning to stasis. Once two breaths have made room for six more, she pulls her stare up from the sink and into the smudged mirror.

"Research," she says to her reflection, sharp and exact.

On her way back to the table where Hunter, somewhat surprisingly, is still sitting, Renee catches sight of Callie sitting at the bar with a handful of women she doesn't recognize. Because of course Callie is here. Naturally. Oddly, Renee feels a sense of calm pass over her, knowing that someone safe—someone who doesn't continually rock her towering walls—is nearby.

"I took a risk and ordered you a beer," Hunter says as Renee sits down once again. "I chose the least offensive option, something that might resemble wine in the slightest bit. It's…" She looks at the menu. "Right. Dionysus's Revenge. It's aged in an oak barrel previously used for wine. Might be a little tart."

Her expression wears a protective shield, one that still exposes the shadow of chagrin beneath it. Renee wants to lean across the table and wipe off Hunter's protective barrier, but she can't fault her for having put it on. Now, she needs to find a way to get her to take it down.

"Thank you. For the record, Hunter, I have no idea what I'm doing. I have no idea what this"—she points to Hunter then to herself—"is. But we've already established that I'm attracted to you so we might as well plow ahead and see what happens."

There, she thinks, satisfied. Actually, she's quite proud of herself for taking that loose brick and heaving it over her shoulder. She'd like to applaud herself but thinks better of it.

Hunter's eyes dance with mischief. *Fuck*, Renee thinks immediately. *What did I say?*

"Actually, we hadn't established that you're attracted to me."

"Yes we did," she says quickly. "The wine and airport night."

"Oh no," Hunter says, grinning. "You said you find me attractive. That, Renee, is a different ball game than being attracted *to* me."

She wants to be flustered. She believes she *should* be flustered. But she's not. Not one bit. Instead, an eerie confidence—a new kind, one she's never felt before—sidles up and takes control.

"Well," Renee says, her tone purposely light and noncommittal, "now you know. I suppose the next move is yours." She raises her beer glass, tries not to cringe, and, never taking her eyes off Hunter, takes a slow sip of the mysterious amber liquid…and promptly gags.

Swallowing takes great effort, but she manages it. She wipes her mouth. Hunter, hand pressed to her lips, is trying not to laugh. Renee rolls her eyes and shakes her head at the same time, which only seems to spur on Hunter's escaping laughter. Renee feels a laugh bubbling up from inside her, tickling her throat as it floats into her mouth. She releases it, lets go of the burden of worrying about what Hunter thinks about her, and gives in to her laughter.

When she pulls herself back together, she realizes Hunter is staring at her, no longer laughing. She feels her cheeks redden. "What?"

"You're beautiful, Renee. I've known that since the first time I saw you. But when you laugh? My God, you're a fucking goddess."

The reverence in Hunter's voice warms every ligament in Renee's body. She pushes her glass toward the center of the table.

"This is disgusting. But thank you. And maybe you should make me laugh more often."

"Challenge accepted." Hunter hops off her stool. "Forget the beer. Let's go to our next destination."

"There's more?" Renee asks, genuinely surprised. She was preparing to forgive Hunter for her terrible choice in drinking holes and call it a night. The thought was disappointing but also somewhat of a relief.

"Did you really think this was all I had planned?" Hunter waves her along, off the stool. "Let's go. We have reservations."

Renee's ears perk up at that word and she follows Hunter toward the exit. Along the way, she spots Callie once again. She definitely sees Renee this time, evident by her expression of shock. Renee waves and Callie lifts a confused hand up in response.

Good, she thinks as she strolls through the door being held open by Hunter. *Gotta keep them on their toes.*

CHAPTER TWENTY-FIVE

Renee stands just inside the doors of the building, feet firmly rooted to the dingy carpet below them. Hunter has gone off to do something important and she was too stunned to follow her. Instead, she freezes by the smudged glass doors, slowly turning her head to take in these utterly bizarre surroundings.

The *noise*. Unforgivably bad eighties hair band music layered on top of intermittent crashing, cheering, and groaning. The repetitive clink of glasses and plastic pitchers knocking onto Formica tables. There's an incessant rumble coming from the far end of the room. Occasional thumps. Boisterous, raucous laughter comes from a very dark room to Renee's left. And somehow, through all of that aural slaughter, she can hear the unmistakable sound of ESPN.

Hunter reappears in front of Renee. She's dangling a pair of beat-up shoes from her fingers and Renee shudders to think about the germs passing between the surfaces.

"No," she says firmly, shaking her head. "I am not wearing those."

"You have to." Hunter swings the shoes toward her but doesn't let go of them. "Come on. You know you want to."

"You honestly think I want to put on a pair of shoes that have been worn by hundreds of other people? Who knows what kind of foot diseases are swimming in those insoles?"

"They clean the shoes, Renee. Come on," she repeats, throwing in a wink for good measure. "Our lane is waiting."

The word "reservations" has only ever meant one thing to Renee: food. And while she imagines there is something resembling food in this establishment, Hunter did not make reservations at the snack bar. No, she made lane reservations.

At a bowling alley.

Hunter has apparently given up on verbally convincing Renee and has assumed she'll follow her. She's right, of course, because Hunter had the foresight to suggest Renee ride with her and now Renee has no exit plan. She has to follow Hunter. She has to put the shoes on.

She has to throw a ridiculously heavy ball down a long brown alleyway and try to knock over foolish white pins that ignorantly stand at the end of the lane, just waiting to be smashed by their nemesis, the weighty globe.

"I can tell my assumption that you've never bowled is correct," Hunter says, her voice painted with amusement, when Renee finally lands next to her on the dented plastic bench.

"Whatever gave me away?"

Hunter's shoulders shake with laughter. "The better question is, what didn't?"

With a huff, Renee slides off her ankle boots and picks up the offending rented shoes. She jumps when Hunter's hand lands on the middle of her back.

"I promise you, they really do clean them." Hunter's lips are alarmingly close to Renee's ear. She nearly leans closer, wanting to feel more of that whispered heat. "Just put them on and tie them."

Hunter's up and at the computer-like-thing before Renee can respond. She stares at her for a moment, wondering how it is that she's let herself come even this far. She blames Hunter entirely. There is just something about her, something Renee can still not—and may never be able to—figure out.

Something so magnificent, so disarming and beautiful and tempting, that Renee puts on the mangy bowling shoes.

Moments later, Hunter turns to her and extends her hand. Renee places her hand in it and allows Hunter to tug her up. To her surprise, Hunter doesn't let go once she's standing. She pulls gently and Renee closes the distance between them.

"Let's go get you a ball, and I'll tell you everything you need to know."

Hunter, possibly a professional bowler, does just that. She fills Renee's ears with general instructions, hot tips, and reminders. Once Renee is outfitted with a sparkling navy-blue ball—Hunter said it complements her eyes, but Renee missed the part of the instructions that said she'll have to put this hulking object anywhere near her face—that once belonged to someone named Crystal, whose name is inscribed along with the phrase "Pindigo Girls," she stands awkwardly at the top of the lane, clutching the behemoth with both hands.

"Remember what I told you," Hunter calls from behind her.

Renee shoots a look over her shoulder. She really cannot believe she's not only wearing used shoes, but now she also has her fingers—her very clean, nicely manicured fingers—thrust into tight, dark holes that have been probed by who knows how many other not-as-clean fingers.

And now, she has to *throw* this aggressively heavy ball. The extent of Renee's athleticism is walking. Strolling while counting steps, making sure she doesn't go over a peeling line on the floor, and heaving a cannonball down a rickety wooden pathway straight to a cluster of enthusiastically stupid white pins is beyond the reach of her skills.

But she will not back down. Not for anyone, but especially not in front of Hunter.

With a deep breath, Renee takes her first step and feels the ancient shoes attempt to betray her. Falling is simply not an option, and she steadies herself, gritting her teeth so hard her jaw aches, before taking another step. One, two, three more, and she swings her arm back, lurches it forward, and yanks her fingers from those obscene holes just in time to fling the sphere onto the runway.

It lands with an earth-shattering thump, earning curiously amused looks from the other bowlers. Renee shakes it off and spins around, trying her damndest to keep her balance, and teeters just once before stalking back to safe ground.

The look on Hunter's face is indescribable, a mix of deep enjoyment, horror, and enchantment. She waits until Renee is right next to her before she opens her mouth.

"That was not terrible."

Renee scoffs. "Is it still sitting where it landed?"

Hunter leans over, her shoulder brushing Renee's hip. "Nope. It traveled. It just, uh, didn't pick up any passengers on its journey." Hunter pauses. "No, wait. It didn't cause any accidents at its final destination." She shakes her head. "Hang on."

Renee laughs and watches as her hand, entirely of its own volition, lifts up and comes to rest on Hunter's shoulder. Her very muscled shoulder. "Leave the analogies to me, okay?"

Hunter turns her head and looks at Renee's fingers before drawing her eyes back up to Renee's face. "Honestly, Renee, I'll do whatever you ask of me as long as you're touching me when you ask it."

The arousal from earlier, now a tantalizing mess of colorful flowers reaching into every available corner of Renee's body, shimmies. The blooms shake in the hot, humid breeze. Renee clenches her thighs together.

"You know," Hunter says slowly, eyes never leaving Renee's, "you have another throw."

Renee drops her hand from Hunter's shoulder and smiles as she turns away. She's certain Hunter is watching her walk toward the ball return, and she gives herself permission to enjoy it. Because, frankly, why not?

After a second similarly horrid throw, Renee retreats to the bench and watches Hunter take her first turn. It's unfair, honestly, that Hunter possesses grace even in a bowling alley.

Her movements are fluid, strong and gentle all at once. Even the way her jeans are rolled up to expose a pair of brightly colored argyle socks is cute. She knocks down four pins on her first throw, wasting no time bowling over the remaining six on her second.

Renee claps as Hunter returns, and Hunter bows from the waist.

"I didn't realize I was playing with a professional."

Hunter gives her a crooked smile. "I'm not a professional, but I did play in a club when I was a kid. My dad was a big bowler."

"And he taught you everything he knew?"

"He tried. I wasn't interested. I really only continued bowling because it gave us time together on the weekends. He wasn't around much otherwise."

Renee's heart stutter-beats. She would like to give Hunter's father a strict talking-to. How dare he not be there for his daughter, who is possibly the most incredible person Renee's ever met? Doesn't he know what he was missing?

The surge of protectiveness surprises her, and for a worrisome moment, she wonders if she sees Hunter as more of a daughter than—

The thought is cleanly interrupted by Hunter turning around and facing her. The look in her eyes sends an electric rush through Renee. No. This is definitely not maternal protectiveness.

"You're up," Hunter says, her words carrying some leftover electricity.

Very aware of the current sparking between them, when Renee stands and moves toward the ball return, she not so accidentally brushes the side of her body against Hunter. She's rewarded with a quiet gasp. *Success*, she thinks with pride…and arousal.

She is not, however, prepared for what happens next.

As Renee stands at the top of the lane, lost in thoughts about how to better extract her fingers from the tight confines of the finger tubes, Hunter walks up behind her and puts her hands on Renee's hips. It's her turn to gasp, and she does so, unable to keep it in her throat.

"Okay if I help you?" Again, Hunter's mouth is dangerously close to her ear. Renee can merely nod in response.

The ghost of a touch at her hips moves down just so. Hunter's hands lay flat against the sides of Renee's thighs. She momentarily forgets how to breathe as she allows Hunter to guide her back two steps.

"I think a little extra space before you launch the ball might help." It's a miracle that Renee can even hear Hunter over the ruckus surrounding them, but she still leans her ear closer to Hunter's mouth. So close that she feels the brush of Hunter's lips against the curve of her ear.

"Easy," Hunter says, and Renee can hear the smile in her voice. "We have a game to finish."

"So help me finish it," she says.

Hunter's reply is the slide of her hands back up to Renee's hips. Her grip is firmer now. Suddenly, Hunter's torso is pressed against Renee's back. She bites the inside of her cheek.

"I'm going to walk with you," Hunter says. "Okay? I'm going to keep my left hand on your hip so you know when to stop, and my right hand"—she moves it all the way up to Renee's shoulder, then glides it down until her fingers encircle her wrist—"will be here. We're going to do a rocking motion, back and forth, and when I say 'go,' I want you to let go of the ball."

"Okay," Renee whispers. She can barely breathe, let alone think. The trajectory of this swing is entirely in Hunter's hands.

Hunter's left hand pulls Renee closer against her, and Renee releases a whimper. She has never whimpered in her life. But the magic of Hunter's body pressed tightly against hers is sending her to worlds and noises unknown.

"Just making sure I have a firm grip." Hunter's lips brush against Renee's ear with each "m" sound.

"Feels firm to me," Renee manages.

"Very." Hunter's thumb detours from her other fingers and swipes at the waistband of Renee's jeans. "Are you ready?"

Renee nods. It's rare that she can't speak, but alas, so it is.

Hunter's pelvis bumps against Renee's butt and she takes a step, Hunter coming with her. They walk in sync toward the line and Renee feels Hunter begin guiding her right arm, making, just as she said, a rocking motion. She could stay here all night, rocking against Hunter's body, but all too soon, Hunter says, "Go," and Renee obeys, sending her ball flying down the lane.

To her delight, Hunter does not release her. They stand together, their bodies dangerously close, and watch Renee's ball journey down the lane. Six pins fall at the point of collision, a seventh giving up the fight at the behest of its friends.

Jubilant, Renee turns around in Hunter's arms. Their noses touch and Renee takes an immediate step back. But just one. One small step, not enough to break the moment or the feelings.

"Nicely done," Hunter says, finally releasing her grip on Renee. "You're a good student."

"It's been a long time since I heard that."

"I have a feeling you'll be hearing it again soon." Hunter smiles, revealing a glimpse of her teeth, before putting more space between them.

The implications are heard loud and clear, and they resonate within Renee for the remainder of their bowling adventure.

To neither's surprise, Hunter annihilates Renee, beating her by sixty-seven points. Normally, Renee would be some kind of pissed about losing, but she's riding high on the very intimate assistance Hunter continued to give her throughout the game. They even split mozzarella sticks and french fries from the snack bar—a true sign of Renee being far happier than normal.

As Hunter drives them back to Harpy so Renee can collect her car, she wonders what comes next. She's given up trying to fight her attraction to Hunter; she can't avoid it anyway, considering she outright told Hunter about it. Had Hunter grabbed her hand and taken her into the locker room at the bowling alley, Renee is pretty certain she would have ripped her own clothes off and offered herself for the taking.

Perhaps she should have tried bowling earlier in her life. She had no idea it could be such an aphrodisiac.

But the tempting thought of in-the-moment bowling alley sex (*good God, Renee,* she thinks, half disgusted with her adolescent hormones but also oddly proud of them for showing up) is very different from the looming end of a date. This is formal, real. Absolute. Unavoidable.

And also, she realizes, fairly unpredictable.

Hunter puts her Range Rover in park and looks over at Renee. "Are you in the parking lot or on the street?"

"I'm right there." She points to her car, safely parked under a streetlight across the street from the bar.

Without another word, Hunter unbuckles her seat belt and gets out of the car. Renee waits, knowing she'll come to her door, and she does, extending her hand for Renee. Hunter keeps Renee's hand clasped in hers as they cross the street with zero rush.

The distance is short, however, and they're at Renee's car in no time. She turns and leans against it, watching Hunter carefully.

"This was an absolutely wonderful evening," Hunter says. "Except for the part where I thought I could get you to like beer."

Renee laughs. It occurs to her right then and there that she's never laughed as much as she has tonight. She swallows the realization. "I hate beer. That won't change."

"And from now on, I promise to respect that."

"Thank you," Renee begins, then shakes her head. "For the beer promise, but also for tonight. I…I don't often let loose."

"I know." So simple, so true, so odd how well Hunter knows her.

"Tonight was good for me," Renee says, her voice an echo of its normal resonance. "Thank you, Hunter."

"Can I ask you something?"

"Yes."

Hunter leans in an inch or two. Renee feels so short around her tonight; without her heels, she's a good six inches shorter than Hunter.

"How are you feeling about your first true date with a woman?"

Renee sucks in a breath. She should have known that was coming. "Good. I had a very good time."

Hunter snaps her fingers. "And just like that, the protective, formal barrier comes roaring up." But her voice is laced with mirth, not irritation. "I should have just kissed you instead of basically asking you to get back in your head."

Renee straightens up. *This is it*, she thinks. "Yes. You should have."

"Renee…"

Oh, that tone. Renee doesn't like it. "Hunter."

Hunter stuffs her hands in her pockets, a movement at odds with her usual confidence. "Are you really prepared for the reality that there could be something between us?"

It's accidental, the way Renee zips up her features. It's her embarrassment, her shame—her sudden confusion. If she's feeling this, how can Hunter not be? She's the one without the experience. Hunter's the professional lesbian here, for God's sake. If she's stuck on "could be," how in the world did Renee fast forward into "there *is* something here"?

"I suppose," Renee begins, "I'll have to figure that out for myself." She doesn't mean for her voice to be thick with steel.

But oddly, Hunter is not deterred. She pulls her hands from her pockets and grabs Renee's hips once again. Her body responds instantly though her brain is going down a different path. She leans in to her own body, hoping to quiet her brain for once.

"Because it really could be something," Hunter says, leaning in.

That *could be* again. Renee tries to shake it off. "It could be," she says, a futile attempt at being cold.

Hunter pauses, her mouth an infinitesimal space from Renee's lips. "Or it could be nothing."

"It could be nothing," Renee repeats, a whisper floating on a breath of anticipation.

And then Hunter's lips are on hers. The softness brings up an ache within Renee. She barely registers her own lips moving in sync with Hunter's, the gentle but impassioned press of their mouths a feeling all its own. Renee loses herself, just for a moment, in the heat and intrigue. She eagerly kisses Hunter, over and over again, the world around them blurring into nothingness. Renee only realizes she's forgotten to breathe when Hunter pulls back, leaving her lips quaking, lungs gasping for air.

Flushing, she presses her hand against her mouth as she tries to compose herself. Hunter is watching her carefully, her lips full and glossed with their kiss.

On another breath, this one sparkling with desire finally seeing the light of day, Renee says, "It's not nothing."

Hunter's fingers stroke her cheek. "No, Renee. It's definitely something."

And then Hunter cups Renee's face in her hands and bulldozes her remaining walls, along with all those blooming, pulsating wildflowers, with five small words.

"You're not ready for this."

CHAPTER TWENTY-SIX

The subtle morning sounds of Jess making their way through the kitchen for coffee and a toasted bagel have dissipated, cloaking the house in silence once again. Renee is thankful that Jess has not grown up to be a loud, careless person. They move with the stealth of a cat (not quite like Mr. Purrington, however, who is oddly heavy-footed for a feline) and other than not regularly using coasters, Jess is low-maintenance and respectful of the house.

The quiet is nice, accommodating. Renee imagines Jess might be louder in their own space; in fact, she has a hunch that when she leaves for work every day, Jess does something irrevocably loud, just to test the sound capacity of the house. They went through a period in their late teens when the only music they listened to was something called "screamo," and it did, in fact, make Renee want to scream. She didn't think that was the point of the music, but whatever the case, Jess's interest in it lasted a scant few months, and then the screaming ceased for good.

It's possible Jess has begun listening to it again. Renee strains to hear any noises from downstairs—she'll never forget the dissonant sounds of screamo—but all she senses is a disappointing mist of silence.

It's a shame, really. Renee pulls her sheet and blanket as tight as possible against her chin. She wouldn't mind dissolving into some screamo right now.

In the thirty-six hours that have passed since Hunter's declaration, no communication has occurred between the two women. Because this is new, this whole dating women thing, Renee has no idea if this is "normal," or if she should be the one to reach out. All she hears when she picks up the phone, however, is the cold echo of Hunter's five words: *You're not ready for this.*

And each time the words bounce freely in her mind, she feels the full revolt of mixed feelings. She vacillates between fury and confusion with sprinkles of flat-out disbelief thrown in between. There have been smears of fear brushed over by languid strokes of "I told you so," but she's not sure who's been telling whom a damn thing. In an unfortunate and unpredictable twist, Renee has absolutely no idea what to say: to herself, or to Hunter. She rarely, if ever, loses her ability to script words into meaningful sentences. But this is new territory, a landscape marred by boulders and jagged ridges. She's already slipped, and like hell will she allow herself to fall.

Actually, she's not sure she has control over that last bit.

One thing Renee is certain she can control is whether or not she gets out of bed today. She's already emailed Audrey with instructions to cancel her classes. This is one of the times Renee is thankful for her secretary missing the compassion chip: She knows Audrey won't ask why she's not coming to work. Those other people in the offices, though—she won't be so lucky there. But she'll deal with that tomorrow.

There's only one thing Renee needs to deal with today, and that does require her to get out of bed. Lying here, blinking in the semidarkness, isn't helping her achieve that goal. With a start, Renee pushes herself up on her elbows. If she doesn't get moving immediately, Jess will realize that she's behind her usual schedule and start asking questions.

"That won't do," Renee mumbles as she gets out of bed and stalks directly to the shower.

She goes through the motions of getting ready, sidestepping her usual professor-wear for something slightly more casual. Again, she's not interested in capturing Jess's attention. A freshly ironed pair of dark-blue pants topped with a cream sweater will be just fine.

Renee avoids her eyes as much as possible as she dries her hair and applies some light makeup. She's certain she screwed up in some secret, monumental way on Saturday night. Perhaps— her eyes widen as she finally looks at herself—she's a bad kisser. In her defense, she's never kissed a woman before, so how was she to know that women are far superior kissers to men? It's been ages since she kissed a man but the difference between *that* and *Hunter* was immediately recognizable. She shakes her head and ties her hair back in a neat low bun. So she's a bad kisser. There are worse things.

Besides, Hunter's right. Renee isn't ready for her, for that, for whatever that is with her. She can easily pack up the experience and ship it off to her memories, never to rip the tape off the box again. And that's fine, perfectly fine.

At least it solves the problem of not knowing whether or not she's supposed to call Hunter and try to convince her that she's wrong.

Renee slaps her hand against her thigh. No. Hunter is right. She's not wrong, she's *right*. Before that obnoxious internal monologue can pipe up and try to convince her otherwise, Renee hurries from her bedroom.

The white colonial home is as imposing as ever, even if the shutters need repainting. Renee drives slowly, arcing her way through the first curve of the driveway, admiring the leaning trees and their multicolored leaves. Sloping lawns on both sides of the home end at the edges of a forest. The setting is picturesque, and the house was chosen for that exact characteristic.

It's also a bit isolated, which Renee hated as a teenager. The house sits on the edge of her old school district's boundaries, and none of her friends were within walking distance. In that challenging period of time after parents are tired of driving their kids to playdates but before those kids are old enough to drive themselves, Renee spent a lot of weekends by herself.

She parks her car at the apex of the driveway and quickly walks up the dramatic brick front steps. Just as her hand reaches the doorbell, she wonders if she should have asked Jess to come along. She has a feeling that Jess would have not so politely declined this invitation.

Moments after ringing the bell, the door swings open and Renee is greeted by Paula, her mother's longtime "assistant." The word is a catchall for too many things to remember, but Paula has never seemed to mind anything Renee's mother has asked of her. She's likely the only friend Margaret Lawler has.

"Well, look at you. Come in, come in."

Renee steps into the warm house, ever surprised at the temperature. She remembers the house as being cold and formal, but either her mother's too old to stand a chill, or her own memories have created a scenario of the past that simply isn't accurate.

Like much in Renee's life at the moment, she does not know what's true and what isn't. It's a mesmerizing and haunting feeling, not being able to trust your mind.

"Margaret will be so happy to see you," Paula says after hanging up Renee's jacket in the hall closet. "She just said to me the other day that she can't remember the last time you visited."

In the place where shame would normally be, Renee feels irritation. Her relationship with her mother has never been one to write home about. She was always closer to her father, Richard, and when he died suddenly when Renee was in her late thirties, she'd half expected her bond with her mother to be fortified. Nearly ten years later, she's still waiting for that to happen.

"It has been a while," Renee allows as she follows Margaret through the expansive first floor. She resists the urge to complete the sentence with "but I imagine she could care less."

"Margaret," Paula calls as they enter the sitting room at the back of the house. Pale morning sunlight streaks through the room and Renee tugs at the collar of her sweater. It must be eighty degrees in here. "Renee is here."

"Oh," comes the reply. Renee steps further into the room and spies her mother sitting in a plush chair, the newspaper clutched in her hands and hiding the lower half of her face. "How lovely."

She knows there's no smile hiding behind the local news section. Just as well; Renee isn't smiling either. "Hello, Margaret," she says, then immediately clamps her hand over her mouth.

"Hello, Renee," Margaret says, not dropping the newspaper. "What brings you here?"

Still reeling from the pinpricked moment of like-mother-like-daughter, Renee takes a moment before answering. "I'm not working today so I thought I'd come see you."

"Oh? It's not a holiday, is it?"

"No," Renee says, then drops into an armchair. "I took the day off."

The newspaper snaps down, revealing a bewildered expression. Margaret's steely gray eyes narrow in on her daughter and the soft wrinkles around her mouth go rigid. "You did what?"

"Did you get the flowers I sent for your birthday last week?" It's a weak diversion, and it won't work but Renee tries anyway.

"I did, yes, thank you. Why aren't you at work?"

Renee flicks her wrist. "I needed a day off. And since I wasn't able to visit you on your actual birthday, I thought I'd come today."

Margaret stares at Renee. There's no empathy, no compassion, just confusion. A bit of annoyance too, maybe. It's the look she wore most often through Renee's preteen years, so at least it's familiar.

"It's fine," Renee continues. "I only have one class today and my students have a significant essay due at the end of the week. I gave them the gift of unexpected work time."

"I see." The paper rises once more, hiding Margaret's entire face.

They sit in silence for several moments, the only sound a ticking clock on the wall. Renee glances around the cheerful yellow room, hoping for something new to notice and discuss, but it appears exactly the same as it was the last time she was here, which was at least six months ago. She'd like to visit more often. No, that's a lie. She should visit more often. But she doesn't, because she doesn't want to. And this is precisely why.

"Margaret," she begins, waiting for the paper to drop, but it doesn't. "Can I ask you a question?"

A huff rattles the paper. "Don't ask a question to ask a question. Just ask the question."

"Right, fine. When did I stop calling you mom?"

The paper stills but remains high and shielding. "You were six."

Renee coughs then clears her throat. "Six? And you didn't reprimand me? Or demand otherwise?"

"Of course I did. But you refused." The newspaper drops a bit, revealing Margaret's frosty white hair. "You've always done things your own way. At a certain point, there was no sense in fighting you."

Renee pulls the collar of her sweater away from her neck, ushering puffs of air down her chest. "It's incredibly hot in here."

"Perhaps you're having a hot flash. I was about your age when I started the change." A rustle of the paper. "I assume you're not planning on having any more children."

The words scald Renee, blistering her and making her ache for reprieve. She could fight; she has in the past. But there's a mountain of other trembling feelings sitting on top of Renee's current shifting feelings for her mother, and she can't reach the ire that she so desperately wants to touch and bask in.

"No, I'm not." Renee stands and clasps her hands in front of her. "I should get going. We'll talk soon."

"Very well. Goodbye, dear."

Renee blindly stumbles to the front of the house, grabs her coat, and leaves without bothering to find Paula.

The sight of her own home draws a much-needed deep breath of relief from Renee. She hurries into the house and goes directly up to the guest room. Or, Jess's room. Renee doesn't even want her guest room back (though she can admit it also doesn't matter because she has two other unused bedrooms on this floor). This room, however: She's finding she prefers it to be Jess's room.

She knocks and without waiting for an answer, pushes open the door. Jess turns in their seat at the desk. They motion for Renee to wait a second.

Unable to sit still, Renee paces the short length of the room while Jess chats amicably with someone on her computer screen. She's so lost in her determined thoughts that it occurs to her much too late that whomever Jess is speaking with can probably see her walking back and forth like a madwoman. Once it dawns on her, she stops in the corner of the room and crosses her arms tightly across her chest.

Soon, Jess slides their headphones from their ears and turns to appraise Renee. "Why aren't you at work?"

"Have I been an absolutely horrible mother?" Renee blurts. "Be honest."

"Umm…" Jess kicks their feet up onto the bed. Renee cringes, seeing their shoes. "Oh good, just checking." Jess puts their feet down and grins. "You seem a little off, but good to know you're still obsessed with my bad habits."

"Answer the question."

"No, you haven't been an absolutely horrible mother. Have you been a little absent?" Jess laughs, seeming to thoroughly tickle themself. "Well, that's putting it lightly, you've been very absent. But physically. Just physically." Jess leans forward, their elbows on their knees and a serious look on their face. "We haven't had an easy relationship. We both know that. But the truth is, Ren—Mom, I have never doubted that you are here for me and support me."

A funny feeling burns at the back of Renee's throat. She clears her throat several times in a row, but the feeling persists.

"Do you…" Jess stands up. "You look like you need a hug."

Renee shrugs as tears make their way down her cheeks. The feel of Jess's arms around her shoulders drops all of her remaining defenses, and she rests her head against her child's.

"You're a good hugger," Renee says, hanging on for dear life.

"So I've been told." Jess squeezes her once more and lets go. "Wanna talk about it?"

"No." Renee clears her throat yet again, to no avail. "But please know that I wanted to be a mother. You have always been wanted, and you have always been loved." She wipes furiously at the tears flying down her face. "I hope that I have never made you feel otherwise."

Jess shrugs. "This hasn't been all roses and rainbows, but I know that you love me."

"Yes, good. Parenting is hard." Renee manages a laugh before holding up her hand to ward off the retort she knows Jess is dying to lob at her. "And I know I left a lot of the parenting to your grandparents. Frankly, I'm more sorry about that than I ever imagined I could be. But you…you made me the one thing I always wanted to be. And, Jess, I am endlessly proud of you, of exactly who you are."

"Ahh," Jess says, nodding. "You went to see Gram."

"I was at work," Renee says, too loudly.

"No, see, I know you weren't at work because one of your colleagues emailed me and asked if you're okay."

"What?" Renee sputters. "Who? And how does anyone there have your email address?"

Jess chuckles. "Callie. Because I gave it to her so I can help her build a website."

"What on earth does Callie Lewes need a website for?"

Jess flicks their wrist and Renee stifles a laugh, loving yet again seeing her mannerisms in her child. "Some editing thing. Anyway. I know you weren't at work, so just admit you went to see your mother."

"Fine. Yes. But we're not going to talk about it."

"No need to, you came right in here and told me everything I need to know." Renee would like to wipe her hand over that cocky smile on Jess's face, but she also kind of loves it. "Anything else you wanna talk about?"

"Nothing." Her throat closes on the word.

Jess studies her, eyes bright and steady. "Okay. I need to get back to work. I'm sure you have busy professor things to do, so how about I make dinner for us later?"

Those awful tears make motions to reappear, and all Renee can do is nod before escaping back to her room, where she allows them to fall freely and painfully.

CHAPTER TWENTY-SEVEN

As it happened, Renee didn't have any classes on Tuesday, so she gave herself another day at home to regroup. Still refusing to open up to Jess about Hunter, Renee has done nothing but Ferris wheel her own thoughts and concerns repetitively, once to the point of making herself so nauseous that she knelt before the toilet and stared into the water, wishing she could rid herself of the conflicted feelings.

When she returns to campus on Wednesday, there's fire in her steps. Gone (or at least misplaced) is the confused sadness. Here to play is the anger.

"Audrey," Renee says as she walks into the office, "my mail."

Audrey snaps her head up. "Dr. Lawler. Good morning. You're back."

"My mail," Renee repeats, her tone frigid. She stalks past Audrey's desk then pauses. "Get me a meeting with the dean. Today."

She doesn't wait to hear the sputtered response. In the safety of her office, Renee drops her shoulders an inch and tries to take a deep breath. It's useless. Her lungs seem to be working at partial capacity, not permitting full breaths. The end result is a prickling sensation that clings to the sides of each half-hearted breath.

It's fine. She doesn't have time to devote to breathing anyway. Her first class begins in an hour and having canceled Monday's, Renee needs to adjust her planned lecture. She has big plans for her two classes today. Very big, very powerful plans.

It seems her students are not excited about her big, powerful plans. Renee's nine a.m. class seems to be sleepwalking. Their lack of engagement only spurs her on, her voice reaching new heights in volume and sharp edges. By the time the clock hits 9:48, the majority of students are staring at her, wide-eyed. She has a hunch it's more out of fear than awe.

Renee finishes her lecture promptly at 9:50, and all but two students waste no time in leaving the classroom. She's really not in the mood for professorial small talk, so Renee does her best to affect an unapproachable air as she packs up her things. It must not be effective enough.

"Um. Dr. Lawler? I just...can I ask you a question?"

The memory of Margaret Lawler's voice pricks the back of Renee's neck. "Don't ask a question to ask a question," she says before she can stop herself.

"Oh. Sorry." The student—Alexa, she of the satisfactory but never mind-blowing work—lets her backpack skim the floor. "I was wondering if I could have an extension on the essay that's due on Friday."

Renee sucks in a breath. She waits a few seconds before meeting Alexa's eyes. "No."

Alexa takes a step back, clearly shocked. Renee isn't known for being laid-back, but she is reasonable. Usually.

"You should have used your extra time on Monday more wisely." Out of the corner of her eye, Renee sees the other lingering student tiptoeing out of the classroom. She resists the urge, just barely, to call that student back and rake him over the coals.

"I...I did. I worked on it for hours on Monday. And yesterday." Alexa pushes strands of dark-blond hair out of her eyes. "I just feel like something isn't clicking. I was hoping we could meet today, and we could—"

"I have no time to meet today," Renee snaps. "This is on you, Alexa. This is a consequence of your poor time management. Additionally, perhaps your struggle is a reflection of this course being too advanced for your current skill set. I urge you to choose courses more cautiously next semester."

Renee fully expects Alexa to tuck her tail between her legs and flee from the scene of the ego-obliterating crime. In a horrid twist, Alexa doesn't move. She doesn't break eye contact, either. Renee is a bit shook.

"I'm confident that I'm prepared for this course, Dr. Lawler." The young woman's voice is level and calm. "What I'm not confident about, however, is this essay. And I was hopeful that you'd be able to help me. I now understand that's not an option. Enjoy the rest of your day."

Alexa turns and walks out of the classroom. Renee gawks, then shuts her mouth and clenches her teeth. *The nerve*, she thinks. *The absolute fucking nerve.*

She has some recognition that she is in the wrong, of course, but the ice covering the pathways of her emotions is slick and dangerous, a glistening luge leading to nothing but troubled awareness.

With all her senses on high alert, Renee sniffs the air before she wrangles open the door leading to the English offices. It smells like a funeral home. She's fairly certain no one has died (not discounting one of the students from her two morning classes) so the scent is out of place and disconcerting.

She throws the door open, hinges screaming from the projection of Renee's continued blistering emotions, and stops in her tracks.

There, perched on the edge of Audrey's desk, is a painfully beautiful floral arrangement. Every single flower is white, glowing against the fern green explosions of leaves and other fillers. It's stunning. Simple but stunning.

Renee filters through ways to avoid accepting this outlandish apology from Hunter. She doesn't want to bring this kind of attention to herself; the idea of explaining who the flowers are from and why they've been sent sends uncomfortable chills down her arms. She's not ready for that—

She stills, her limbs caught in defensive position steps from Audrey's desk. Right. Hunter was right after all. She's *not* ready for that.

Resolved, even if the resolution brings with it a new surge of ire, Renee takes the remaining steps until she's standing right in front of Audrey's desk. Audrey hasn't looked up yet and Renee both loves and hates this.

"Throw them away," she says, her voice low and clipped.

Audrey looks up, confusion evident in her features. "Dr. Lawler? Hi. I'm sorry, throw what away?"

Renee points a single finger at the floral arrangement. "This. I don't want it."

"Oh. I—no." Audrey hunches her shoulders, looking like she'd like to disappear into herself. "They…Dr. Lawler, they're not for you."

The fire consuming Renee's organs spreads fast and furiously. She doesn't blame Audrey for trying to protect her, but now is not the time to lie. "Of course they are." She knows she sounds indignant, but why shouldn't she? "Fine," she acquiesces. "You can keep them. I don't want them."

Renee leans her hands on Audrey's desk, bringing her face dangerously close to Audrey's. The young woman doesn't back up, and Renee remembers why she hired her.

"I'm asking you to—"

"Renee."

One word, one voice. The soft but commanding tone plows through Renee's embattled barriers. She feels her shoulders drop but her hands don't lose their tense grasp on the desk.

"Renee." Softer, but more commanding. She lets her wrists relax.

No one speaks. The air in the room, which is small to begin with, ripples with spiky tension. Renee senses the walls closing in and her urge to sprint to her office is high and strong. She steps to the right and jumps back when her arm collides with Kate's chest.

"Come with me," Kate murmurs. It doesn't matter if Audrey hears her—Renee has done enough damage for the day, possibly the week—but Kate has the grace to be quiet about her direction.

And Renee, nearly twitching as she feels her chest tighten and her eyes water, knows she would do anything Kate asked her to do in this moment.

They make their way to Kate's office and Kate shuts the door as Renee primly sits down in the leather chair. She's suddenly exhausted and has to prop her head up with her hand. Kate's office is like that, though. Whereas Renee's is all business and little personality (perhaps Franklin was right and it is drab), Kate's space is bursting with her personality, even if it's all subtle. The space exudes calm authority.

"Don't," Renee says lamely as Kate sits down next to her instead of behind her desk. "Don't do your thing with me right now."

"What thing?"

"The quiet thing. The waiting me out thing. Just ask whatever it is you want to ask."

Renee doesn't want to look at Kate, but she can feel that discerning gaze wash over her. Some of the panic in Renee's chest starts to loosen.

"What is going on with you?"

Renee nods, knowing she's deserving of a blunt question, even if it's not Kate's usual style. Before she can piece together an answer, Kate goes on.

"You've been exceptionally harsh on Audrey lately. She has her quirks, but we both know she's a fantastic secretary and there's no reason for your brutality."

Renee snaps her head up, but keeps her eyes trained to the floor. "Brutality? That seems extreme."

Kate releases a held-in breath. "It is. I'm sorry. I'm…I'm worried about you."

Renee plops her head against her right hand once again and flicks her left wrist with little enthusiasm. "No need for that."

"No, Renee. There is a need." Kate scoots closer. Renee feels her heart drum up a faster beat, staccato and loud. "Your absence the last two days did not go unnoticed. Nor did the fact that you didn't return my texts. It's not like you to disappear. And truly, your…well, there's no other way to say it. Your behavior has been unusual and concerning."

"There's nothing going on."

"I know that's not true. Is this related to Jess?"

Renee shakes her head, strands of loose hair brushing her ears. She's jolted back to the bowling alley, Hunter's lips ghosting against her ears. "No." She waits for a new guess, but nothing comes.

When Renee finally dares to meet Kate's eyes, she's hit with a swell of emotion. Her friend is looking at her with compassion and concern. But that's not the cause of the swell.

Renee nearly laughs out loud. She feels a giggle rising in her throat and presses her fist to her lips. She may be at a point of completely unwinding, but she won't let herself—

A knock at Kate's door causes both women to turn toward the sound. Neither says a word but the door creaks open anyway, and Callie's head appears in the crack.

"Oh, hey. Sorry to interrupt." Callie steps into the office and walks over to Kate, dropping a hand to her shoulder and squeezing. It's subtle intimacy, and Renee laps up every moment of it. She watches the way Kate's face brightens, the gloss in her eyes illuminated when she looks up at Callie. Callie's cheeks are pinched pink, and her smile is dazzling. The love between them is palpable.

"Just wanted to thank you for the flowers," Callie says, eyeing Renee before leaning down and pressing a quick kiss to Kate's cheek. "They're beautiful." She whispers something in Kate's ear, and Renee isn't sure if she's sad or relieved that she can't hear it.

Kate's cheeks flush and she grabs Callie's hand, squeezing her fingers. "You're welcome. We'll talk later."

Callie nods and goes to leave but Renee calls out to her.

"Wait. Wait." She looks back and forth between Kate and Callie. "Those flowers on Audrey's desk. They're from you? To Callie?"

Kate cracks a half-smile, one without humor. After all, she witnessed part of Renee's flower-induced breakdown, apparently knowing it was as unhinged as it was unnecessary.

"I see." Renee bites the inside of her cheek and looks away. She steals another glance at Kate, and the same feeling from before Callie interrupted loops up her throat.

Callie leans against the closed door. She's watching Renee carefully. "Ahh," she says softly. "Well, it's about time."

Kate shoots a confused look at her girlfriend. "What are you talking about?"

Callie, grinning now, points to Renee. "Ask her."

Renee is certain her face has either imploded with an explosion of fuchsia or lost all color and she's turned into a ghost. Her emotions are so topsy-turvy that she genuinely has no idea which it is.

Not wanting to go down this path, really wanting to avoid it at all costs, Renee shakes her head. Vehemently.

"You thought the flowers were for you," Callie says gently. Gently, yes, but Renee can't help but fantasize about darting across the room and wrangling her out the door.

"Oh no," Kate says, her tone equally gentle. Really? What is it with these two? "Renee…"

She holds up one hand to stop Kate from continuing. "It's not what you think."

Callie straightens. "Actually, I think this is a conversation you two should have without me."

"Who did you think sent you flowers?" Kate surely means this in a kind way, but Renee momentarily hates her for asking such a bold question.

Callie scuffs her shoe against the floor. "Kate," she says softly, waiting until Kate turns to look at her before continuing. "You…you really haven't picked up on this?"

"I have no idea what you're talking about." Kate looks back at Renee. "Do you?"

Renee can now feel her ears burning. She assumes her face is also a lovely shade of red. "What did you mean—" She stops and clears her throat. "When you said it's about time?"

Callie crosses one ankle over the other. She's the picture of calm, and Renee, knowing what's begun knocking at her doors of awareness, is surprised because she now knows exactly what Callie was referring to. She just wants to hear it from her.

So she doesn't have to say it herself.

Callie unceremoniously gestures to Kate and Renee. "I meant that it's about time you realized you have feelings for my girlfriend."

Kate gasps; Renee sighs out a laugh. There. Relief. She didn't have to say it.

Realizing it was enough admission for one day.

"And I guess you also thought she sent you flowers?"

Renee shakes her head. "No, of course not. Why would she send me flowers when you're in a relationship with her, and she and I are just friends?"

Callie shrugs, the picture of not being threatened by this big reveal. Renee admires her for it, truly. "That's the part I can't figure out."

"Wait a minute." Kate's voice cuts through their back-and-forth. "You?" She shakes her head, seeming to try to clear her head. "What are you two talking about?"

"I didn't think Kate sent me flowers." Renee needs to clarify that; she refuses to be a splinter in this healthy, happy relationship between two people she genuinely likes and cares about. "As for the other part…It was an accident."

Callie laughs. "Yeah, I know the feeling. I'm gonna go, let you two talk." She hesitates with her hand on the doorknob. "On second thought, maybe this is a conversation you'd rather have outside of work?"

Renee takes one look at the bewildered expression on Kate's face and nods her agreement. Callie leaves and the two women sit, staring at each other.

"Kate, I—"

"Wait. I think we both need to sort through some things before we continue this conversation." Kate's voice is back to gentle and warm, though she still looks stunned. "Tomorrow night? We've already planned to have dinner at Courtney's."

"You..." Renee sighs inwardly. "We need Courtney as a buffer?"

"No," Kate hurries to say.

"I've made you uncomfortable."

"Not at all." Kate reaches over and skims her fingers over Renee's wrist. "Just very, very surprised."

Renee hums. "I suppose Courtney is aware of it too."

"If Callie is, we can guarantee Courtney is."

Renee sits with that. She does need some time to navigate through the realization and the announcement, even though the vocal admission doesn't mean much. She doesn't want to be with Kate. Perhaps if Kate were single, then...yes, perhaps. But Renee's heart has latched on to someone else, even if that certain someone else still has not made any effort to contact her.

Not even with flowers.

CHAPTER TWENTY-EIGHT

Renee inspects the charcuterie board while Courtney and Kate are holed up in the kitchen, having some sort of secret spy meeting. She imagines it's about her and the small tremor that Callie initiated yesterday. Renee isn't looking forward to having this discussion—though she does appreciate that Courtney will be present because she'll provide much-needed comic relief—but she's pleased that the amount of time it took for her to wrestle herself through her thoughts and feelings about Kate was far less than she'd expected.

It's simple, really. Renee has had a crush on Kate for years. She just never realized it because Kate didn't give her the opportunity to. She has easily chalked it up to thinking Kate's brilliant and beautiful, a sublime combination, but not one Renee was interested in beyond a coworking and friendly relationship. Sure, she looks forward to seeing Kate. She likes being around her. Maybe she even felt some things here and there, deep in the buried recesses of her libido. But nothing ever solidified into something she could present to Kate—not that she would, given that Kate's very much taken. The attraction simply sat between her ribs, sparking into light every so often, but largely dormant and unaddressed.

The unfortunate offshoot of this realization is the Hunter stem. Hunter gave Renee the space, the opportunity, the electric moments of being faced with a mutual attraction. And after testing that connection with a single, achingly arousing kiss, Hunter took it all away.

Renee picks up a piece of chipotle cheddar cheese and takes a bite. The spice hits slow and low, a rolling fire of smokiness. She savors the taste, using it to dispel her increasing agitation about Hunter.

"How's that cheddar? Here, try it with one of these cracked pepper wafers." Nick Rodriguez, Courtney's husband, breezes into the room with a basket of crackers. He sets it down next to the meat and cheese board, then puts his hand on his hip and sighs. "Courtney went a little overboard with the meats and cheeses. No room for the crackers."

"It's fine," Renee says. "Delicious."

"Yes, *but*," Nick says, annoyed, "everything should be *on* the board. Not sitting over here in these horrendous baskets we got as a wedding gift."

"And they definitely weren't on the registry," Courtney adds as she and Kate come back into the room and sit down. She grabs a handful of crackers and tosses them onto a plate. "Thanks, Nick. See ya later."

Nick gapes at his wife, hand still firmly on his hip. "Excuse me? You're dismissing me after I spent hours in the kitchen putting this masterpiece together?"

"Yes."

Kate stifles a laugh, and Renee can't help but to smile. She loves the dynamic of this marriage. Poor Nick never stood a chance of being in charge.

"So I'll miss all the gossipy girl talk?"

"Exactly." Courtney pushes her socked foot against his shin. "Goodbye."

Nick releases a loud sigh, throwing both hands against his thighs. "Cruel," he mutters as he saunters back to the kitchen.

"Much better." Courtney leans back in the oversized chair next to the fireplace. It's not quite cold enough for a fire, but Renee wouldn't mind it for the ambiance. "Help yourself to wine, ladies."

Kate wastes no time in pouring a glass. She holds it out for Renee, but Renee shakes her head. She doesn't miss the look that her friends exchange.

The conversation quickly rolls into work talk. The end of the semester showed up before Renee was ready for it, and they're celebrating the final day of classes. All three will need to go into their offices next week as each of them is teaching a winter session course, but they're avoiding that discussion for now, focusing instead on the more gossipy tidbits of the semester. Now that Renee's gotten the budget ironed out, Courtney is set with a TA for next fall and she's calmed down. Renee does miss those bouts of anger from her, though.

"And the Viola situation? That all worked out?" Courtney grabs another handful of crackers and makes a neat pile of assorted meats next to them.

Kate laughs lightly. "You could say that. According to Callie, she took care of it, and Viola is apparently dating a thirty-year-old man now."

"Well how does that work?" Renee sputters, coming back into the conversation after having drifted a bit into tense thoughts about Hunter.

"Which part?" Courtney asks around a mouthful of food.

Renee hesitates. She doesn't want to be in charge of this part of the conversation, but she also wants to get it over with, so might as well plow ahead. "She was obsessed with Callie but now she's with a man?"

"I don't know the specifics, but she told Callie she's never been attracted to a woman before. Until she met Callie, that is." Kate shrugs, unbothered. "I can't blame her for that."

"Ew," Courtney mumbles into her crackers.

"Oh, like you've never found yourself suddenly attracted to a woman," Renee says with a roll of her eyes. "Honestly, Courtney, I thought you were a lesbian when I first met you."

"Renee," Kate says, a warning.

Courtney waves them off. "Everyone does. It doesn't bother me."

Renee leans forward. "You've truly never been attracted to another woman?"

With a deep sigh, Courtney relents. "There was a girl on my basketball team in college. She was more competitive than I am, which I know is difficult to believe. We were constantly at each other's throats, and it's possible I had what I now realize was a small, confused attraction to her."

"But you never acted on it?"

"Nope." Courtney shrugs. "Never even crossed my mind."

"Really? No lusty locker room fantasies?"

"Here we go," Kate mutters.

Renee sits up straighter. "We're not going anywhere."

Courtney eyes the two of them. "Should I ask?" she says, clearly directing the question toward Kate.

"It's in your best interest not to."

Renee eyes the wine bottle before pouring herself less than half a glass. "That's not for you to decide, Kate."

Courtney echoes her snippy reply immediately, mimicking Renee's voice with startling accuracy.

"Do you practice that?" Renee asks, staring at Courtney.

"Roughly twice a week, but only when Nick demands a Dr. Renee impression." Courtney pops a piece of cheese into her mouth. "But carry on, take us wherever we're going."

After exchanging a quick look with Kate, who remains the picture of coolness, Renee takes a sip of wine before speaking. "It has recently come to my attention that I've had a bit of a… crush on Kate." She shuts her eyes after the confession, waiting for Courtney's reaction.

When she doesn't hear any bodies hitting the floor after fainting from shock and intrigue, Renee opens her eyes to find Kate sipping her wine and Courtney slicing a piece of the chipotle cheddar off the block.

"Did you hear me?"

Courtney shoots her a look as she continues piling cheese onto her plate. "Of course I heard you."

"So you…There's nothing you want to say?"

"What do you want me to say?"

Renee huffs and pushes her hands through her hair. "Don't be an ass, Courtney."

She laughs in response. "I'm not being an ass. Not on purpose, anyway." Courtney nods toward Kate. "I'm guessing you already shared this with her."

"I did," Renee says, nodding. "But I'm failing to understand why you're not surprised."

"Were you surprised?" Courtney asks Kate.

"I was," she says evenly. "But it wore off quickly."

"Right." Courtney nods. "I mean, I saw it a couple months after Kate started at Pennbrook."

"You *what*?" Renee exclaims, trying not to shriek. "Does everyone know? Have I been that obvious?"

"Oh, no. Not at all." Courtney puts her plate down and gives Renee her full attention. "I just pick up on stuff like that. I saw the Kate and Callie romance brewing the moment they laid eyes on each other." She shrugs. "My vibe detector is strong."

"If you're so aware," Kate begins, looking pointedly at Courtney, "then why didn't you ever mention this to me?"

"I did." Courtney's tone is exasperated, as though she can't believe she has to mediate this attraction bullshit between the lesbian and the questioning-maybe-a-lesbian. "You said I was 'so out of touch' and changed the subject."

"Well, it's irrelevant," Renee says loudly. She doesn't need to hear the ways Kate would have denied her had she ever proclaimed her attraction to her. "Now that I know I've some feelings arise for Kate, I can squelch them and it'll be like nothing ever happened."

"Is that how it works, Renee?" Kate sounds amused.

"Yeah, is that what you did with the electrical engineer? Just stomped out your—"

"Courtney," Kate says, interrupting. Her eyes look a bit wild, which is odd for her. She's normally very placid, almost to a fault.

Renee may be more book smart than people smart, but she knows exactly what's happening here. She crosses her arms, more for effect than a need to protect. "I see you two have been colluding."

"Three," Courtney corrects. "Callie has been an omniscient fountain of information."

"Oh my God," Kate mumbles. "She's going to murder you."

"Who? Callie or Renee?" Courtney grins wickedly. "Look, Renee. We've only been *colluding*"—her tone reeks of sarcasm—"because we care about you."

"And we've been worried about you," Kate adds.

Renee releases her arms. "And what sorts of information have you gathered?"

The other two women exchange a guilty look and Courtney presses her finger to her nose. "Not it."

"You're such a child," Kate says. She turns to Renee. "The basics, really. There seems to be an attraction between you and Hunter, and you have spent some time with her. Off-campus time," she clarifies. "Oh, and you had a bit of a fight with her."

"Which was clearly your attempt at pushing her away in order to not deal with the fact that you're into a woman," Courtney tags on. "Apparently you really were in the dark about your Kate-crush."

"I was," Renee says slowly. "Had I not met Hunter, I don't know that I ever would have become aware of my feelings for Kate."

"Okay, wait." Courtney has an odd expression on her face, a bit of panic mingling with sadness. "You still have these feelings for Kate? Are you going to try to break her and Callie up?"

As Renee says, "Don't be ridiculous," Kate says, "Courtney, relax."

Renee tucks her feet under her. "I will always admire Kate. But I would never try to get in the way, because I also admire and respect her relationship with Callie."

"Thank you, Renee," Kate says. A genuine smile breaks over her face.

"So we can put that whole thing to rest?" Courtney asks.

"Yes," Renee and Kate say in unison.

Courtney exhales dramatically. "Thank God. Honestly, you two would make a terrible couple."

Renee tunes out whatever Kate is saying to Courtney because her phone is buzzing against her leg. She stares at the screen, dumbfounded.

Hunter's name, right there in white against dark gray. Two options sit at the bottom of the screen and after only the slightest hesitation, Renee presses her pointer finger against the one that says "decline."

The discomfort that rises within her is nothing new; it's a carbon copy of the way she's felt for days now. Unmoored, irritated. A bit curious but mostly certain that Hunter was right, and Renee is not ready for anything that comes along with continuing to date her.

She hears her name in the mess of Courtney and Kate's words and mentally shakes off her Hunter-haze. She tries to focus on their conversation, but her phone buzzes again, just once. A text. A text she absolutely does not want to open. Not knowing is better. She's certain of that.

And yet, her stomach aches in a way that cannot be attributed to hunger. With more hesitation than it took to send Hunter to voice mail, Renee slides the tip of her finger over her phone and unlocks it, revealing Hunter's words: *I'd like to talk to you. Please call me back, whenever you're ready.*

It feels like a breakup and they hadn't even begun. If this is what lesbian relationships are composed of, Renee would prefer to slip back into her predictable, unattached life that did not involve any acknowledged attractions to women.

"More wine?" Courtney asks, crashing into Renee's thoughts. She nods. "Just a little."

Renee does her best to mute the Hunter-focused side of her brain, turning her attention instead to Courtney and Kate, who artfully dodge the very topic Renee is on the brink of opening up about.

CHAPTER TWENTY-NINE

In the handful of days that have passed since the evening with Courtney and Kate, Renee has found that she's unable to continue avoiding the topic of Hunter. She didn't bring Hunter up after the missed call and the text, and for reasons unbeknownst to her, Courtney and Kate went easy on her and didn't mention her either.

Renee isn't the kind of person who thrives off opening up to others. It's a miracle that she's able to be open at all, having spent her formative years being taught to avoid her feelings at all costs. It's one of several adaptive childhood behaviors that continue to hang over her head, swinging gently in the breeze of personal growth—something that she never resolved with her father before he died, and something she isn't sure she wants to discuss with her mother. Renee doesn't entirely see the point of digging into old, buried parenting failures, but more precisely, she knows how Margaret would respond and has no desire to face that outcome.

And so, Renee has continued swinging violently back and forth in her own brain. In one moment, she's convinced she never needs or wants to see or speak to Hunter again, and in the next, she's craving her in ways she didn't know a person could crave someone else. At times, the very name *Hunter* causes her organs to clench into tiny fists. But at night, the image of her face, her mouth, the soft reminder of her kiss consumes Renee, luring her to vow to seek Hunter out once she wakes and faces the next day.

So far, she's managed to brush off those desires in the morning.

Today, however, is proving to be more difficult than usual. Renee wakes—there's no other way to say it—in the pulsing heat of arousal. The only hands she can picture on her body are Hunter's. The only mouth she wants caressing her own is Hunter's.

A cold shower doesn't help. She marvels at learning now, at the age of forty-seven, how sensitive her nipples are and how thoroughly they respond to arousal coupled with cold water. How much else is left to learn about herself?

When Renee makes her way into her office, cursing the fact that she agreed to teach a winter session course, she feels the relief of Kate's presence but avoids her, not wanting anyone to see what she's certain is a flat-out "fuck me" expression on her face.

Dismay hits her as she looks at her calendar and sees that a student is coming by to meet in less than ten minutes. It's a meeting Renee arranged, one that needs to happen, but she's concerned that her visceral desire for Hunter will refuse to be shoved aside for the sake of professionalism. Alarmed, Renee quickly pulls up the most boring academic website she knows of and spends nine minutes staring at her screen, dragging her unwilling brain away from Hunter and toward the land of literary theories of *Beowulf*.

"Dr. Lawler?"

Renee looks up, thankful that her body seems to have taken a break. "Alexa. Come in, sit down."

Alexa, wearing an expression of distrust and uncertainty, obliges. She perches on the edge of the chair opposite Renee's desk and waits.

After several thoughts poke their way through Renee's brain, she gets up from behind her desk and sits down on the chair next to Alexa.

"This is better, isn't it?"

Alexa, now dumbfounded, nods.

"Thank you for coming in to meet with me. I'm sure there are plenty of other things you'd rather be doing with your time off."

The young woman shrugs, then tugs at the end of her ponytail. "I'm working all break, so I'm on campus."

Renee tilts her head to the side. It's rare that she gets to know her students on a personal level, but it's not unheard of. She knows little about Alexa but is struck by this comment.

"You're not going home for the holidays?"

"Uh, no. I'm not."

"That's unusual," Renee remarks. She's not sure where to go next.

Thankfully, Alexa takes the lead. "My parents asked me not to come home. We had...We had a bit of a falling out, I guess you could say." She pushes her bangs out of her eyes. "So I'm on a break. From my family."

"I'm sorry to hear that." And she is. Though she may lack some of the compassion that others have, Renee knows how difficult it is to have a strained relationship with one's parents. "Would you like to talk about your essay?"

Alexa smiles but it doesn't reach her eyes. "Anything other than my parents. Yes."

Renee walks Alexa through her final essay, not bothering to abbreviate her opinions. In their post-class conversation a couple weeks ago, Alexa proved that not only can she handle Renee, she also wants to improve. She's essentially a dream student. Even though the semester's over, Renee is happy to help guide Alexa through the avenues of improvement, especially since she'll likely end up in another one of Renee's classes down the line.

Renee hands the essay back to Alexa, who tucks it into her backpack. "One more thing, Alexa. I want to apologize for how I handled things at the end of the semester." She pauses, clears her throat. "I'm afraid I let my personal life affect my classroom life, and you were caught in the cross fire."

Alexa keeps her fingers wound around the strap of her backpack. "I was dealing with some heavy stuff," she says, her eyes never wavering from Renee's. "So I may not have handled myself, academically, very well at that time."

Renee rests her hands on her lap. "Seems we were both off-kilter."

The young woman finally breaks into a real smile. "It happens." She stands and goes to the door, turning to say, "Thank you, Dr. Lawler. I appreciate your time and help."

Alexa leaves the door ajar. Renee stays in the uncomfortable wooden chair, thinking about seeing if Kate's available for coffee. It's annoying her, knowing that if she wants to talk about Hunter, she has to be the one to initiate the conversation. Honestly, what's happened to her nosy, busybody friends?

Renee pushes herself off the chair and crosses to the door, grabbing her coat off the hook. As she walks down the hallway toward Audrey's desk, she notices that Kate's office is dark. She checks her watch. Right, she's in class. Renee faintly remembers Kate saying she'd be leaving right after her morning class; she and Callie are hosting Callie's parents this evening.

The rest of the office is deserted, not unusual for the winter session. Renee checks her mailbox out of habit and walks to the door, pulling it open. She halts.

There, wearing an unreadable expression, stands Hunter.

"Oh," Renee says, the word barely audible. She instinctively wraps her arms around her torso. "You're here."

"You realize you left me no choice," Hunter says, cleanly bypassing a polite greeting. It chafes Renee in an alarmingly pleasurable way. "You won't answer my calls or my texts."

There have been more, of course, after that initial attempt last week. Renee has always found an excuse to decline and ignore. And she's regretted it each time.

"Not here." Renee takes a step back.

Hunter peers into the office. "Looks pretty empty to me."

"It is. But I need fresh air for this conversation." Renee steps into the hallway, jerking the temperamental door shut behind her.

Campus is desolate, flaked with day-old snow and the hush of missing students. Hunter and Renee walk slowly, neither talking for some time. Just as Renee is angrily accepting the fact that she needs to be the one to begin the conversation, Hunter speaks up.

"I'm sorry," she says plainly, her hands stuffed deep in her jacket pockets. "The way I ended our date…Renee, that's not like me. It really isn't."

"I wouldn't know," she replies icily.

"No, you wouldn't. And I've already asked you to trust me, and you have. Then I go and act like a complete fucking idiot, make a shitty statement, and disappear on you."

Okay, great. This is going very well, Renee thinks. "And why did you? Disappear?"

Hunter blows out a breath, the crisp air catching it and turning it to steam. "I like you too much."

Renee nearly trips over an invisible crack in the sidewalk. Hunter grabs her arm, but Renee pushes her away.

"What does that mean?"

"Exactly what it says. I like you," Hunter says, turning to catch Renee's eye, but she stares straight ahead. "And I like you too much. There are significant differences between us, and I don't know that you're—"

"You are not the one to tell me what I'm ready for and what I'm not ready for." Renee bites off each word.

This time when Hunter grabs her arm, she doesn't pull away. She allows herself to be stopped and turned to face Hunter. The expression on her face is searching, open. Renee's breath catches in her throat.

"Are you? Are you actually ready to date me?"

The earnestness of Hunter's words and voice nearly breaks Renee. "I don't know," she says, her tone lacking some of its earlier ice. "I truly don't. But how am I supposed to know unless I'm given the opportunity to try?"

Hunter stares at her, blinking her beautiful, soulful, cocoa-brown eyes. "How do you feel?"

Renee tries to laugh but it comes out as a choke. "I can't stop thinking about you, Hunter. Is that what you want to know?" She taps the side of her head. "I cannot get you out of my head. You're everywhere. I can't escape you."

"Those are all thinking words."

"Jesus Christ, Hunter. I'm trying here. Can't you see that?" Renee pushes her tongue against the back of her teeth. "I have told you that I don't do this. And this? This is exactly why. I can't do this. I'm too cerebral. I'm too unfeeling. I don't connect with people in the ways that they want me to connect with them." *No,* she thinks. *Do not cry.* "You want to know how I feel? I feel you. That's it, Hunter. I feel you everywhere inside of me. You've taken up space in my body, pushed yourself into places no one has ever been. When I say I can't escape you, I mean it." She motions to her body. "You're in here, making me feel. And I hate it. I fucking hate it."

Hunter's hand comes to rest on Renee's cheek, cupping it lightly. "You hate it?"

"Yes. So much." She shivers.

"Do you hate me?"

Renee locks her eyes with Hunter's. "No. I hate the not knowing."

"Not knowing what?" Hunter's voice is low, dangerously so.

"Not knowing if you feel this too."

The silent landscape around them closes in, boxing out the rest of the world. Hunter's hand slides down, her fingers drawing lines on Renee's neck.

"Only one way to find out," she whispers.

CHAPTER THIRTY

By silent agreement, the two women have returned to Berringer Hall. In the few words they exchanged on their walk back, Hunter mentioned something about going to lunch and Renee thinks she agreed.

"Let me just get my things," she says as they approach the English offices. Hunter nods, holding the door open.

The overcast day provides little illumination, but Renee has a worn path to her office and has no need for the overhead lights. Once in the safety of her space, she presses her hand to her chest and tries to calm her racing heart. Nothing happened. There's no definitive cause for the increase in her heart rate. She's learning that simply being around Hunter at this point causes her body to react in all kinds of unfamiliar ways. Not unpleasant. Just new.

"Everything okay?"

Renee jumps at the sound of Hunter's voice and turns to see her silhouetted in the doorframe. "Yes. Perfectly okay."

"Do you always move around your office in the dark?"

"I know it so well I don't need light," she says, putting her laptop in her bag.

"Huh." Hunter enters the office and walks over to a floor lamp, flicking it on. Renee loses her breath once more when she sees the desire clearly shining in Hunter's eyes. "I like a little light every now and then."

Renee feels her bag drop to the floor. She remains standing at her desk, watching Hunter move through her office, inspecting books and pictures.

"I'm surprised you don't show more of your personality in here," Hunter says casually as she skims her fingers over the spines of several books. "Wait, I take that back." She throws a smile over her shoulder. "This is your personality."

Renee feels her spine seize into steel. "What exactly do you mean by that?"

"Strong, assertive. Brilliant. No-nonsense." Hunter turns and draws her eyes up and down Renee's body. "Secretive."

"I'm not secretive." That's not the word that sticks in her brain, though. *Assertive* rings loud, clear, a bell that won't be ignored.

"That's not the right word, then." Hunter is in front of her now. Her hands hang loosely at her sides and Renee stares at them. "Protective."

"Of what?" Her voice is thick but quiet.

"Yourself."

It shouldn't affect Renee so strongly, the way Hunter knows her in ways that seem obvious but aren't. She doesn't know this woman, not as well as she wishes she did, but she can't deny the electricity burning between them. If this is her one opportunity to know what Hunter's feeling, to see if they match or need to shuffle and draw again, Renee isn't willing to avoid it. *Research*, she reminds herself. She doesn't permit herself to think twice before she closes the distance between them and presses her lips to Hunter's.

Hunter responds immediately, her hands grabbing Renee's hips and pulling her closer. Renee finds her own hands suspended in uncertainty, then moves them to rest on Hunter's shoulders.

As her lips melt against Hunter's, she feels her body pounding awake, not that it had ever really slept after the thick arousal that greeted her upon waking this morning.

A flash of memory whispers to Renee and she pulls away, leaving Hunter mid-kiss.

"Am I a bad kisser?"

Hunter cocks her head and studies Renee. "I'm not sure yet. I need more evidence."

That's as good as a no for now. Research, after all, is a comfort zone for Renee. She leans in and kisses Hunter again, gasping when Hunter captures her bottom lip between her teeth. She presses harder against Hunter's mouth, her tongue a whisper against Hunter's. Renee feels her mouth open wider, bringing Hunter with her, the speed and intensity of their kiss accelerating wildly.

Hunter slowly backs them up until the backs of Renee's thighs hit the edge of her desk. Hunter's mouth slips from Renee's, her lips skimming tender spots on her neck, behind her ear. Renee, looser now, scrapes her fingers down Hunter's arms. She hesitates when she reaches Hunter's waist. Her torso feels taut, strong. Renee kneads her fingers to Hunter's back, finding the curve of her lower spine to be a delectable spot to touch, even through her sweater.

Hunter pulls back, making quick work of crossing the room and firmly shutting the door. She strides back to Renee as she yanks her sweater over her head, revealing a tight white T-shirt straining against her breasts.

"It's hot in here," she remarks before her lips graze Renee's jaw.

Renee hears her, fully feels the movement of her lips, but she's consumed by this less-clothed version of Hunter. Her hands move over Hunter's ribs and stomach with a gentleness she didn't know she could possess. She feels a tiny tremor ripple through Hunter.

Before she can react, Hunter's hands grip her hips and the next thing she knows, she's sitting on her desk, her legs wrapped around Hunter, who stands in front of her. After pushing loose hairs away from Renee's face, Hunter drops her mouth to Renee's once again, their kiss taking off at the exact heated spot it had been interrupted.

When Hunter's fingers begin a cautious, divine dance against Renee's collarbone, she leans in slightly, giving a silent yes. To her dismay, Hunter takes her time unbuttoning each button on Renee's shirt. Only when the shirt is completely unbuttoned and pulled off of Renee does Hunter yank it, ball it up, and throw it across the office.

The action makes Renee laugh and it's then that she realizes she's on her way to being half-naked on top of her desk. Her laugh stops short as her nerves reenter the scene.

Hunter grazes her fingers over the swell of Renee's breasts. Renee looks down to watch Hunter's knuckles brush against the fabric of her bra, teasing Renee's extremely hard nipples. She gasps and her hips, on a ride of their own, buck forward.

A murmur of a laugh comes from Hunter as she leans down and moves her mouth over Renee's exposed skin. In a swift movement, Hunter unclasps Renee's bra and it too flies away, lost in the dark corners of the office.

"You are stunning," Hunter says as she cups Renee's breasts in her hands. Her mouth closes over Renee's nipple and she barely contains a scream. Hunter's tongue swirls against her, teeth scraping. The pressure of her mouth holding Renee's nipple captive is too, too much—and somehow not at all enough.

Craving friction, Renee grinds against the surface of her desk. She grips Hunter's arms as she continues to suck and bite Renee's nipple. In the dim light of the room, Renee can make out their bodies and every point at which they touch.

She needs more.

But more than needs, she wants. She can feel her body finally giving in, cresting over its tightly formed boundaries, ushering in this rush of anticipation and hunger.

"Renee," Hunter says suddenly, her face level with Renee's chest.

It takes her a moment to come back from the euphoric feeling of Hunter's mouth on her breasts. "Hmm?"

"What are we doing?"

At that, Renee pulls back. She looks down at herself, her nipples wet with Hunter's saliva and protruding, begging for more.

"We—" She knows, of course, but saying the words out loud is a step she has yet to approach.

Hunter takes a step back and Renee sits up, grabbing her hand to ensure she can't leave. "Don't go."

"I'm not going, but I...Are you sure you want to do this?"

Assertive. She hears it again and decides she can be more assertive than she's ever been before. Renee stands up and unbuttons her pants, sliding them down to the floor. Hunter's mouth gapes softly as she watches Renee stand before her in nothing but black satin bikinis.

"You and I could talk everything to death." The words come out of Renee's mouth like a gentle rainstorm, one that threatens to become so much more. She shimmies back onto her desk. "Or we could give in to what we both desire and see if our bodies match as well as our minds."

Flickers of previous conversations dance in the back of her mind but she extinguishes them. She leans forward, tugs Hunter closer, and kisses her passionately. Still holding Hunter's hand, Renee guides her to where she wants her. The thrill of Hunter groaning into her mouth nearly sends her over the edge. The room collapses into silence, deafening the sound of their breathing. The feeling of Hunter's fingertips gently rubbing against the outside of Renee's underwear is overwhelming. Any hopes of containing herself are evaporating by the second.

"Please," she hears herself whisper. "Hunter, please."

"You're sure you're ready for this?" Hunter asks. She's staring at Renee as her knuckles begin to press harder. "We could stop."

"God, no," Renee exclaims, pressing herself into Hunter's touch. "Don't you dare stop now."

Hunter grins, hovering above Renee's mouth. "I wouldn't dream of it."

The underwear is gone in a flash, leaving Renee very naked and very exposed. On her desk. She recognizes this fact obliquely, like a fading memory she knows she should hold on to.

Hunter kneels down in front of the desk. Her hands are warm on Renee's skin as she grips her hips once again and pulls her to the edge of the desk. Renee's eyes are glued to Hunter's and neither one breaks eye contact, even as Hunter leans in and slides her tongue over Renee's clit.

She cries out, her body unraveling further at every one of Hunter's touches. Hunter's mouth feels like silk, her tongue strong as it concentrates on circling Renee's clit. The sensations are overpowering. Renee grabs for something to hold on to and comes up empty. She can only arch her back to press herself further into Hunter's mouth.

It isn't long before Renee feels tiny sparks of explosion beginning, their trail lighting up fast and furious until she storms into an all-consuming orgasm, her body shaking and pulsing with each rip of pleasure. She barely has time to come down from having her ceiling smashed open before she feels Hunter enter her.

The sensation is nothing like those of her past. Hunter glides, thrusts, curls. Renee's head drops back, her body submitting. She feels Hunter pull her closer, her free arm wrapping around Renee and holding her as she fucks her to a second, very different crash of rapture.

Hunter's fingers continue gently rocking inside Renee. She reaches down and holds her there, not ready to let her go. As Renee slowly spirals down back to earth, she opens her eyes and is met with the sexiest expression she has ever seen on another human being.

Still wildly aroused and encouraged, chucking aside her fear of inexperience, Renee sits up just enough, clenching around Hunter's fingers to let her know she can't leave yet. She unbuttons and unzips Hunter's khakis. The staggered breath coming from Hunter spurs her on. She slides her hand down Hunter's navy-blue boy shorts and takes a ragged breath, shocked to discover wetness so similar to her own.

"You don't have to," Hunter says, her voice a scrape above a whisper.

"I want to," she says, already stroking her finger over Hunter's clit.

Hunter's reaction is immediate, her body tensing and driving down on Renee's movements. As Renee's strokes increase in speed, Hunter begins a gentle thrust of the fingers still inside Renee. They move together, limbs bumping and breathing strained. Each time Hunter emits a strangled gasp, Renee presses harder. She feels her own orgasm building and suddenly it's right there, tumbling wildly through her. She manages to keep her own movements going and not long after Renee's cries fill the office, Hunter groans and Renee feels the pulsing ripples of her orgasm.

Moments later, Hunter leans down and kisses her, hard. It's a bruising kiss, the kind they'll both feel for hours afterward, touching their fingers to their lips in a haze of memory. Renee pulls Hunter as close as possible, then gives up and stands, wrapping her arms around Hunter's waist.

"So," Hunter says after they finally break for air. "Does that satisfy your curiosity?"

The intensely pleasurable mist of sexual connection evaporates instantly. Renee reels back. The words hit like miniature buzzing daggers, as though Hunter has captured the hive from Renee's stomach and thrown it, furious bees and all, directly at her.

Hunter must see it because she takes Renee's hands in hers and tugs them. "Hey. Look at me. I didn't—that wasn't meant to sound the way it did."

Retorts choke to dust on Renee's tongue. All she can do is stare at Hunter...until she remembers she's stark naked. She wrestles her hands from Hunter's grasp and goes about finding her clothes, hastily pulling them on.

"Renee, wait. Please. Wait."

She shakes her head. Distantly, she registers the sound of Hunter zipping up her pants. A veil of shame settles over her.

"Please talk to me," Hunter tries. "I know this is intense for you. That's why I kept asking if you really wanted to do this.

The last thing I want is for you to dive into something that you don't feel ready for." Renee hears Hunter sigh, the scrape of her shoes on the floor. "I'm making this worse, aren't I?"

Renee can't reply. There's a painful awareness surfacing inside of her and the harshness of it drags Renee down to a low, cruel place.

"It doesn't matter." Her voice is clipped, and she looks at Hunter briefly before focusing on the wall behind her. "This was—this was an experiment. You're right, Hunter. You satisfied a curiosity. And now we both know what this really is."

She can't bear to look at Hunter. The buzzing between her eyes won't let up and it reaches a stinging crescendo when she realizes that she's alone in her office.

CHAPTER THIRTY-ONE

The soft glare of fresh snow normally makes Renee feel at peace. It's soothing, the way it covers everything and forces the world to slow down. Considering it's mid-January, the teasing midpoint of snow season in New England, the current inch or so on the ground is only a preview of what could come over the next two and a half months. Though she loathes shoveling, Renee wouldn't mind if a blizzard hit in the next hour, burying the city and stopping time.

As she strolls through campus, Renee feels nothing but the emptiness of winter. It pales in comparison to the emptiness she's been growing within herself. Like a sourdough starter, it expands, bubbles, and falls. Each cycle hurts, one no more than another. She has grown accustomed to the pain—it's her own fault it's there, so the least she can do is accept it.

Perhaps the worst part of the empty pain is the fact that she can't hide it. It seems to ooze from her. It's affected Jess, who spent a week back in Brooklyn over winter break, just to "get in some clear space with better energy." Renee didn't even have the energy to be upset about it, or convince them to stay. She felt like a forlorn ghost, wandering the hushed halls of her own house while Jess was gone. They've been back home for a few days now, but the silence continues to shroud Renee.

If she had the courage to open up about the self-inflicted internal wounds, she knows Callie and Kate would be there to listen and guide her through a healing process. But she hasn't been able to bring herself to utter more than, "My research failed me," a paltry statement that cannot encompass the magnitude of her fuckup. Kate, polite as ever, hasn't pressed for more information; Renee is both grateful for and despondent over this.

She inhales the frosty air, willing it to exorcise the stubborn pain in her chest. Renee has only admitted to herself that she does not know what to do. Her research—and she knows she has to stop referring to it as that—provided crystal clear results: She is intensely attracted to Hunter. And beyond being attracted to her, she likes her. Really likes her. Likes her to the point of wanting to tear down her own walls just to let Hunter get closer, no matter what that looks like, no matter what it means.

But her research also failed her because it brought an end result she wasn't expecting and certainly wasn't intending.

Renee hurt Hunter. She knows this without being told. She can, shockingly, *feel* it. It's a terrible, vacuous feeling. It doesn't matter that she didn't mean to hurt Hunter; it happened, she is at fault, and she is the only one who can fix it.

But it's been weeks now. Weeks of silence. Renee is quite aware that the ball is in her proverbial court. But she's frozen, much like the landscape she's currently carefully stepping through in boots with a heel not meant for this type of weather.

She wishes her feelings, like the icy puddles land-mining the sidewalk, could freeze over before melting away into nothingness.

Renee looks up to the sky as she approaches Berringer Hall. The cloud cover is thick and unrelenting, the kind of gray that promises more snow. Maybe she'll get that blizzard after all. She would like to be at home, safely wrapped in a blanket in front of the fireplace. The thought of returning to the building that currently contains numerous people who either need something from Renee or are perceptive enough to realize she's a shade of her usual self is unpleasant. She just doesn't want to go in there. It's music, an entire concert's worth, she doesn't want to face.

Alas, there is a job to be done, and Renee Lawler will not allow her current state of emotions to prevent her from doing it.

"You're home." Renee slips off her jacket and gloves. "Are you hungry?"

She's not sure how she made it through the day. She felt like she was curling her toes around a tightrope every time she was in the English department offices. Thankfully, no one seemed to need her, which would normally be a thorn in her side but today it was an absolute blessing.

Now that she's home, the earlier image of a blanket and the fireplace still appeals. But first, maternal duties, which are a fantastic distraction from her stupid, painful emotions.

"I could eat," Jess says from their perch at the kitchen counter. "But how about I make dinner? You look like you could use some comfort food and some rest."

Thankful that her back is to Jess, Renee presses her hands against her abdomen, trying to push down the sadness rising rapidly inside her. The tears start before she can get her hands to her eyes to stop them. As it turns out, her lack of an immediate response gives her away.

"Mom? Don't hide, okay? No one knows you better than I do, and I've never seen you like this."

Overlapping measures of sadness jam up in Renee's throat. No stopping the tears now.

"I hate this," Renee mumbles, furiously pushing the tears from her face. "I do not like feeling things."

"Well, yeah, of course you don't. You spent forty-some years telling yourself you can't feel things, so now your body's revolting with, like, the most intense feelings possible."

She'll ignore the irritating reality of Jess's words for now. "How do I make it stop?"

Her child is at her side now, nudging her until she looks at them. Jess's smile is tinged with sadness. They cup Renee's shoulder and squeeze gently. "Bad news. You can't. You can only lean into it."

"That is"—she pauses to take a deep, shaky breath— "unacceptable."

"Get used to it. It's how feelings work." Jess crosses the kitchen and begins looking through the refrigerator. "You don't need to tell me what happened, but have you thought about how Hunter might be feeling? Wait. I'm assuming this is about Hunter. Is there someone else?"

The thought of "someone else" makes Renee taste bile in the back of her throat. No, she doesn't want someone else; for God's sake, she's spent her entire life avoiding the concept of "someone else" until Hunter Ciccone showed up, doing everything and nothing other than existing to throw Renee into a state of questioning her entire nonacademic existence. "It's Hunter," she says quietly.

"Okay, good. I was a little worried you'd thrown yourself into this whole thing and started meeting all kinds of women." Jess looks over their shoulder and grins playfully. "Plus, I like Hunter. But think about it, Mom. I mean, if you're this torn up, she must be having an equally hard time."

Renee's stomach clenches. Yes, she has thought about it. Far more than she's ever considered anyone's feelings, as a matter of fact. And each time she tries to roll out a map detailing the paths she can take to resolution, she takes wrong turns that nudge her back into despair and embarrassment.

"Look. Level with me." Jess closes the refrigerator and leans against the counter. "What happened?" They make an X with their fingers. "Do not give me dirty details."

Renee looks at her child, wondering how they grew up into such a compassionate, perceptive young adult—one with very vocal, very strict parental boundaries. She could, she realizes, talk to Jess. She's done it before. There's an internal pull to continue handling her wild mess of emotions by herself, but her rational voice reminds her that she's gotten nowhere on that solo journey.

Maybe she doesn't have to figure everything out on her own.

Renee clears her throat and avoids Jess's eyes. "We slept together."

The noise that comes from Jess is a groan mixed with a strangled laugh. They shake their head several times, as though trying to wipe any unfortunate imagery from their mind. "I just said—"

"I'm not giving you dirty details, Jess. But that's the problem. We slept together and then things went downhill."

"Like, immediately after? Or the next day?"

Renee draws circles on the countertop with her fingertip. "Immediately. There was a bit of a postcoital miscommunication, I suppose. It spiraled from there."

"Okay. That's easy. Call her."

It's cute, the way young folk think a phone call can solve everything. Renee chuckles darkly. She's not sure Jess's advice is wrong, but it doesn't feel like the fix she's searching for.

"Honestly, Jess, I doubt she even wants to talk to me."

Jess raises an eyebrow. "You gave her the Dr. Renee Lawler treatment, didn't you?"

It's an old family joke, one her mother cobbled together after hearing too many stories of Renee's interactions with male colleagues and fellow academics. "Blunt," Margaret likes to say. "Your sharp mouth can steer anyone out of your path."

She'd like to tell Jess they're wrong, but...

"It's possible." Renee sucks in a breath. "I told her that our time together was an experiment."

"You did *what*?" Jess gapes at their mother. "What the fuck were you thinking?"

"I wasn't. I think that's clear. Hunter—she said something off-handed that rubbed me the wrong way—"

"After she rubbed you the right way," Jess interjects with a cackle.

Renee swats their shoulder. "We agreed no sex-talk. I should wash your mouth out with soap."

"Get my brain while you're at it."

With a shake of her head, Renee sighs. "As I was saying, Hunter made a comment after we...you know." The image of

Jess hiding their face behind their hands brings a smile to Renee's face. "She was being Hunter. I know that. She backpedaled immediately; I guess she saw the look on my face. But her words reminded me of my own actions. My own plan."

"Plan? Oh no." Recognition dawns on Jess's face when they drop their hands to the counter. "You came at this with an agenda, not feelings, didn't you?"

"It was only because I needed to protect myself," Renee hurries to say. "I am not built for vulnerability. You know that."

"Yeah, I do, but Hunter doesn't. Not really, anyway." Jess stares at Renee. "You fucked up."

"Believe me, I'm aware."

"Good. Now you need to fix it."

Renee swishes her wrist through the air. "I am also aware of that."

Jess seems to collect their emotions before launching their next statement at Renee. "But before you fix it, you need to figure out exactly what you want with Hunter, because dragging her through your big sexual awakening and dismissing her as an experiment is possibly the worst thing I've known you to do."

There's no argument that Renee could prepare and present to her child. Jess is absolutely correct, and the truth of their statement is providing the heavy lump in Renee's heart. Her awareness of every element of the situation, barring Hunter's current emotional status and feelings toward Renee, is present and accounted for.

Fresh tears gather in the corners of her eyes. She's too wrung out to wipe them away.

"That's just it, Jess. You and Kate are right. I let my brain dictate everything. I've treated Hunter horribly because I can't get out of my head." She drops her cheek to her fist. "I'm terrified of letting my heart do anything other than pump blood."

"I don't think you have much of a choice anymore." Jess almost sounds apologetic, and Renee appreciates the sentiment. "But the bigger problem remains."

They don't need to finish the statement; Renee is well aware that how she handles this, and Hunter, moving forward is likely the biggest problem she'll face in her romantic life…if there is to be one.

"You realize," Renee says dramatically, "this is exactly why I've avoided love for my entire life."

Jess's eyes pop. "Love? Whoa whoa whoa. You're in *love?*"

"No!" Renee stands up. "No. I am not."

"Mmhmm." She does not care for Jess's wicked tone. "But you're at least admitting there's a chance for love, yeah?"

"Have you decided what to make for dinner? I'm suddenly quite hungry."

The wickedness carries into Jess's delighted laugh. "Spicy veggie mac and cheese." They dash around the counter and surprise Renee with a tight hug. "Find a way to talk to her when you're ready. And if she doesn't listen to you and see how honest you're being"—their voice drops to a whisper—"I'll kill her."

Renee squeezes Jess as tightly as she can. At the very least, if things don't work out with Hunter, she now has a safe place to land.

CHAPTER THIRTY-TWO

"You're incorrigible."

Renee barely contains herself from rolling her eyes. Having avoided him for nearly an entire month, she finally got snared into the trap of Franklin's office to discuss a litany of issues he deems important. She's finding his list to be underwhelming and petty.

"I know my staff well, Franklin. Perhaps you should try trusting me for once."

His fist thumps against his desk, a darling little tantrum. "Imani Frances is brand-new. What makes you think she can handle the demands of a graduate-level course?"

"Have you seen her teach rhetoric?" She knows he hasn't but can't resist driving in a dig at Franklin's laissez-faire approach to the inner workings of the department he claims to be dean of. "She is dazzling." Renee pictures Imani and her new braids, the layers of blues and whites she says symbolize the onslaught of winter and promise of blue-skied days ahead. The woman is a vision and a visionary—not to mention a phenomenal instructor of writing. "I'm not arguing this. She's getting the 400-level course in the fall."

"And Dr. Wincheck-Rodriguez is okay with that?"

Renee balks. "Courtney? She'd give Imani her left leg to get out of teaching any writing course."

Franklin grunts and types something into his computer. "Fine. Anything else?"

"I'm afraid not," she says gaily, standing and pressing the lines out of her black pencil skirt. "Pleasure, as always."

She doesn't wait to hear his cranky response before leaving the stuffy office. Renee waves at Donna and takes a deep breath once she's beyond the office door.

She has to find Hunter.

Time has done its work as Renee has done her deep examination of her feelings. Yes, she's gone there. It wasn't pretty and it wasn't enjoyable, but she did it, and largely on her own, which she is overly proud of. She even wrote notes and drew up some graphs, including a pie chart. That one she shared with Jess, just because she was so thrilled with her ability to do something mathematical. She didn't even care when Jess informed her that she did it incorrectly. It was the meaning behind the chart that was more important, anyway.

It's been a challenge for Renee to come to terms with the fact that something has always been missing from her life. She tried to thwart the emergence of the void by having Jess at an early age, assuring herself over and over again that she could be a good single parent—that she didn't *need* someone else in her life. And while she's still reckoning with her absence during Jess's childhood, Renee feels her relationship with adult-Jess is solid. She doesn't even want them to return to Brooklyn, though now that it's late February, Jess is getting a bit antsy and using the term "the city" far more than they did when they first arrived in Chestnut Hill.

It was a bit shocking, really, when Renee allowed herself to realize that a child is not a substitute for a romantic partner. Perhaps that works for some people—she surely thought she was "some people"—but it turns out it does not work for Renee.

And it may have worked had Hunter Ciccone not appeared in Renee's world the very moment she did. Had Hunter never walked sideways over Renee's firmly straight path, Renee may have never known what she's been missing.

But now: She can't not know. She can't unknow.

Renee is confident that the puzzle pieces of her life fit snugly, neatly. She loves nothing more than the clean snap of a jagged piece into position. But she also knows that she sometimes hurries to shove pieces together. She doesn't inspect the bigger picture, often because she doesn't want to spoil the surprise of the end product. It's taken time for Renee to understand that she and Hunter move differently: Hunter from the inside out with a keen eye on the bigger picture, Renee from the outside in with odd confidence that everything will work out without being inspected too carefully. Hunter is cautious where Renee is impulsive. Hunter sees the bigger picture for both of them; after all, she was certainly not wrong when she told Renee that she wasn't ready for "this." While Renee will always prefer the smaller details, she respects Hunter's ability to see past them. In fact, she's observed enough relationships to know that these personality traits snug together nicely.

Wait. No. She cannot get ahead of herself.

Certain that she's done the necessary overthinking required by women who love women, Renee is ready to face herself and Hunter. She's ready to slide Hunter the last piece of the puzzle and wait for her to snap it into place.

If only she could find Hunter, that is.

Or if she could work up the nerve to initiate communication with her, that is.

As Renee makes her way to the first level of Old Main, she halts on the landing of the second floor. There, down the hall, as if she summoned her. Renee squints. Yes, that must be Hunter.

Mustering up all the confidence she can, Renee walks with purpose toward the middle of the hallway of the second floor. Hunter is crouched down on the ground, peering at a row of papers.

Once she's standing behind her, the courage that flew into Renee departs with a wave. She feels shaky and uncertain, but like hell is she going to let this opportunity flee with her bravado.

"That looks interesting," she says, hoping she doesn't sound as awkward as she feels.

"Not especially."

Renee nearly laughs, but she's too confused to make any noise at all. When Hunter stands and turns to face Renee, she blinks several times, trying to figure out what's going on.

"Have we met?"

The voice is decidedly not Hunter's, not even close. But everything else about this person is so very Hunter...except, Renee now realizes, for the very flat chest and somewhat skimpy shoulders and arms.

The person peers closer at Renee, then a lightbulb must go off. "Oh, right. You've gotta be that English professor."

"What a marvelous introduction." Renee combs through her memory. "You're Hunter's brother."

"Renzo," he says, offering his hand. She shakes it, disappointed by the lack of firmness. "Lookin' for my sister?"

Any flags bolstered by the sight of Hunter have sagged in the recognition of Renee's misstep. Before she answers, she takes a good look at Renzo. Yes, the resemblance is uncanny—something Hunter could have warned her about. They even have the same eyes, though Renzo's lack the *look* of Hunter's.

All systems go, Renee waits for the strike of attraction. And she continues to wait. She peers at Renzo again, ignoring his curious expression. Sure, he looks more "male" whereas Hunter has that androgynous sexiness, but truly, they are practically carbon copies of each other.

Except for their energy, Renee realizes. Renzo has a distinct male air about him. And Hunter...Hunter's energy is feminine with a masculine edge. She emits calm control, strength, and sincerity. And, yes, a playfulness and smoldering fire of—

"Oh God," Renee whispers behind her hand which has flown up to cover her mouth. "I do believe I'm a lesbian."

"Sorry?"

"No, nothing." She nearly bursts into laughter but controls herself. "Yes, I am looking for Hunter. Where can I find her?"

"Brooklyn."

Renee's stomach drops. She was anticipating a jaunt across campus, not one to another state.

"Family emergency," Renzo tags on. "Not sure when she'll be back."

With that, he returns to his papers on the ground. Renee stares at his back for a moment, then hurries from the scene of her final awakening.

"So call her."

Renee grips her phone tighter against her ear. "But that's so, so…"

"Oh my God, stop making excuses and do it." Jess crunches on something. "We're out of carrots, by the way."

"Then go to the store and get some," Renee snaps.

Jess laughs. "Chill, Mom. She'll be back. Or you could hang up with me and call her."

Renee can't explain what it is that holds her back from pressing Hunter's name on her phone. It's impersonal, somehow. She wants to see Hunter. She needs to see Hunter. This conversation isn't one she fancies having over the phone.

"I can wait," Renee says as she pushes open the door to Berringer Hall. "She'll be back."

"I hope for your sake it's soon. Huh. And for hers, because you owe her the biggest apology—"

"Thanks for the chat, darling! Goodbye!" Renee hangs up and walks down the hall to the English offices. The halls are pleasantly empty and sounds of professors professing slip out from beneath closed classroom doors.

Audrey is, as usual, on the phone. Renee waves at her. She's been trying to be kinder. Audrey doesn't seem to see her, however.

There's quite a bit of noise coming from Courtney's office. Renee pauses a few feet from her door, wondering if she feels up to joining the party. She decides on no, but remembers she needs to meet with Callie before she goes off to her next class of the day.

Callie's office door is shut, and when Renee knocks on it, it swings open and the person standing before her is definitely not Callie.

"You're here," she says, an echo of another day, a different charged moment.

"I am." Hunter crosses her arms over her chest then steps into the hallway, closing Callie's door behind her.

"Your brother said you were in Brooklyn."

Hunter raises her eyebrows. "Did you hunt him down for that information?"

"Of course not. I ran into him." She hesitates, then plunges ahead. "I thought he was you at first."

"Yeah, we could be twins."

"Except that you're a woman."

A laugh escapes Hunter. "You do know that twins can be… Of course you do." Hunter tilts her head. "Ah."

"Don't 'ah' me," Renee fires back, but there's no real anger in her voice. "Look. Hunter." *Don't let this go*, the little rational voice yells. "Can we talk?"

"Not here," Hunter says in a low voice.

"Right." Renee, unsure of what to do with her hands, clenches her fists at her thighs. "Not here."

Hunter waits. It's a surprise for Renee to discover she doesn't want to be in charge of this, whatever *this* is, whatever it may become. But in order for that to happen—if the chance even exists—she has to step it up, and now.

"Tonight?" She whacks the question from her voice. "Tonight. If you're available."

"I am. What do you have in mind?"

An excellent question, one Renee is not prepared for. She isn't like Hunter, masterful at crafting surprising and unique outings. And while she's tempted to try the Hunter Ciccone Dating Method, she's learned through her recent reckonings that Renee has to be Renee Lawler, faults and all.

It should be noted, she thinks, that the fact she can now admit she may have some faults is magnanimous all on its own.

"Actually," Hunter says, interrupting Renee's frantic thinking. "I have some time now, and I'm starving. How does lunch sound?"

"Lunch sounds perfect."

CHAPTER THIRTY-THREE

A short time later, the two are nestled into a booth at a nearby café. Renee swirls her spoon in a bowl of roasted tomato soup, hoping she doesn't forget a single word of her planned speech.

"How's your soup?"

"Hunter, I am so beyond sorry," Renee blurts. "I was awful to you, simply awful. You are not an experiment. You never were. You took me by surprise, and you have been so patient, so gracious with me. And I was horrible to you."

Hunter spoons lentil soup into her mouth. After she swallows, she says, "That's odd commentary about soup."

"It wasn't about the soup."

"I know, Renee." Hunter leans back in the booth. "I'm not sure how to handle this."

Renee's stomach clenches uncomfortably. Her speech is forgotten, as are the rest of her known words.

"You're right," Hunter continues. "I was patient. I knew I had to be. And while I don't regret it, not in the way you think,

I wish that evening in your office hadn't happened." She holds up her hand before Renee can sputter a rebuttal. "I wish it had happened differently, later. I knew it was too soon for you."

Renee's soup spoon clangs in her bowl. "You cannot make decisions for me."

"I know. Believe me, I'm very aware of that. But honestly, Renee." Hunter runs her hand over her forehead. "I've been here before. You haven't. I just wish we'd had more conversations about that. It may have saved us both some heartache."

There it is, the admittance of pain. "I know I hurt you," Renee says. "And please know that I am deeply sorry about that."

"I believe you."

"But more than that." She picks up her spoon again, needing something to hold on to. "I think you should know that it hurt me to know that I hurt you."

Hunter sits with that. She eats more of her soup, giving Renee space to do the same, even though her tomato soup feels like lava pooling in her belly.

"That's significant," Hunter finally says.

"I know." She plows ahead. "I've done a lot of thinking. Too much, maybe. And I'd love to tell you I've reached new heights of self-awareness. I think," Renee says, dropping her spoon once again, "it's a work in progress. And I don't love that."

"No, I imagine you don't."

She cracks a small smile. "It is both disconcerting and exhilarating, seeing the ways in which you know me."

"It feels that way sometimes, too."

"Have I ruined this completely?"

Hunter sips her water. As she places the glass back on the table, she shakes her head. "No. I don't think so. But you really were an asshole to me."

Shame spirals through her. "Hunter, I know. I know. I have replayed that night so many times in my mind and I hate myself more every time."

"Hopefully just because of your final words." There's a shake of uncertainty in Hunter's voice and Renee would like to lunge across the table and smooth it away.

"Yes," she says emphatically. "Only because of my final words."

The sounds of the café overtake their space. Clinking dishes, jostled ice cubes, shredding napkins, and a wide range of voices and laughter. Renee sifts through her brain, relying on it just to help her bring back her speech. She has more to say. At least she thinks she does.

"I'm not going to make you squirm your way through this." The words bring Renee out of her mind with a pleasant rush. "I can see that you're sorry. Plus, I had insiders updating me on how miserable you've been." Hunter's smile is warm and wide.

"Who?" Renee demands, thinking, *those assholes*.

"People who care about you." Simple. Factual. It'll do. "People who want to see you happy."

Happy. It's a new concept—or at least it has new meaning, meaning Renee is finally ready to face and accept.

"I'm not an…easy person," Renee says.

Hunter looks at her, a serious look sharpening the already prominent edges of her jawline. Slowly, her cheeks redden, paving the way for full-facial blush.

Renee peers at her. "Are you breathing?"

Hunter shakes her head slowly, the red evanescing into something more purple. She bites her lower lip and her eyes begin to water. A tiny sound escapes the miniscule part of Hunter's lips, apparently enough to allow her coloring to begin returning to normal.

Renee squints. "What is wrong with you?"

Hunter leans her head back and exhales deeply. "I'm trying like hell not to laugh, Renee." She takes a moment to compose herself before meeting Renee's eyes. "Not for a single moment have I, or would I ever, consider you 'easy.' In fact, I'd claim you're the exact opposite of easy."

"Okay, I get it, you can stop."

"No, you don't get it." Hunter reaches across the table and takes Renee's hand in hers. "You're not easy, and I like that about you. Very, very much. Because beneath that not-easiness? You're a stunning human being, the very woman I cannot stop thinking about."

"Good," Renee says firmly. "Because as it turns out, I can't stop thinking about you."

"That works out in my favor." Hunter presses her thumb against Renee's finger. "So we're doing this?"

"Yes, please."

The chuckle in Hunter's throat is low and decidedly sexy. Renee wants to hear more of it. "You want to date me, Dr. Renee Lawler?"

"Yes." She purposely leaves off the please, unwilling to give Hunter that pleasure...at least for right now.

"And you're okay with people knowing that we're dating?"

"I am." Renee sits up straighter. "As it so happens, I've recently discovered I'm probably a lesbian, but at the very least, I know that I'm very attracted to you. As a bonus, I also like you."

She knows how it sounds, but she also knows how Hunter will take it, and she laughs, just as Renee hoped. "Lucky, lucky me. Renee." Her name sounds like a warning and Renee shifts in her seat.

"Just say it," she says.

Hunter's shoulders drop a tiny, nearly imperceptible, bit. "Just be honest with me, okay? That's all I ask."

Myriad fears and worries flit around in the unspoken words. Renee sees every one of them and knows her actions will determine how and when they are extinguished. "I'm ready," she says, her voice smooth and filled with a warmth that surprises both of them.

"Good." Hunter nods. "Great."

Renee grins. "Awesome, one might say."

Hunter's features relax and she sends Renee a look, one she will come to know very, very well. "Awesome, indeed."

EPILOGUE

With an exasperated grunt, Renee shucks off the simple black dress she thought would be perfect for this evening's event. She's been given strict instructions not to go "over the top," but everyone knows Renee will do just that. It's in her blood, after all.

She hears a commotion downstairs and Mr. Purrington zooms into her room. She glances at the clock before looking at the cat, who has made himself comfortable on Renee's bed. Jess has decided to stay in New Hampshire indefinitely, and Renee is very happy about her continued company—but honestly, she's also come to love the cat.

"Too loud for you? That's okay, you're safe up here with me." She pets Mr. Purrington's soft head, smiling at the sound of his absurdly loud purrs, before returning to her closet and pawing through her dress section.

"It's a fine line," she says to the cat, "between being too dressy and not dressy enough. I don't want to upstage the guests of honor, of course, but to be honest, Mr. Purrington, one of those guests of honor is not known for an exceptional sense of style. I'm afraid whatever I wear will put her to shame."

"You could wear a burlap sack and upstage her."

Renee spins around and looks at Hunter. "You're supposed to be waiting for me downstairs."

"And yet, here I am, interrupting your tête-à-tête with Mr. Purrington." She crosses the room in quick steps and takes Renee in her arms. "Besides, it's cruel that you won't let me watch you get dressed." Her hands caress Renee's ass, gripping her in a way that means only one thing.

"That's because," Renee says, half-heartedly wiggling to escape Hunter's grasp, "you know very well what happens when we're in a bedroom together."

"Especially"—Hunter begins kissing a path down Renee's cleavage, extra buoyant in her dark-red bra—"when you're wearing scandalous items like these." Her right hand slides under Renee's matching underwear, grabbing the flushed flesh beneath the thin lace.

Renee looks at the clock again, calculating how much time they have. She knows it's not enough, but she can't pull herself out of Hunter's hold. Her body betrays her need for punctuality, her legs spreading to encourage Hunter to move her hand.

"Not yet," Hunter whispers. "I know how much you hate to be late." Her touch vanishes from Renee's skin, and Renee can only glare at her, though she knows it's weak.

"Fine. As long as you're here, pick something for me to wear."

Hunter brightens. "I thought you'd never ask." She flips through Renee's selection of dresses, stopping on a midnight blue number with a plunging neckline that Renee never thinks of wearing. She's always considered it too sexy, but with Hunter on her arm, it feels right. "This one. With those fuchsia heels you love so much."

"I'm fairly certain you love them, too." She must, considering the several times she hasn't let Renee remove them while they've been intimate.

Hunter must be thinking the same thing because she winks at Renee and leaves the room. Had she stayed, they both know, they would have certainly been beyond late to the party.

"I'd say you're not overdressed," Hunter says in Renee's ear as they walk into the restaurant where Courtney and Nick are hosting their twenty-year anniversary party. And Hunter is right: the crowd is dazzling. She vaguely remembers Courtney complaining about Nick's extended family being "over the top," and that much is obviously true.

As they continue walking arm-in-arm through the restaurant, Renee subconsciously digs her fingertips into Hunter's arm. It's a move of gratitude, a silent hello, an acknowledgment. Over the three months that Renee and Hunter have been dating, Renee has been taking in loads of new information about herself. One of the best discoveries is that she is actually a highly sexual being and thoroughly enjoys all types of intimacy with Hunter. An odd discovery, however, is that she does not enjoy holding hands. What she does love, and what Hunter enjoys in a prideful sort of way, is the way Hunter takes her arm whenever they enter a public space. Renee has come to appreciate and enjoy the feeling of being taken by Hunter.

No one is more shocked by this than she is.

"Drink?" Hunter asks as they near the bar.

"Just a glass of wine." Hunter nods and walks toward the bar, leaving Renee to slowly spin around and take in the crowd. It's not long before a familiar face appears in front of her.

"I see you took Courtney's advice seriously," Kate says, eyeing Renee's outfit.

"Advice? It felt more like a threat to me."

Kate grins. "Have you seen her yet? She looks incredible."

"Is she..." Renee leans in, inhaling Kate's clean, soothing scent. She's pleased it no longer affects her; it seems her crush has stepped aside to make room for Hunter. "Is she wearing a dress?" she whispers loudly.

"God, no. She flat-out refused. Callie found her a very cute pantsuit with a nice feminine flair. Nick seems to like it quite a bit."

Renee scans the crowd for the couple and spots them off to the side, surrounded by a gaggle of young women who must be Nick's cousins. From what she can see of Courtney, she does look wonderful, aside from the current smirk on her face.

A glass of wine presses into her hand and Renee smiles. She feels Hunter's arm encircle her waist. She leans into her touch.

"I have to say, Hunter," Kate begins, and Renee braces herself. "You've really done something to this one. And I mean that in a good way, if an incredibly unexpected way."

"Wait a minute. Are you insinuating that I've changed?"

Callie sidles up next to Kate. "Ooh, I'm just in time for the show."

Renee shoots eye-daggers at her. "There will be no show. Kate, answer the question."

Kate pretends to think deeply, eyes rolling to the ceiling, finger tapping against her chin. "Have you changed…" She rolls her eyes back down. "Professionally? Not one bit. I know that's what you're worried about."

It's true, but Renee needs to know more. "And personally?"

"You're softer," Callie says.

Renee gasps. "You take that back."

Callie holds up both hands. "I cannot."

"She's right." Kate looks at Callie with such endearment that Renee swoons a bit herself. "You are softer. And it's been lovely to watch unfold."

"I can assure you both that she still has her edge." Hunter presses her palm against Renee's hip. Her swooning increases.

"Whoa, no." Courtney, who appeared out of nowhere, waves her hands in front of her face. "We do not talk about sex in this group. Okay? No sex. Ever."

"Prude," Callie mutters, barely dodging a friendly punch in the arm.

"Shut up. Now someone tell me how nice I look because I swear to God, you will never see me this dressed up ever again."

"Except," Callie says, tapping her finger against her chin, "at your funeral."

Courtney stares her down amidst the snickers from the others. "Why am I friends with you?"

Later in the evening, once the dancing has sped off to a remarkable intensity, Renee and Hunter escape to the back patio for fresh air.

"I love your friends," Hunter says as they get comfortable on a bench. "The banter gets a little intense at times but it's highly entertaining."

"Colleagues," Renee corrects.

"Oh, please. Those are your people."

One thing she really likes about Hunter is how she handles Renee. She makes it look easy, but they both know Renee is anything but. She's right, too. Those are her people. Perhaps they were once just colleagues, but over the years, each of them has rooted a little deeper into Renee's heart.

"So."

Renee looks over at Hunter. She's staring straight ahead at a line of twinkling lights. "What?"

"Are you enjoying dating me?"

"Good God, Hunter, what do you think?"

She grins and bumps against Renee. "Just checking to see if you're still into me."

"Do you really doubt my interest?"

"No." Renee hears the relief in her response, and she feels it roll through her. "You don't give me the opportunity to doubt anything about you."

"Yes, well, you're welcome for that."

Hunter presses her lips against Renee's temple. "Are you ready to make it official?"

"You mean we aren't officially dating?" Renee feels her forehead wrinkle in confusion.

"I meant official beyond dating. You know, a committed relationship."

Renee leans back to stare at Hunter. "Are you implying you haven't been committed to me?"

"My, my. Someone sounds defensive." Hunter grins. "Are you sleeping with someone else?"

"No!" Renee gently pushes Hunter. The thought tangles in her brain. TruSystems wrapped up their work at Pennbrook a month ago, sending Hunter back home to Vermont. They've spent every weekend together since, but... "Are you?"

"Tell me when I'd have time to even think about another woman when we're together every opportunity we have. And when we're not, you're enticing me with provocative text messages."

Renee huffs. "I can't be blamed for our scintillating sexual chemistry."

"Oh, no. There's no blame to be had or made." Hunter nudges Renee again. "So? Wanna be my girlfriend?"

Renee can't help but to smile. Of all the ways Hunter could have presented this proposition, this one is entirely her, beautifully and perfectly in line with their contrasting sides of the coin.

"All right. If you insist."

"A rousing agreement." Hunter tilts Renee's chin and kisses her deeply. "Happy one second anniversary."

The sentiment heats Renee through and through, quieting any leftover uncertainty that may be stored in the recesses of her heart. Hunter is absolute. She is steady, patient, kind, and intoxicating. She's everything Renee never gave herself the awareness of lacking. But now that she has her, she knows for sure Hunter is the piece her life has been missing.

"I'm ready to leave if you are."

"I am." Hunter rakes her eyes up and down Renee's body, sending shivers in all the right places. "I'm also ready to take that dress off of you."

"And the heels?" Renee points one foot and turns it back and forth, giving Hunter ample time to enjoy the show.

"No," she says simply, pulling Renee up. "The heels stay."

More Titles from Bella Books

Mabel and Everything After – Hannah Safren
978-1-64247-390-2 | 274 pgs | paperback: $17.95 | eBook: $9.99
A law student and a wannabe brewery owner find that the path to a fairy tale happily-ever-after is often the long and scenic route.

To Be With You – TJ O'Shea
978-1-64247-419-0 | 348 pgs | paperback: $19.95 | eBook: $9.99
Sometimes the choice is between loving safely or loving bravely.

I Dare You to Love Me – Lori G. Matthews
978-1-64247-389-6 | 292 pgs | paperback: $18.95 | eBook: $9.99
An enemy-to-lovers romance about daring to follow your heart, even when it's the hardest thing to do.

The Lady Adventurers Club - Karen Frost
978-1-64247-414-5 | 300 pgs | paperback: $18.95 | eBook: $9.99
Four women. One undiscovered Egyptian tomb. One (maybe) angry Egyptian goddess. What could possibly go wrong?

Golden Hour - Kat Jackson
978-1-64247-397-1 | 250 pgs | paperback: $17.95 | eBook: $9.99
Life would be so much easier if Lina were afraid of something basic—like spiders—instead of something significant. Something like real, true, healthy love.

Schuss – E. J. Noyes
978-1-64247-430-5 | 276 pgs | paperback: $17.95 | eBook: $9.99
They're best friends who both want something more, but what if admitting it ruins the best friendship either of them have had?